Praise for
The Killing Club

"The twists twist well, the characters have just the right amount of depth, and Malone's splendid use of detail enables him to create a fascinating, multidimensional community."

—*Booklist*

"[A] readable, entertaining effort."

—*Library Journal*

"If 'author' Walsh is killed off on *OLTL*, she can always make a new career writing readable, enjoyable mysteries."

—*Publishers Weekly*

THE KILLING CLUB

THE KILLING CLUB

BASED ON A STORY BY JOSH GRIFFITH

MARCIE WALSH
with MICHAEL MALONE

HYPERION

New York

Mass Market ISBN: 0-7868-9094-0

Hyperion books are available for special promotions
and premiums. For details contact Michael Rentas,
Assistant Director, Inventory Operations, Hyperion,
77 West 66th Street, 11th floor, New York, New York 10023,
or call 212-456-0133.

FIRST MASS MARKET EDITION

10 9 8 7 6 5 4 3 2 1

For Shelly Altman

THE KILLING CLUB

1

JAMIE

HERE'S THE IDEA, Christmas comes but once a year. In Gloria, New Jersey, it comes for five months. Red-nosed reindeer are running across the roofs as soon as the ghosts come off the porches. Christmas trees get dragged out to the curb, dumping a trail of tinsel and needles, after the Valentine candy goes on display at Solly's Drugs. In Gloria, the good parents hide Santa's loot in the crawl space by late September and they're still paying for it in July.

I'm Jamie Ferrara, Giovanna Lucia Ferrara. No kids, not married, less than a year to go before I'm thirty. People don't think that I'm Italian, both sides, because I have blue eyes and strawberry-blond hair. But my family's stayed 100 percent Italian since they first came to this harbor town. They were here when the mayor changed its name from Deep Port back in 1927. Gloria was the mayor's wife's name. The high school where we all went was named after her too, Gloria Hart High School. We figured the mayor must have really loved his wife, although from her picture in the hallway it was hard to tell why.

A lot of us who went to Hart still live in Gloria, even if we're always saying that someday we're going to leave. I'm one of that any-day-now set. For me, there're not many strangers here. So driving along River Street, I knew Pudge Salerno was headed back from the planning board meeting when I saw him park his new Lexus in front of his family restaurant. I knew the Virgin Mary and Joseph had gone to Dockside Tavern to warm up when I passed the gazebo on Etten Green. They'd left a sign hanging on the manger wall: BACK IN TEN MINUTES. There was no one left guarding the wooden Jesus in the crèche but two plywood shepherds, a plastic camel and a cow. No one was going to steal him either; he had a bicycle chain around his belly.

It was a Friday, early December, bone-cold, dirty snow frozen in lumps in the gutters. A nasty wind was flapping through that one crack, right at the back of my neck, in the canvas top of my Mustang. I admit it, a 1968 Ford Mustang Shelby GT-500 is not a practical car. But I like my convertible, and life is short. I was about to be reminded of that lousy fact.

I'd been in court all day, testifying for the state in an aggravated assault case, and now I was headed for a birthday dinner with Rod Wolenski, chief of detectives at Gloria Police Department (GPD). Rod moved to town five years ago from Philly. He's my boss. For three years, he's been my fiancé too. The same everybody who disapproves of my Mustang—and that's various relatives, including my older brother—thinks a three-year engagement is two years too long. In Gloria, girls from Italian families get married before they're thirty, even if the girls are detective sergeants who love their jobs. Especially if the girl could marry a good-looking man from a Catholic family who, while not Italian, was not out of a job, not an alcoholic and not already married to somebody else. Seven months till my deadline.

I was a little early for our reservation at the Ironworks Inn so I headed west, away from downtown and the river, and drove to a mid-nineties subdivision called Glen Valley (there was not much glen, and no valley in it). I wanted to take a look at what Ben Tymosz had done to his house this year. I'd been thinking about Ben today because of an odd phone call from him that afternoon. I'd known him since we were teenagers but we had never been close and I don't think I'd said ten words to him in the last couple of years. So his phoning and making a formal appointment to come see me in my office the following morning had felt odd, especially since he wouldn't tell me what he wanted to talk about.

In Gloria, Ben is famous for his Christmas show; it spreads from his roof down across his yard, covering the small lawn in plastic icicles, wreaths, reindeer, elves, nutcrackers, Victorian carolers, giant candles and peppermint sticks, all rigged to blink in waves of red, white, blue, green, orange, red, white, blue, green, orange. It's about as tasteful as an Atlantic City casino, and uses about as much electricity.

So when I first saw the sky, I didn't think fire; I thought, wow, Ben's really outdone himself this year. He was always a

believer; we were already in fifth grade when he socked
Garth McBride for saying there was no such thing as Santa
Claus. Now Ben played Santa for the Rotarians in a plastic
igloo in Appleton Mall. Shopping with my nephew, Clay, I'd
seen Ben there in full costume a week ago, telling a long line
of kids that if they were good, they'd get what they wanted.
Clay, thirteen, had laughed. "Yeah, sure." In Ben's case, it was
hard to argue with Clay's pessimism: Ben had wanted to go
to college on a football scholarship and had never made it.
He'd wanted to live in one of the big houses on the river and
never got there. "Just not good enough," he used to tell us
and nobody had argued with him.

Turning into Glen Valley, I could see the smoke, then
smell it. As soon as I took the right onto Windsor Lane, I
knew it was Ben's house on fire. When I saw how bad it was,
my hands went hot on the wheel. Our big red ladder truck
and the pumper had pulled up onto the lawn. Black and
whites blocked off the street. Neighbors stood watching
from the sidewalks. EMS was in the driveway and two paramedics were lifting a gurney with a body lumped on it into
the back of the van. Half of the bright yellow, two-story
clapboard Colonial was a charred shell. Firemen were still
hauling out wet sooty furniture. Everything was steaming in
the frozen air.

I drove past a brand-new black Mercedes sedan, still
with its dealer plates, across the street. The guy who owned it
was talking on his cell phone in the driver's seat. I recognized
the aggressively handsome profile of Barclay Ober, who'd
built Glen Valley. I wondered why he was there.

Nearby, my fiancé, Rod, was walking the chief of police
to his car. Even in a New Jersey suburb, there was something

about Rod's way of walking that made him look like he was headed through an open stretch of dusty sagebrush to rope a wild horse. Chief Warren Waige depended on Rod. But Rod gave everybody that feeling—that you could lean on him and he wouldn't fall over.

The chief drove away as I got close enough to shout out the window, "Rod! Is it bad?"

He nodded, hands hunched in his suede jacket pockets.

I called again: "Is it Ben?"

He nodded.

For our date at the Ironworks, I was wearing a short dress under my parka, and I was tripping in the hard snow in red Ferragamo knockoffs that spend most of their time in a box on my closet shelf. It was a rare enough sight for my fellow GPD detective Danny Ventura to grab the flattened fire hose, shake it at me from between his legs and whistle. "Hey, Giovanna Lucia, you're a *girl!*"

"Give it a rest, Danny." I threw him the finger. It didn't mean as much with my padded gloves on.

He made a kissing face. Danny Ventura and I had gone out once, years ago, when I first joined GPD. Once was enough. He was good-looking in a sleazy sort of way. He was a good detective too, though not a smart one, but dogged and observant. Everything else about him—well, let's leave it at that.

Rod told Danny to back off. Danny did. Rod is his boss too.

"You catch it on the radio?" Rod pulled me under his arm and hugged me. He's lanky, but as solid as a tree. He's close to a foot taller than I am.

"No, I was just driving by. How bad is it?"

"Bad." Rod still wears his hair longer than the current style. Most people in Gloria are a little behind the times. I could smell the smoke in his hair when he said, "Ben's dead."

I'd figured somebody was, from what was on the gurney. "Oh Jesus. Megan and the girls?"

"No. We couldn't find anybody else in the house. Haven't reached her."

"Electrical?"

He walked me over to the front walk, guiding me out of the snow patches into which my heels were slipping. "Looks like he fell down his basement steps, went down probably because some fuses blew. Kicked over a gas can. I'm sorry, baby. I know you two go back."

"God, *Ben*?" I watched the bulk of the body bag sliding through the white doors. "*Ben Tymosz?* In a basement? I still think of Ben three feet off the ground."

As I said it, I was thinking back to a night almost a dozen years ago. Hunched on the sidelines of a scruffy football field in a rainy December, I was pointing a beaten-up zoom lens at a teenager with *Tymosz* on the back of his jersey. He was twisting his thick body high in the air in the end zone, his pockmarked face earnest, his big hands red and raw around the football. Touchdown!

HART HIGH SCHOOL CHAMPS! flapped the banner over Main Street until that April, although the truth was, we lost that final game. And, like I say, Ben didn't make it through college. And he hadn't been very good at selling insurance either. And we'd run out of things to talk about and had lost touch.

I felt bad about it all, standing there looking at the sign

Ben had stuck in his lawn for his daughters: SANTA, STOP HERE. KATHIE AND KRISTIE HAVE BEEN GOOD ALL YEAR.

"Not sure I follow you, three feet off the ground." Rod had that puzzled look he gets sometimes when I forget that he can't be as inside my head as I am.

"Football. Ben was the running back for Hart High. For a big guy he could jump."

Rod nodded, hugged me again, headed me toward the blackened house.

"So what's Barclay Ober doing here?" I pointed at the Mercedes across the street. Barclay was a local, around my age, but rich, really rich. He'd married my sister.

"Ober called it in." Rod and I looked at the man in the hundred-thousand-plus car as he finished his cell phone call. "Said he was driving by, dropping his son off at a friend's, saw flames shoot out of the basement window, Ben's car was in the drive, so he called 911."

"He didn't try to get in the house, do something maybe?" I don't like Barclay Ober. My sister, Gina, would have been thirty-one, like Barclay, two years older than I am, but she'd died a week before her twenty-sixth birthday. Cancer. Clay, her only child, was eight years old when she died. We had to drag him out of my dad's attic to take him to the funeral. Later I found out Barclay was cheating on Gina the last year of her life. It didn't surprise me.

I looked at the burned front door, hacked off its hinges, thrown over the juniper shrubs. Rod said, "Barclay tried to get in but it was locked. He broke a window and was about to crawl through when the whole thing just blew. With the wind, it went fast."

"Yeah? So he sat in his Mercedes."

"Okay, well, let's give him a break, Jamie."

I headed toward the car. Barclay saw me and waved like we'd run into each other at the beach. But then he drove quickly away, though I suspected he knew I was coming over to talk to him.

Nobody had been able to reach Ben's wife, Megan. The woman next door said the two Tymosz girls had gone to a birthday party with her daughter. The neighbor was going to take them over to Ben's mother's house until we could find Megan and tell her the news.

The house stank of burned furniture. I recognized most of the volunteer firemen dragging it out of the living room. There were too many stuffed chairs and couches, most of them velour. Too many knickknacks. Framed family photos. Dozens of kitschy clocks (one of a lighthouse, one of Betty Boop). Assorted teddy bears now wearing Santa hats. A charred spruce tree, eight feet tall, ornaments and lights melted to the branches, lay on the wet carpet of the pine-paneled family room. Already at its base, piles of wrapped presents, safe in fire-retardant metallic paper. A recliner in front of a huge television. Dinner on a tray on the seat. It was probably pepperoni pizza.

I looked down into the black hole that had been the basement. The bottom of the steps and most of the rail were burned completely away.

I asked Rod, "Are you here because the fire guys suspect something?" As chief of detectives, he headed all divisions, including arson. "Insurance? Fire got out of hand?"

"No. Just checking. Looks like an accident." If things had to go wrong, Rod preferred them to be accidents. He'd come to Gloria after ten years in Center City Philadelphia, where he'd worked at the job that burned him out and brought him to a small town where he had some distant relatives. He'd been running a South Philly youth bureau, dealing with criminal offenders seventeen or younger. Just hearing his stories was rough.

Our volunteer fire marshal came over. He had a report ready to write up about what they figured had happened to Ben.

One of the giant stars on the Tymosz roof blew, shorting out the reindeer lights. Inside, the house went dark. Ben lost ESPN from the overload; according to the neighbor, Ben's lights blew almost every Christmas. He felt in the dark, lit a couple of holiday candles, headed for the basement circuit breaker box, tripped on something at the top of the stairs, fell, kicked over a can of lawn mower gas. He was knocked out and the fire had a field day in the combustible junk heaped against the basement walls.

Rod signed off on how GVFD (Gloria Volunteer Fire Department) was going to write up its report and then the marshal went away.

I didn't like the theory. "Why wouldn't he get a flashlight?"

Rod shrugged. "Maybe he couldn't find one. Those dumb Christmas candles were all over the place."

"You're going with accident?"

"Accident, Jamie."

"I didn't tell you this, but Ben called me out of the blue today, wanted to talk to me tomorrow."

"About what?"

"He didn't say."

"Accident. Jamie, rein it in." As Rod looked up at the burned-out ceiling, the tilt of his face let you see the little bit of Leni-Lenape Indian in his wide cheeks and strong nose. It was a good face. Robert Dominick Wolenski is a thoughtful, fair-minded man, and that's not a bad thing in a chief of detectives. But if he always thinks everything's an accident for as long as he can, I figure I'm paid to consider the other possibility. I tell him it seems like a reasonable basis for a marriage.

"Hello there, Jamie. You gotta be cold." It was Gert Anderssen, our GPD medical examiner. "Watch your step in those silly shoes." Gert's sixty, and six feet tall. She still has the blue-eyed gaze and broad-shouldered body you can see in her old photos. She didn't wear silly shoes forty years ago either, when she transferred to U Penn from a college in Sweden and by the next spring had won the national women's heptathlon. She is a really good medical examiner—sharp, patient, creative—and had somehow managed to hang on to kindness after a lifetime of cutting open dead bodies.

She tapped the back of her head. "This was not the inhalation. This was the cranial blunt force." Gert has never lost her accent, with its singsong shifts in pitch, and she sounds like an old Greta Garbo film on my dad's movie channel. She looks like an old Greta Garbo too, except with cropped white hair and wearing blue jeans. Gert's been having an affair with Chief of Police Waige for decades. For decades most of Gloria has figured she was a lesbian because of her athletic ability. I like her more than I do Chief Waige.

"What?" I asked Gert as we walked back into Ben's front yard. The ambulance had left, and so had the pumper and some of the neighbors who'd been watching from across the street. "Ben's feet went out from under him and he hit the edge of a step?"

Gert smiled tolerantly. "That is reasonable. But I am going to my home now, so good-bye."

As she strode off, swinging wide of Danny Ventura, he called to her, "Hey, bah-dah-boom to the chief tonight," but not so Gert could hear. She wouldn't have known what he meant anyhow. Or if she did, she'd ignore it.

THE SCREAM WAS so loud, it startled even Rod, who wouldn't twitch if a cat landed on his back. Ben's wife, Megan, whose car was pulled up onto the sidewalk, with its door flung open, fell to her knees, pounding her head into the dirty snow. Her scream went on so long it was like it pushed all the air out of her. Danny Ventura was leaning over the blond woman, trying to help, but believe me he's the last person I'd want to get that kind of news from. Megan shook him off and started yanking at her hair, rubbing her heavy makeup and mascara in it. There was a lot of hair, bleached and permed. And there was a lot of Megan now; she looked to have gained ten pounds just in the last six months. My dad—not always the most tactful man—had asked her at this year's Halloween parade if she was supposed to be Jayne Mansfield. Megan had no idea who Jayne Mansfield was.

Rod knocked Danny out of the way and hauled Megan to her feet. Then he just held on, till she wore herself out and her voice hoarsened to a whisper. "Goddamn, Ben, I'm so fuckin' sorry!"

There was something weird about the way she kept

telling her dead husband she was sorry, and asking us to call Father Connor at Immaculate Conception. But I figured she just felt guilty because she hadn't been home when it happened so maybe she could have saved him. Except where had she been? Exercising at the new gym in Appleton Mall, she told us. I wondered why a married woman would wear so much makeup, a sleazy sequined blouse and big, blinking Christmas bell earrings, just to drive home from a workout in a gym.

I told Megan how sorry I was, but that I had to ask her if she knew why Ben had wanted to talk to me tomorrow, why he'd said it was important. Her face first looked horrified, then shut down completely. "I got no idea," she told me.

Keith Connor, a priest my age, arrived and took Megan to Ben's mother's house to pick up her daughters; I headed back downtown to tell Pudge Salerno that his best friend was dead.

As for Rod's birthday dinner at the Ironworks, we'd do it another night.

"It's okay," Rod said as I kissed him. That's what he says every time I put off setting a wedding date.

Rod knows me. The only thing on my mind now was finding out what that "important" thing was that Ben had planned to say to me.

2

PUDGE

PUDGE, I'M REALLY sorry I had to tell you this way. Step outside, come on." The restaurant was busy and loud, like always. But I couldn't get Dante "Pudge" Salerno to move.

"You can't lie to me. You know that. He's not dead, Jamie, don't screw around, Ben's not dead." Pudge just kept smiling, shaking his head to encourage me to admit I had made the whole thing up for a sick joke.

Eleven years back, on that rainy December night when Ben's touchdown took us to the final quarter of the state championship and no farther, Pudge had said the same thing to me. "Don't lie."

That night everybody in the stadium had just laughed at

him because his pants had fallen down as he'd marched off the field at the end of the halftime show. Pudge had played trumpet in the Hart marching band and he hadn't wanted to quit on Bon Jovi's "Livin' on a Prayer" in order to grab his trousers. So he lost them when his big safety pin broke.

"Just shoot me," he said that night, tears splotchy under the high white hat with its gold GHHS. "I'll never in a trillion years live this one down."

"Sure you will, Pudge." I pulled him to the sidelines, patted his chest; the brass buttons gaped on the dirty white jacket. "Nobody really noticed."

"Nobody really noticed!?" Pudge bulged his large brown eyes, the lashes of which were the subject of periodic envy in the Hart High girls' bathroom. "The giant marshmallow man from *Ghostbusters* drops his pants on the fifty-yard line at the state finals and he's wearing zebra-striped bikini shorts, and nobody really noticed?!"

"Okay, maybe a few people noticed."

"Right, Jamie, maybe only seven thousand five hundred and ninety-nine people noticed. Maybe you weren't looking because you were checking out the stands for stupid Garth McBride."

"Fat chance of seeing him there," I admitted.

Pudge grinned, wiping tears away with a plump pink fist. "Fat chance of his giving you the time of day if you did see him."

"Everybody noticed your pants fall down. They'll be talking about it for centuries."

"Did Eileen Terry see it? Don't lie to me. Only real Italians can get away with lying." Because of my coloring, Pudge would never believe I was pure Italian, the Ferraras from

Bologna and the DiMauros from Venice. "Don't even try," he told me fiercely.

SO IT WAS WEIRD THAT Pudge said the same thing now, almost a dozen years later. But he knew I was telling the truth; he was just trying to hang on to disbelief a little longer. His friend Ben, whom he'd idolized since pre-K and stolen food from his parents' restaurant for, and shared pot with, and lent his car to, and bought more insurance from than he could ever use, was dead.

Pudge leaned on a booth, his face almost the color of the green vinyl, breathing heavily.

I tugged at him again. "Let's go outside, it's too crowded in here. Get your coat."

"I don't need it. This better not be true, Jamie."

"It's true. I'm sorry."

Pudge had inherited the landmarked storefront diner on River Street from his mom and dad. They'd named it Dante's after him, their firstborn. His parents had served only takeout, but Dante's had grown into green-checked tablecloths and vinyl booths and was now a real restaurant. All year round, there was always a fresh pink rosebud on every table; it was to Pudge a sign of "class." But the motto (on menus and cardboard buckets) was still "Take It Home," and the portions were so big, you had to. Pudge was generous. He loved his customers. To him they were all family. His restaurant was cheerful and cheap and crowded. And the food was so good he had write-ups on the walls from newspapers as far away as Philadelphia. You had to wait for a table, you had to take a number for an order to go, but nobody minded. It was the most popular restaurant in Gloria.

Pudge and I sat at one of the little iron tables chained outside under the awning. In the nice weather, you could watch the town go by. Now there was nobody around, except that across the street on Etten Green, the Virgin Mary and Joseph had returned to their manger. They stood hunched over Jesus, warming their hands in their armpits.

"Pudge, Ben called me today and said he wanted to come in, talk to me. I hadn't heard from him in ages. Do you know what it was about? Was he okay?"

Pudge seemed about to say something. His lips, pink and full, opened, but then tightened. "I don't know. You ought to talk to Megan about it."

". . . Okay. I will. And I'll let Debbie know, but you can call Amanda."

"Life's just not fair," Pudge sighed. "Ben was the nicest guy in the world."

No, he wasn't. Pudge was the nicest guy in the world. But I nodded, sat with him, gave his knee a rub every now and then.

My baby brother, Dino, drove by too fast in a Ford Ranger that didn't belong to him, and he had Clay with him. It wasn't the first time I'd seen them riding around Gloria together. But I wondered what Clay was doing with Dino after his father, Barclay, had said he'd "dropped him off at a friend's." The truck was shaking from Pink Floyd on the audio system. Dino pretended not to see me but he did slow down. Dino's twenty-four, a stoner, living in a time warp, headed for a Black Sabbath concert that happened years before he was born.

Either the Ford or the wind knocked down one of the cardboard shepherds. Joseph ran over to pick him up.

"It's cold out here," Pudge finally admitted. He had on his Christmas blazer, Kelly green, and he pulled the lapels around his neck.

"You don't know why Ben would want to see me tomorrow?"

"No." Pudge hesitated, then added, "But I don't think he was happy. I think he was having money troubles and maybe troubles with Megan too. He was going to church a lot."

"I never saw Ben. Why would he come to me with his troubles?"

Pudge shrugged. "I don't know. Connie's with Megan now?" Father Keith Connor was already head priest at the largest local Catholic church, Immaculate Conception, the one Ben apparently often attended; we'd called him Connie since we were in high school together. I nodded. "And somebody ought to call Garth, Jamie."

"Garth?"

"He'll want to know about Ben. I mean, he started the club."

My legs were freezing. I wasn't used to wearing a dress. "That was a long time ago. I don't even know where Garth lives."

"Manhattan, East Sixty-eighth Street."

I was surprised. "You keep up?"

"Christmas cards. He was Ben's friend, sort of. Maybe it'd be too tough on you to call him. I'll do it."

"Why tough?"

"You know." In Pudge's world, once you felt something, you never stopped. Just because I'd once been a plump sophomore so desperate for Garth McBride it hurt my chest to have him suddenly amble past my school locker, why should that mean anything to me now? Now I was Detective Sergeant Giovanna Ferrara, Investigative Division, Gloria Police Department, currently engaged to marry the good and good-looking and very patient chief of detectives, Lieutenant Rod Wolenski.

"Forget it," I said. "I'll call Garth tonight. Leave me his number. I should go. It's Rod's birthday."

"Oh, happy birthday. You want a cake?" He waved his hand at the restaurant. "I got a nice double fudge. I could write something on it."

"That's sweet of you but thanks anyhow. You okay, Pudge?"

"It's hard to take it in." He shook his head. "I guess I'll go see Megan. Did somebody tell Ben's mother?"

"I don't know. Megan probably did. Anyhow—"

"We ought to, I don't know, take up a collection or something."

I said okay. Then he talked a while about funeral arrangements at Immaculate Conception. Megan would want to do the service there. Father Connie would say the Mass. And the Rotarians would want to do something. Ben would like a lot of flowers. My guess was, Pudge would pay for them.

At the manger, the wind blew the shepherd over again. This time Joseph propped it up against a stone mile-marker that had stood there in the green since before the Revolutionary War. I could hear the Virgin Mary from all the way across the street. She didn't sound much like the Mother of God. "It's too fucking cold out here! My tits are ice! Can we just like go?" Joseph pulled a plug on an orange industrial cable. The crèche went totally dark.

It was getting late. The early crowd was leaving Dante's, waving to Pudge as they walked out. Looking at his customers was like taking a census of Gloria. Ninety percent white, most of them of Italian, Polish, Irish or German backgrounds. A few blacks, a few Hispanics and very few Asians. Merchants, truck farmers, teachers, Ober construction workers, tile setters. Gloria had started out building ships; now it built subdivisions. And made face cream at the Kind Lady Cosmetics factory.

Pudge pulled out a fresh pack of Marlboros. I grabbed it away from him. "What are you doing? You quit smoking five years ago."

He shrugged, lighting up. "I'm doing the gum again but it's not totally working for me." He flicked open a lighter that looked like it was made out of gold. It had his initials on it.

"I guess not. Is that lighter gold?"

"Yeah. Eileen gave it to me way back when." He stared at it.

I tossed the pack into the iron trash container near the crosswalk. I was surprised I made the shot. "I bet she doesn't know you're smoking. Or your kids either. Jesus Christ."

"Come on, Jamie, cut me some slack."

"Well, Jesus, Pudge, I care about you."

"You look pretty, by the way." He gestured offhandedly at my legs and shoes. Obviously this new look was something to consider if things blew apart with Rod and I needed a date.

"Thanks," I told him. "I'm freezing my butt off."

"You should go. So you said it was like Ben's lights blew? What, he was electrocuted or something?"

I guess Pudge had been so upset he hadn't heard me. "No, I said he died from the fire."

"Fire? His house caught on fire?"

Now Pudge asked for details.

"What it sounds like, the main fuse blew, Ben headed down to the basement, tripped and fell down the steps, maybe had a candle or something with him, and somehow he set off a gas can."

Tossing his cigarette onto the sidewalk, Pudge frowned at me like I'd made fun of his dead mother. "That's not funny."

"What's not funny?"

"Everything you just said."

I didn't know what he was talking about. He couldn't believe I didn't remember. "The Killing Club. The first murder Ben made up. That's how he was going to kill Mr. Payton."

It took me a minute even to place the name. "Mr. Payton the geometry teacher?"

He pulled thin wool gloves from his jacket, blew warm air on his big supple hands, then put the gloves on. "Yeah, for flunking him for cheating on the exam."

I smiled. "Ben did cheat on that exam. You gave him the answers. We all got grilled about cheating. You're just lucky Ben didn't tell anybody you were helping him or you would have flunked out too."

"Jamie, you're not listening. It's exactly the same. It's what Ben wrote in the Death Book. For the club. How the killer ran a wire across the top of the basement stairs, and then when Mr. Payton went down there in the dark, he tripped and fell."

"No, I don't remember, and I don't see how you possibly

could either. That was over ten years ago. More. You're talking about those stupid Death Books we wrote stuff in?"

Pudge looked sheepish. "I remember that one because I made it up for him. He didn't really think of it." Pudge's explanation came out quickly, the way things always did with him when he felt bad about what he was saying. "Ben was worried he couldn't think of a good murder. And I really wanted him to get in the Killing Club, plus Garth really wanted us to be able to meet at the old theater, and it belonged to Ben's dad, so I figured it would make Ben happy and Garth happy, and I made up a murder for him."

"Oh, Pudge. You were always cheating for Ben!"

He gestured with his shoulders. "He's my friend."

I rubbed his hands. The black wool gloves looked weird with his green blazer. "Did you make up all Ben's murders?"

"Yeah, pretty much. But I just told him what to say. I made him write them up himself in his own words. But I remember the first one, Jamie, it was a basement fire."

As he told me the details, the story came vaguely back to me, Ben's sloping careless handwriting in the Death Book in which our high school Killing Club had written out imaginary homicides. In these murders we disposed of the people who were ruining our lives.

Pudge was saying, "The killer runs a wire across the steps, then he bashes in the back of Mr. Payton's head with a baseball bat, pours gas on him and lights a match. There's no way that's a coincidence."

"We all thought Ben's entries were pretty lame." Ridiculously, I apologized to Pudge. "Not the ideas, the writing."

Leaning over, Pudge pointed his gloved finger in my face. "Maybe he wasn't a brain, but Ben was never clumsy.

He didn't fall down his own steps like that. Those steps had a rail. He would have grabbed it."

"People fall. It happens."

"Jamie, he would have had a flashlight with him. What's he doing walking down to the basement with a fucking candle?" Well, I'd asked the same question myself.

A Salerno cousin in a waiter's T-shirt labeled DANTE'S TAKE IT HOME came pushing through the crowd of young couples in the doorway and hurried over to us. He said that Pudge's wife, Eileen, was looking everywhere for him, that she'd just gotten a phone call and was very upset.

Pudge jumped to his feet. "Oh shit. That was probably Megan calling about Ben. I gotta go. But we need to talk about this fire thing. You think about it, Jamie. You think about it." Pudge pulled off a glove and took out his phone as he ran inside, I bet to call Ben's wife, Megan. It was hard for him to make his way quickly through the people waiting to get into his restaurant.

I thought about it.

3

GARTH

IN THE BEGINNING, tenth grade, there were only four of us, and Garth McBride named the club the Sign of Four after the Sherlock Holmes story. When we let more kids in, he changed the name to the Killing Club and called it KC. The club disbanded in our senior year.

Garth was always starting things, trying to get something going in Gloria, wanting it to be bigger and more interesting than it was. Now he's something of a local celebrity because he's on a television news show in New York that gets carried by cable and dish here in Gloria.

A widow, his mom ran day care out of her house. I was dropped off there for years with my sister, Gina (who giggled or cried all the time), and our baby brother, Dino, who smiled all the time like he was already stoned. Our other brother, Joe Jr., was out on his own, on his way to becoming the jerk he is today.

My sister was the same age as Garth's sister, Katie, and they didn't have much use for me, so I tried to hang out with Garth, but he didn't have much use for me either. I spent a lot of hours spying on him. He's probably the real reason I'm a detective. Unnoticed—or so far as I knew—I watched him pretending to be Han Solo and Indiana Jones and Bruce Springsteen, and once I saw him trying to pee into the gas tank of his mom's Datsun. The first time Garth was nice to me was when he found out my dad was a cop and I told him I'd bring over his Python .380 to look at. I knew it wasn't going to happen because my dad kept the revolver locked in the liquor cabinet when he was home. I just said it to show off.

The original Sign of Four was Garth and me, Pudge, and Garth's best friend, Lyall Hillier, who committed suicide our senior year. They let me join, even though I was a girl, because my dad got Chief Waige to give us a tour of the police station.

Appointed secretary, I dutifully wrote down the rules. They hadn't changed when the Killing Club maxed out at a dozen members in its final year: You had to be an outcast— meaning you didn't sit at the lunch table with the in-crowd, you didn't hold school office and you didn't hang with the athletic crowd (until Pudge got us to invite in Ben Tymosz). You had to be funny and hold the world in ironic contempt. As for an ostensible purpose, we discussed mysteries and horror books we'd read (or at least had seen the movies), and we tried to scare one another by any means possible— leaping up from the backseat of a dark car, forcing the startled driver to spin off the road, for example—then whispering to our victim, "*Death has come to your little town, Sheriff,*" from the movie *Halloween*. When that got old, we started coming up with ingenious ways to kill people we didn't like—which was pretty much everybody we knew.

The Killing Club met in an old brick warehouse out on the east edge of Gloria, near some abandoned docks, that for a while had been Ben's father's movie theater. In the late eighties, Mr. Tymosz, who'd gotten run out of business by the cineplex, leased the building to the Pine Barrens Players, a local community theater that did too many plays (like *The Iceman Cometh*) that nobody in Gloria much wanted to see. "The *Iceman* Cometh and Wenteth" reported *The Gloria Gazette*. The building, still labeled Pine Barrens Playhouse, had stood empty ever since, with a faded FOR LEASE sign on it. I used to be sure that Garth had let Pudge's friend Ben into the club (when he failed to fit the profile—he played football, he didn't read mysteries and his idea of humor was a loud fart) only because he had a key to the padlock on the empty playhouse. We rode our bikes out there at night and held our meetings on the empty stage, sitting in old canvas director's chairs. When new members were initiated, they got a copy of Ben's key so they had access to the theater. Connie made the keys at his dad's hardware store.

The real irony of the Killing Club was that by our final year, the in-crowd at Hart High (many of whom we'd imagined murdering) was knocking on our door, wanting to join us because we wouldn't let them do it.

We did let in Barclay Ober the first year, though he was part of the in-crowd and nobody really liked him, because he had a very nice car. I think he was there for the pot and a girl named Amanda. But he didn't stay long. We were sophomores and he was already a senior, already dating my sister, Gina, whom he knocked up and then married the summer after they graduated. Gina had absolutely no interest in the Killing Club.

We invited three other girls to join in one swoop. Debbie Deklerk, my best friend, because she had the first nose stud in Gloria. Amanda Kean, because she was beautiful and the guys all wanted to sleep with her, and some of them did. Wendy, I don't remember why. I stayed secretary the whole time. Garth stayed president.

In the beginning, the Killing Club was mostly just an excuse to hang out, drink the Lambrusco that Pudge would steal for us from Dante's, listen on a huge boom box to Echo & the Bunnymen. As mainstream as we got was Stevie Nicks and John Mellencamp. We'd smoke Lyall's dope and bitch about how much we hated Hart High School, our homes and our lives.

But Garth kept the murder theme going: We had to write down our homicides in a spiral notebook that he called the Death Book and that I kept hidden in my closet at home. Each fall we'd start another one. We voted on who was most likely to get away with these imaginary murders. Every month we gave a Best Murder prize (a six-pack of beer or a rock album or a bag of pot). Garth won seven times; his were the most intricate and imaginative crimes. Next was Debbie—maybe just because she had more entries than anybody else; she appeared to want to murder everybody she knew. Then Connie; he always had the best "backup" plans, as he called them, sometimes two levels deep (the cover story to cover the cover story). I didn't win that often, but I was the best at finding the flaws in other people's crimes. It was

Garth who first suggested, "Why don't you go to cop school? Then you can arrest people instead of just bossing them around."

The Killing Club fell apart in the winter of our senior year when Lyall Hillier committed suicide. He was reported missing the day after that football game for the state championship where Ben had scored a touchdown that almost won the game and where Pudge had lost his pants.

Lyall had been at the game with Garth. He was always with Garth. Well, not at the game—not in the stadium stands where (Pudge had been right) I was looking for Garth—but in the parking lot, where Lyall and he were sliding blue sheets of paper under the windshield wipers of everybody's cars. The printout called on the people of Gloria to sign a petition condemning something the government was doing. Trash cans were stuffed with hundreds of these blue sheets.

That night was the last time I saw Lyall. Sometime before dawn, he had left a note in his coat on the docks near Pine Barrens Playhouse, saying that he was going into the river and hoped his parents would forgive him. Deep Port River is fast and cold even in summer, and at this time of year there was already a border of thin ice spreading out from the embankment. Lyall had torn the ice apart jumping in. They said he couldn't have survived in that water for very long. They never found him.

We were even more freaked because our first year Barclay had actually "killed" somebody in the Death Book by passing off the homicide as a drowning. According to Garth, Barclay had just lifted the idea from his favorite movie, *Chinatown*, which he'd admitted to liking for the men's clothes, not the mystery.

We wondered if Barclay's "murder" had actually given Lyall the idea of how to kill himself. But finally we decided he had been thinking about suicide for a long time—because of odd things he'd said and done. In any case, Lyall's goodbye note; his mother's terrible crying at the memorial service; Garth and Ben hurrying Keith Connor, who started vomiting during the last prayer, over to the riverbank in the cemetery; and then back at Hart High, the dead boy's daily absence from our lives—it all made the Killing Club too real.

Overnight, imagining murder stopped being fun. There were no more meetings. Before long, we were graduating from Hart High, headed into the future, losing touch along the way. Barclay, who had infuriated his mother by marrying my sister, flunked out of Princeton. Garth built an anti-apartheid shack on Etten Green, moved into it, got arrested, went to Princeton, hated it, transferred to NYU, went into television. He never came home to Gloria. Or so I thought.

Like many of the others, I never left. Keith Connor was ordained a Catholic priest and moved up the church ladder at Immaculate Conception after Father Cooke died to become the youngest priest to run a church that size in his diocese. Amanda got married for a living and moved up to the top of her own ladder as the wife of the CEO of Kind Lady. Others stuck closer to home: Debbie worked in her dad's bar, Ben sold insurance for his wife's father, Pudge worked in his family's restaurant. And I finished up at Rutgers and joined the Gloria Police Department, where my dad had been a cop. Joe Ferrara never made detective, never wanted to. He was a uniform, thirty-three years, till some punk robbing a convenience store put him in a wheelchair. So promotion to detective, passing him by, was a hard bar for me to clear. I'd flunked the exam twice before my dad told me I wasn't doing him any favors.

I lived at home. It's what good Italian girls do until they get married, but that wasn't why I was still there. My dad's wife had left him; I didn't want to do it to him too. Not to a guy who was in a wheelchair because he'd jumped in front of a couple of strangers to stop some crackhead from unloading an automatic at them. Dad watched a lot of movies on TV and I watched with him.

IN THE ATTIC "junk" room on the top floor of my house, I finally found the Death Books tossed behind the box I'd thought they'd be in, one labeled HART HIGH STUFF, with old programs and term papers. The attic was a mess; every time I went up there I vowed to clean it out. Dino's old junk was thrown everywhere; Clay had played up there for days on end when he was younger, and now Joe Jr. periodically ransacked the place for anything he thought he could sell on eBay.

There were three notebooks, different colors, for sopho-more, junior and senior years. As secretary, I'd kept the records. As a "saver," I'd carted them to the attic when I left for college. In the final book, I'd taped the printout I'd given everybody of the complete list of names of the club members, along with their phone numbers. My phone number was the same. The names were:

> Jamie Ferrara, Secretary
> Garth McBride, President
> Lyall Hillier, Vice President

Pudge Salerno, Treasurer

Ben Tymosz

Barclay Ober

Amanda Kean

Shawn Tarrini

Debbie Deklerk

Wendy Schumacher

Jeremy Zumwald

Keith Connor

I didn't know what had happened to Wendy and Jeremy. Like Garth, they'd moved away. Nobody had mentioned them for years. Of the six of us still living in town,
when I called them with the news about Ben, none could tell
me where Wendy and Jeremy had gone, or whether they
were married or not. I wasn't married. Garth wasn't. Debbie and of course Father Connie weren't. Barclay had married my sister. Shawn Tarrini had married Amanda, the
prettiest girl in the club, after her first husband had suddenly died of a heart attack. Shawn himself had died in a
car crash two summers ago, heading back to Gloria on the
Atlantic City Expressway. Amanda was on her third husband now.

Three of the Killing Club dead before they turned
thirty. Twenty-five percent. That was out of the norm.
Wasn't it?

On the red cover of the original Death Book, decals of
skulls, drawings of bloody daggers and the black-stenciled
words THE KILLING CLUB had faded. I'd taped my copy of
the old Yale lock key to the back of the cover. Carefully I
turned brittle pages, looking for Ben's first entry. I found it

scrawled in pencil, no more than five words to a line. It was pretty much as Pudge had described it:

MR. PAYTON

I make it look like an accident. A house fire. I go over to his house and hit him over the back of the head with a baseball bat. Then I throw him down the basement steps and he breaks his neck. Or maybe I rig a wire at the top of the steps so he trips and breaks his neck. I'm not even there. I'm somewhere with an alibi. Then I soak everything in gasoline and set the house on fire. The police figure it's an accident.

Ben Tymosz

The anonymous comments (I recognized my own handwriting on the longest one) were not complimentary: "Stupid." "Ditto." "Give me a break."

But now it was the way Ben had died.

AFTER GETTING GARTH'S NUMBER from Pudge, I sat by my bay window in the blue armchair. Downstairs I could hear Dad's TV, the easygoing lecture of The History Channel. For twenty minutes, I sat looking at the phone in my lap, sipping a glass of wine. Below me in the front hall my mom's family's grandfather clock bonged ten times. She had left the clock behind, along with everything else.

"This is dumb," I finally concluded, and dialed the Manhattan number Pudge had given me. A machine picked up quickly. A brisk woman's voice. "Ashley and Garth. Leave a message." The machine clicked off, wasting no time. It could have meant Ashley and Garth should leave a message, or Ashley and Garth wanted you to leave a message. "Ashley" sounded like she didn't care one way or the other.

I talked quickly, as if she might cut me off. "This is a message for Garth McBride. Garth, this is Jamie Ferrara. From Gloria? Pudge Salerno gave me your phone number. He thought I should call you. I don't know if you remember Ben Tymosz. But he died today in a fire. Like I said, Pudge thought you'd want to know." I couldn't think of anything to add so I mumbled, "Thanks," and punched END.

The phone rang the minute I set it back in the cradle. Was Garth just standing there in his doubtless chic Sixty-eighth Street apartment beside his answering machine? But it was Rod calling me, asking how things had gone with Pudge. We talked a while and then he said he had something new on the death of Ben Tymosz. "Gert called in from the morgue. She talked to his doctor. The guy had pancreatic cancer. She says it was pretty bad. Maybe that's what he wanted to talk to you about tomorrow, you think?"

"Oh, God. Did Megan know?"

"She said no. Said she had no idea. I called this Doctor Tischman. He says he didn't tell anybody but Ben and that Ben didn't want anybody to know about it. He said there wasn't much they were going to be able to do for him."

"Any chance it could be suicide? Depressed about it? Insurance?"

"It's too crazy a way to try. No, makes no sense. Throw yourself down the stairs? You couldn't even count on breaking your leg."

"I'll tell you what's crazier."

Rod patiently listened to me read him Ben's first entry from the Death Book, in which, a decade ago, Ben had "murdered" his geometry teacher in a basement house fire.

There was a pause while Rod thought over what I'd told him. Then he rejected my request to open an investigation. "I still say accident. So see you tomorrow. Eight okay?"

"Eight's fine. Don't buy me any sticky buns!"

"Love you lots."

"Love you too."

Rod and I meet most mornings at Broad Street Bakery. I have a black coffee and an egg-white omelet. He has sticky buns and two cappuccinos. I gain weight. Rod keeps using the same worn-out hole on an old belt. Life, as Pudge pointed out, just isn't fair.

I WENT DOWNSTAIRS to the kitchen, pulled a strip of pasta off the Dante's lasagna that I'd brought home with me and ate it as I walked down the narrow side hall to the front room. My dad was there asleep in his wheelchair, already in the pajamas and plaid robe that the nurse helped him put on after she helped him bathe. His hands rested on top of the remote control in his lap. They were hands I loved, familiar hands. They had liver spots on them now, and two of the fingers were crooked with arthritis.

As I walked in, he came immediately and fully awake. It had never been possible to slip out of the house past my father the cop. "You okay?"

"Fine, Dad."

"So how was the Ironworks? You sing Rod 'Happy Birthday'?"

"We didn't go. Maybe you heard on the news? Ben Ty-mosz?"

"Yeah, what a shame. You can't mess with electricity like that." He pointed at our Christmas tree. Like always it was a thick fat tree of crowded long-needle pine boughs. It had been in place in front of the window since December first and would stay there until the sixth of January. The tree had every ornament we'd ever owned on it, but each year my father threw out all the strings of electric lights and bought new ones at the after-Christmas sale at Solly's Drugs. "You want something else to eat, Pumpkin?"

"I'm fine, Dad. Let me ask you something?"

"Sure. One second." Not tall but big-backed and strong-armed, he wheeled into the little entryway, checked his quartz watch against the grandfather clock there. His hair was thick and bright white, wavy—giving me hope I'd go white too in another thirty years or so. "Dino back?" he asked.

"You kidding?"

My baby brother, Dino, and I still live where we grew up, where my dad grew up, on the corner of Fourteenth and Dock Streets, the bad end of town, only two blocks from the river but still out of the reach of the gentrifiers. We're at the end of the row of long, thin 1870s four-story clapboards, with a bay on each floor, so we get three sides of light. I live there because I don't want to leave my dad. Dino lives there because it's free. He works at Jonesy's Marina during the day and at night he plays rhythm guitar with a heavy metal cover band at the retro rock clubs in Atlantic City when they can get the work. Dino is always in trouble with Dad, who has no patience with his way of living hand to mouth—our hands, his mouth.

"Dino doesn't sleep, Dad, you know that."

"Your mother didn't sleep. I slept like a log."

It's been twenty-three years. He hasn't stopped talking about her. There is a studio photo of her four decades old in the curio cabinet still. "Bella DiMauro at the Poseidon Lounge, Atlantic City. Nitely." Dino probably figures he'll run into her some night. I figure she's long gone.

"Shoot," my father said. "Ask away."

I sank into the big sloppy black leather couch, Dad's extravagance that I hated and he can't sit in anymore, and pulled his wheelchair closer. "What do you think the odds are, you could write up an accurate description of how you'd die over a decade later?"

"Slim." He sipped from the one little glass of grappa he lets himself have every night. It's a ritual he likes me to share when I'm around. We clink the glasses and he says, "Tomorrow. One day at a time."

And I say, "We're doing great, Dad."

"So," he asked, "who wrote this accurate description? Ben Tymosz?" I nodded. "Why'd he write it up, how he would die? And how come you know about it?"

My dad was a cop and he asked questions, which had been a drag when I was growing up, but had probably been good training.

I told him a little bit about the Killing Club (which I'd never really talked about to him before), then I showed him Ben's entry in the Death Book. "You kids," he said. "Too much time on your hands."

We talked it through, but in the end my father agreed with Rod's view that Ben's death was a freak accident. The parallels with the Death Book were finally just a coincidence (albeit an unusual one). And as he headed for bed, he left me with his old warning. "Don't let your imagination run away with you." When I was little, he would tell me that. So often, there was a time when I was scared of my imagination, as if it could grab me out of my bed, cart me off someplace from which I couldn't find my way home. As if it had been imagination that had taken my mother away. Because why else would a mother leave her kids behind?

"Lock up," he told me. "Turn off the lights and the tree and be sure you get Sam in." Our big gray cat, Sam (named by my dad for Sam Spade in *The Maltese Falcon*), was a night prowler when he got the chance.

"'Night, Dad."

I walked back to the green pine kitchen table where my father's pill bottles (for high blood pressure, for high cholesterol, for half a dozen other problems that worried me) sat neatly on the painted wood lazy Susan, along with salt and pepper shakers, olive oil and vinegar. At this table, Dad had sat us down to tell us Mom had to go somewhere and that she'd be gone for a long time. I was six. Gina was eight. She cried. I told him I hated my mother. Dino just smiled and drooled on me. He was eleven months old. Joe Jr. was seventeen. He said she was a whore and he didn't care what she did. Dad knocked him into the refrigerator. It was the only time, as far as I know, he ever hit any of us.

My dad had a rough time for a while, and a worse one when we lost Gina, and started searching in a bottle for answers that weren't there. I think it was like losing my mother again. Gina looked like her and had tried in a way to make up for her by offering domestic gifts to my dad—flowers and candles on the table, cakes baked, towels and sheets beautifully folded. Her relationship with our father was mostly nonverbal (unlike mine) but so close that he would let her gunk up his hair with gel and comb it into different styles. Her death hit him harder than anything else in his life. The priest at Immaculate Conception, to which we'd belonged but hardly ever gone, Father Cooke, a good man, reached out for my father like he was hauling him out of the ocean, with Dad kicking at him the whole way. For months in a long, awful summer, Father Cooke came by our house almost every night, always bringing some of the beautiful roses he grew in the church garden. He just sat there with my dad, sometimes watching TV with him. Slowly the priest replaced the Scotch with his kindness.

Later on, Joe Jr. told me our mother had run off with a guy in the record business. In the years to come, I used to look for her albums in stores, but I never saw any. She had a beautiful voice. As our dad kept reminding us.

THE SHRIEK OF THE TELEPHONE scared me awake. The heavy hardcover book I had been reading fell off the bed onto the oak floor and scared me again.

"Hello?"

"Jamie? Hey, sorry. I woke you up."

"Who is this?" I don't know why I said it. I knew who it was.

"Is this Jamie Ferrara?"

"Yes."

"Sorry. This is Garth McBride. You left me a message about Ben Tymosz? About the fire?"

"Yes." I slid down out of the high bed, paced around it. "Pudge said to call you."

After a decade, it wasn't an easy conversation. We didn't know each other. I'd seen Garth a few times on the news after Martha (the woman his sister, Katie, lived with) pointed out his picture in a news ad in *TV Guide* in her dentist's office. But I wasn't sure now whether he really already had been told by his sister that I was a detective with the GPD and that I was engaged or he was just pretending he knew.

We agreed it was weird that we hadn't run into each other even once, because Garth said he took the train down to Gloria every few months, quick visits to Katie and her partner, Sweets, Martha's nickname. As for my bumping into him in New York, it wouldn't happen. On big nights Rod and I go to Philly, where he knows good places to eat and listen to music and dance.

We agreed it was weirder still that Ben should die by fire. "Lyall by water," Garth said. I'd always wondered if he had blamed himself for losing Lyall, for not knowing how far into despair his friend must have fallen. But we'd never talked about it.

I said, "That's three. Lyall. Ben. And Shawn." I told him how a few summers ago Shawn Tarrini had gone into the embankment on an expressway ramp, totaled his car, died at the scene. How he'd been alone, on the way home from A.C., apparently having had too much to drink.

"That must have been tough on Amanda," Garth said.

It was amazing. My muscles tightened with a body-memory of when I'd learned he was steadily dating Amanda Kean. Garth and I had always spent plenty of time together (I'd grown up in his house, at least five afternoons a week, after all), but the summer and fall before that, before Lyall had died, we'd actually gone out on what I'd thought of as dates—two movies, three jazz clubs, one outdoor rock concert and half a dozen coffeehouse talks—plus there'd been several sessions of mild-to-heavy petting in his car. But clearly none of it had meant as much, or had meant something else, to him.

He added, "I always figured Shawn was the one Amanda had a real thing for."

"Maybe. Shawn was her second husband. She's on her third."

"Really?"

"Really. She's got a kind of plant loyalty to her though. Like her own little union shop. All three of her husbands worked at Kind Lady. Well, the current one owns it."

"You never liked Amanda."

"Well, certainly not as much as you did." Why was I even talking about this? Calling Garth was stupid. Pudge's idea about Ben's death and the Killing Club was stupid. I was stupid.

Garth surprised me. "I'm coming home to see Katie. You call me as soon as you get some details about Ben's funeral. And look at the book."

"What book?"

"Shawn killed somebody with a car. I think he was imagining it was me. You know, because of Amanda. Have you still got the Death Books?"

"Yes."

"I figured. You always kept everything."

"Except for the stuff people stole from me, like my jazz albums."

He ignored the old accusation. "Look in the second book. Or maybe it's the third, the blue one." He'd always had an amazing memory—for some things. "See you in Gloria. Will I recognize you?"

There was a full-length mirror on a mahogany swivel stand in a corner—another of my mother's left-behinds. I checked myself out. White sleeveless T-shirt, white bikini underpants. I've always had great skin and I was in the best shape of my life. I weighed twenty-two pounds less than the last time he'd seen me. Since Garth had left Gloria for good, I'd gone to college and the police academy and had solved a dozen homicides. I'd had seven years of training in Tae Kwon Do, and in ten seconds I could put five shots from a .45 caliber pistol pretty close to a bull's-eye at twenty-five yards. "I doubt it," I said.

"Then carry a sign. 'Bye, Jamie Ferrara."

He was gone. The way he always had been gone. Vanished behind the locked door of his bedroom, around the corner of the Hart High hallway, out of town and into the crowded limitless world.

WHEN I COULDN'T sleep, I felt my way back downstairs to the kitchen, where I'd left the old spiral notebooks on the green table. The one labeled "III" was blue. Garth had been right. Shawn's last "murder" before we disbanded was a hit-and-run. In his entry, he'd described how he could hot-wire a car from Fair Deal Autos, run the car over the guy who was sleeping with his girlfriend, then steer the stolen vehicle off the steep incline at the top of Boar's Head Turnpike and walk home. As a crime, it wasn't bad. And it was so unlike the simple car crash that had really happened to Shawn that it seemed far-fetched of Garth to try to connect them. The realization made me more sympathetic to my dad's and Rod's skeptical responses to the idea that Ben Tymosz's dying in a house fire had to be connected to an imaginary fire in a club's "Death Book."

I heard tires squeal, then a long blast of a car horn, then the doorbell rang. *Bingbong, bingbong, bingbong, bingbong, bingbong.* It was two A.M. It had to be Dino, who could never remember his keys. One of his friends had dropped him off. I tried to get to the door before he hit the doorbell again and Dad started yelling from his bedroom.

I swatted Dino's outstretched finger away just in time. "Be quiet! You're going to wake up Dad!"

"Sleep of the dead. Doan worry 'bout it."

Our cat, Sam, scooted around my legs, shot through the open door and bolted down the street. He'd come back in the morning, probably with a squirrel.

"Damn it, Dino, where are your fuckin' keys?"

"Doan know." He grinned that goofy smile he'd had as an infant. I was a sucker for it. Dino looks like a stoned angel smeared with black machine oil. Tall, slim, neon-blue eyes, tight bronze-colored curls that he sprinkles gold glitter on when he performs. "It makes me stand out in the light," he tried to explain to our father. Under his parka he wore his vintage KEEP ON TRUCKIN' T-shirt with dirty cut-up jeans.

He had on a Led Zeppelin cap, his whole outfit an ad for seventies rock. His brightly painted guitar case leaned against the iron stoop rail.

"Well, for God's sake, use the key under the brick like Clay does. Okay? Don't wake people up!"

"I forgot. Merry Christmas Merry Christmas. We got anything good to eat?" He pretended to be skateboarding down the ramp built on the side of the porch stoop for our father's wheelchair.

"Dino!" It was important to say his name firmly in order to get his focus. He'd been that way since he was a baby. "Where'd you get that new black truck you were riding around in with Clay, and what were you doing with Clay anyhow?"

"Clay? Oh that was earlier, yeah. He needed a lift from a bud's." He slipped backward, caught himself on the rail. "That's Ramon's truck. You know Ramon, works with me at Jonesy's?"

"Yeah, I know him."

"I love you." He tried the grin again.

"I love you too. And I hope Ramon told you you could borrow his truck. I hope I'm not going to see your ass hauled into the station again." I pushed him ahead of me back into the house.

"Jamie, doan be so mean, 'cause I love you so much." He turned to hug me, smelling of pizza, marijuana and beer.

"Listen to me, Dino. I don't want you speeding around town with Clay. Especially when you're 'borrowing' a car from a 'friend.' And don't *ever* let me find out you're giving him beer and pot."

"Me? He's the one with the money. I get it from *him*."

"He's thirteen!"

"Yeah? That's what you think."

I was about to close the door when I noticed a manila envelope lying on the doormat. It must have fallen from inside the screen. Maybe it was what Dino had slipped on; he'd left the heavy tread of his hightops across it. There was no address on the envelope. Inside there was a single piece of cheap lined paper, torn from a spiral notebook. The words looked as if they'd been cut (some letter by letter) from a magazine and pasted on:

death has come to your little town, Sheriff

4

ROD

NEXT MORNING, before breakfast with Rod, I drove over to Glen Valley. On a gray, drizzly December morning, at seven-thirty, it was still fairly dark, but in first light Ben's gutted house looked spooky, rising in the mist behind the yellow police tape.

Inside the house I thought I saw a silhouette move past a window. I found a flashlight in the glove compartment of my Mustang, and crawled in through a side window.

"Anybody in here?"

Listening hard, I eased the .380 out of the shoulder holster I was wearing beneath my parka. Every morning at breakfast Rod asks me, "Got your gun?" (When I mentioned that Rod believed in accidents, I should have added that he believed you had to be ready for them.) I always have the gun. I was a cop's daughter. This pistol was a BF10 Olympic Magnum that my dad had given me. In a cop family, even an Italian girl can get a single-action snub-nose for Christmas.

"Police! Anybody here?"

Moving slowly through the Tymosz house, trying not to make noise, I listened hard but heard nothing. Maybe the shadow had just been the odd half-light of dawn coming. The rooms that hadn't already been boarded up with plywood were empty now. They stank of charred damp carpets. Megan's brother, who owned a local moving company, had come over last night with a truck and a crew, carted away anything that might have been worth stealing and piled the rest like a funeral pyre in the driveway.

I'd come to check out the entry to the basement.

The door itself had been removed; crossed one-by-fours had been nailed over the empty space. Down on my knees, I checked the blackened residue on the doorjambs. About six inches up from the floor, there was an almost undetectable pinhole of raw wood. Above the spot, I could feel a slight forked indentation, as if someone had used a hammer against the wood to pry out a nail. At the same level, on the opposite jamb, a nail was still visible, bent and broken, its head gone, but new. The nail was where it would have been if a wire had been stretched across the top of the stairs in order to trip someone. Like the wire in Ben's story.

I HATE THE new Gloria police station; I think I'm the only one there who does. Maybe those who moved over from the old station are right; if I'd ever had to work squeezed in with forty other cops on a single cramped drafty floor of the old town hall, with its loud clanky radiators and its flaky plaster, I too would, as Rod says, appreciate the upgrade. "I like not having to stick a curtain rod in a window to keep it from falling down on my fingers. I like doorknobs that don't come off in my hands. I like a urinal that doesn't come loose from the wall. I like—"

"Okay okay." So I don't argue with him. But the fact is, the very modern new Dixon Police Building is hideous. It's even more horrible that they squeezed this monstrosity in between the 1872 town hall (stone, neo-Gothic) and the 1834 County Courthouse (white frame, Federal). "Well, baby, you're just a weird history buff," Rod says and kisses me. Hey, if it hadn't been for weird history buffs, the Liberty Bell would be gone too.

Gloria's town hall is still where the hall of records is, rows of tall, musty, flaky leather boxes I used to look through, waiting for my dad. Even now sometimes I go there on a rainy day off. That's how I was the one who found the original London Company charter, stuck in a nineteenth-century tax assessment ledger, authorizing Captain Thomas Ricks in 1741 to strip the forests bordering Deep Port in order to build ships from the virgin oak and pine. Everyone made a fortune. While the woods are pretty much gone, the town's still here. The charter I'd found now hung in the foyer under an oil painting of Captain Ricks that Barclay's mother had commissioned of her distant relative. There was absolutely no way to know what the man had actually looked like, but that hadn't stopped Mrs. Ober. Nothing did. Except maybe, for a while, Gina.

In the new police station's detective bureau we all have

our own cubicles with our own computers, and the squad room is big and sunny with comfortable office chairs on rollers. I spun one of these chairs around in a circle because Rod was shaking his head at me. He slid my digital printouts back across the desk. I hadn't said anything to him till I'd gotten the blowups made and now I'd made my case. But I could tell it was going to be a hard sell.

He dutifully studied the magnified image of the nail hole in Ben's doorjamb. "This is why you were late to breakfast?"

"That nail was pulled out *after* the fire. Look at the coloration on the wood. And the nail still in there looks brand-new. Why would it be like that?"

Rod frowned. "Earlier today you were talking suicide for the insurance. I checked it out. It was a million-dollar accidental death policy."

". . . Okay."

"But now you're off in a different direction. Somebody trip-wired Ben, poured gasoline on him and torched his house to cover up a murder?"

"I'm just saying it's possible."

"Sure. Anything is." Rod had been curious about my story, but seemed more focused on our long-ended Killing Club meetings at the Pine Barrens Playhouse than my theory that Ben's death might have been a homicide. Apparently he shared my dad's view that the members of that club had had too much time on their hands. Especially the time I'd spent with Garth.

He asked me a little more about the club members. Pudge, Debbie and Barclay he knew pretty well because we ate at Dante's and Deklerk's, and Barclay was not only the richest guy in town, but an up-and-coming power in local politics. Amanda he'd met. Plus she was in *The Gloria Gazette* a lot, doing worthy things for the environment, and winning equestrian prizes. Garth, he'd heard of. And not just from me. (Even if you'd never seen a television, Garth's sister's partner, Martha, boasted about him all the time, and Martha had the biggest dental practice in Gloria.)

"So this guy Garth, the one you used to go out with?"

I shrugged. "Briefly."

"The one that dumped you for Amanda Morgan."

"Well, to be fair, I don't think he saw it that way. I don't think he figured there was anything *to* dump. She was Amanda Kean then. Then Bryce, Tarrini, Morgan. But yeah, that Amanda."

"What a stupid guy." It wasn't meant as a compliment. It was just, in his view, the truth. There were reasons why I was engaged to Rod Wolenski. His saying things like that was one of them. "You tell your old friend Garth about this threatening note on your front stoop?"

"I didn't get it till after I'd talked to him."

He held up the cut-and-pasted page of letters, now encased in plastic. *Death has come to your little town, Sheriff.* "This guy Garth had you thinking dreaming up murders was fun?"

"It got us through some tough times."

"I guess. The suicide. Why'd he throw himself in Deep Port River?"

"Lyall? I don't know. I think drugs were involved. Kids do it. How many times have you seen it?"

I knew Rod had seen it too often. He'd been the one telling the parents while they sat there trying to take it in.

He slid the evidence bag toward me across the big

table. "The note's a problem. Most likely somebody's just got a sick sense of humor. But talk to your 'club' members. Find out which one did it. And why. Tell them it's not funny. . . . What you and Danny got open on the board today?"

"Nothing much." Homicide is supposedly my specialty (at least I've been the primary investigator on local murders since my promotion to detective). But then, we've averaged only two homicides in Gloria a year. So usually I work a more general caseload.

"I'll talk to Pudge and the rest about the note," I promised Rod.

We kissed good-bye. He slid onto my desk edge and pulled me between his legs. We were kissing when Danny Ventura made loud porno moaning noises at the door. "Excuse me? Who's always saying 'This is a police station, no personal business'?"

Rod looked at him, his arm around me. "This isn't business."

Stepping away, I gave Danny the finger.

"You do that a lot. It's vulgar."

"Not as vulgar as you, Danny."

I waved good-bye to Rod. "I'm still going to look into Ben's death," I called to him as I headed out to take the note back down to the forensics lab.

He grinned. "No fooling."

IT WAS A QUIET AFTERNOON in the squad room. Together, Sergeant Danny Ventura and I make up the whole Investigative Division of the Detective Bureau of GPD. We investigate anything that could be a felony—robbery, domestic violence, narcotics, whatever happens in Gloria that's worse than a misdemeanor. Today we arrested two twenty-year-olds who'd run off with the Salvation Army Christmas bucket from in front of Sam's Club. Lucky for us, they'd sat in their truck in the parking lot to divide the money. Nothing much else was happening to distract me from a possible homicide.

I spoke again to the five other members of the Killing Club who still lived in Gloria. They all felt bad for Ben and were all coming to his funeral next week. They all denied sticking an anonymous note behind my screen door with a quote pasted on it from the movie *Halloween*.

The sky cleared and the afternoon was one of those brilliant winter days of blue sky, white clouds and sun. After I logged out at GPD, I decided to take a jog before getting ready for my date with Rod. It wasn't that cold and I was feeling a weird sort of restlessness coming out of a past I hadn't thought about much in a long time. I ran along Schumacher Creek, the tributary that wound beside the town cemetery, and then started up the hill. The light slanted across crooked tombstones and crosses. Near the path, my great-aunt Betty Wurtz, in her eighties, was kneeling on her green plastic gardener's knee-rest, brushing snow off the grass at a graveside. I didn't know Betty well; she was from my mother's side, the DiMauros, and my mother, as ought to be obvious, hadn't been much of a family person.

"Hey, Aunt Betty."

"Hey, sweetheart." I had no idea if she really knew who I was, or called everybody my age and younger "sweetheart."

I stopped beside her. "Were you close to Sam Lorenzo?"

"Never heard of him." She gasped, short of breath from her labor, and wiped her hands on her slacks. Her thin hair was as pink as cotton candy, and it matched her rubber boots.

I pointed at LORENZO engraved in the stone. "Well, it's nice of you to take such good care of his grave."

The small old woman scooted closer, pulling her plastic knee-rest with her. She stared through thick lenses at the letters. "Shit!"

I tugged her to her feet and, shaking her head, she made her way down the slope to the next row of graves, where her husband Isaac Wurtz was buried. I'd been told by my dad that Elizabeth DiMauro had been "thrown out of her family" for marrying a Jew. My mother had married an Italian but then had "abandoned" him, so she'd been "thrown out" of the DiMauros as well. As a child, I wasn't sure what being "thrown out" meant, but I recall that I'd agreed with the Di-Mauros' turning on my mother for deserting us, but had thought they'd been wrong to reject Aunt Betty for marrying Mr. Wurtz, even though, when I met him, the couple was already living at Harbor House, the extended-care center, and he had no legs and was very crabby.

Nearer the water, sunlight reddened the fifteen-foot marble obelisk that had been erected by the great-grandchildren of the town's founder, Captain Ricks. (They had the money to do it after razing the primeval forests of New Jersey.) Some tall guy in a long loose coat was stretching his leg on the side of the obelisk. It seemed a little disrespectful; not that Captain Ricks had anything going for him worth respecting, except that he'd been around for a couple of centuries.

I trotted up the hill toward him, then dug in my heels on the gravel path when the man suddenly turned, saw me and took off the sunglasses. His coat was cashmere, like his turtleneck (trust me, Italians know good fabric), and his blue jeans fit with the same rumpled easy perfection that Garth McBride had always managed.

"Jamie? Jamie Ferrara?"

Here's what's ridiculous. My first thought: I may be freezing but at least I'm wearing Spandex, not a sweat suit. My second thought: The weirdness of my breathing pattern is easily attributable to a long jog, not the sight of an old boyfriend who hadn't even realized he was a boyfriend.

"What are you doing here, Garth? The funeral's not till next week."

He laughed. "Yep. Jamie Ferrara. You want to say hello?"

He was always telling me I forgot to be polite. "Sorry. Hi. How are you, Garth? It's been a long time. Happy to see you. What brings you to town? Long time no see."

"Okay. Okay. I'm on vacation." He ruffled his hair, an old gesture I recognized. "You look great."

"Thanks."

"Life's good?" He seemed really to want to know.

"Life's good."

He folded his arms. "I guess so. You're a detective, you're engaged, you look great."

"That sums it up." Glancing off to the side, I noticed that near the water's edge, beneath the weeping cherry, leafless now, there was a large spray of roses leaning against Lyall's granite cenotaph, a headstone his parents had put there even though searchers had never found the body.

Silent, we walked toward the headstone. I think the last time Garth and I had been in this cemetery together was at Lyall's memorial service. I wondered if he was there blaming himself for not guessing what his best friend's problem was, for not fixing it.

It was right after Lyall died that Amanda Kean had made her major move on Garth. And he just let her. But I'd seen it coming. I'd seen them all leave together the night of that state championship football game. Garth and Amanda, with Lyall tagging along as usual, all shoving into the back-seat of Barclay's car. Already married with a child, Barclay hung out with the old crew to be around Amanda. Or so I figured. Ben was squeezed in beside Barclay next to Connie, who was to be ordained into the priesthood six years later. Connie, still in his football jersey, leaned yelling out the shotgun window, "Fuck the fucking world!!!!"

LYALL HILLIER

1974–1992
Beloved Son

I straightened the dark red roses, brushed some old snow off the rough ledge of the gravestone.

I said, "Lyall's been dead eleven years. That seems very strange, doesn't it? Eleven years."

"He missed out on a lot of crap."

We looked for a moment at the engraved name and dates. Then Garth finally shrugged, turning toward me. He was even better looking than he'd been in high school, his hair longer, his face leaner.

His eyes hadn't changed. I avoided them, studied the

roses, almost black against the white granite. "So," I asked him after another silence. "You come back early to spend the holidays with Katie and Sweets? They talk about you all the time. I saw Sweets a few weeks ago. Broken filling. She showed me an interview with you in some New York paper. Pretty ironic."

"Ironic times." He just kept looking at me.

I said, "What are you looking at?"

He smiled. "You."

"Me? Why, what's the matter?"

"Nothing. I think I came back early to see you."

Anybody who's ever sat in the first car going over a steep drop on a big roller coaster knows what I felt like.

My next mistake was looking straight back in his eyes. Then "Shit!" I told myself, sounding just like Elizabeth Di-Mauro Wurtz.

WE WERE WALKING OUT of the cemetery when we passed Aunt Betty headed for her car. She was offended when I asked her if she still had her driver's license. "You're the one needs a license. A marriage license. Why don't you marry this man here?" She poked at Garth with her plastic knee-rest. I introduced them.

She pointed back up the hill. "My husband, Isaac Wurtz, is up there. He was in real estate. He got a great deal on our plots."

Garth laughed.

"Laugh now," she told him.

5

BEN

GLORIA IS A SMALL TOWN but it has four Catholic churches. The following week Ben Tymosz's funeral took place at Immaculate Conception, the biggest and oldest—a block's worth of double-spired massive gray stones rising straight up from the sidewalk atop an incline on the other side of Etten Green from Dante's, cattycorner to the town hall.

I saw Father Keith Connor's name listed on the glassed-in announcement board to the side of the doors, now the pastor at Immaculate with two priests under him. He'd be the one leading Ben's funeral mass. Except for the very slight and I suppose stereotypic ruddiness of his drinker's face, Father Connie still had the Irish good looks and buff body that had made girls at Hart envy Mary Beth O'Faolain, with whom he'd gone steady halfway through Georgetown, at which point he'd left her to join the priesthood—to the surprise of everyone who knew him, except presumably Mary Beth. I didn't see him much, not being a churchgoer, though my dad had become a regular in the Father Cooke days.

Police business nearly made me late to the service. When I tiptoed inside, blinded after the winter light, Connie's homily about Ben's virtues was almost over. Big as it was, its vaulted roof so high and smoky with incense that you couldn't see the ceiling, Immaculate Conception was filled to capacity that morning. In the only Escada suit I ever saw at the local discount mall (was I wearing it for Ben, or for Garth?), I slipped into a side pew near the door as Connie was telling the congregation that the lavish way Ben decorated his house at Christmas, the way he played Santa Claus at the Rotarian igloo in the mall, all spoke to the generosity of his heart. The fact that Ben had carried on with both, knowing how ill he was—though he'd told no one else of his cancer—spoke to a courage that his wife Megan wanted acknowledged here today. The same courage he'd once shown on the football field of Hart High, when it had been Connie's honor to play that game with Ben. And then there we were, back at that famous game, which the whole town seemed to misremember as a victory in the state championship.

After his homily, Megan's cousin, Father Connie's old girlfriend Mary Beth, married twice since, and possibly unaware that she was still in love with a priest, sang "My Heart Will Go On." She stood in front of the casket, which was heaped with hundreds of long-stemmed pink roses that must have cost Pudge a fortune. The church itself was simply decorated for Advent, with white candles and plain green pine wreaths, and in contrast the vividness of the floral displays was like a reminder of what an extravagant waste death could be.

Ben's widow sobbed herself hoarse in her brother's arms. Her two little girls looked at her, puzzled. Ben's mother, herself a widow, reached out to embrace them.

I couldn't find Garth in the crowd. It had been four days since our meeting near Lyall's grave, and I wondered if he hadn't hung around for the funeral after all, but had instead gone back to New York. Since he'd made that stomach-churning remark to me in the cemetery ("I think I came back early to see you"), I hadn't heard from him. He'd just smiled and walked away—the way he always had.

There were dozens of Rotarians seated in one cluster of the old wood pews. In another, near the front, sat what looked like a reunion of the surviving members of the Killing Club: Pudge, with his whole extended family, was close to Megan. Not far from Pudge I saw Amanda and Debbie—a study in contrasts: Amanda wore a sable hat and Debbie had spiked purple-black hair. Seated behind Amanda, and periodically leaning forward to whisper to her, sat my rich, perfectly dressed former brother-in-law, Barclay. He was having a rough time with his son, Clay. My nephew has my sister's eyes; that may be why I always feel a surge of affection whenever I see him. Clay had grown four inches from age twelve to thirteen; he'd gone from chunky child to thin teenager and was now as tall as his father. He was making it clear he didn't want to be at the funeral. Barclay kept hauling him out of a slouch so deep you couldn't see his head from the rear of the pew. Clay kept slowly sinking again out of view. It was an old family war. There'd been a time when Barclay had slugged it out with his mother, Gloria's grand dame Meredith Etten Ober, in even more dramatic ways—like marrying Gina—but they'd long since called a truce. Mrs. Ober hadn't had to push her son into local politics; he'd flung himself there as if across the tape at a finish line. His almost clichéd good looks (like a cross between Christopher Reeve and a Ken doll), with his toothy smile and jutting chin, could be seen in the local paper at least once a week. It was obvious to me that some party was going to run him for some office sooner or later. Sooner, if his mother had her way.

After Connie swung the thurible over Ben's casket, the pallbearers gathered to hoist it by its shiny brass rails. That's when I saw Garth. He was one of the pallbearers, bent to the labor of lifting the heavy box, standing between Barclay and Pudge. Once they'd maneuvered the coffin into the hearse, Garth surprised me by crossing over to Connie, moving him away from the crowd the priest was greeting as they left. I could see that some people had recognized Garth and were pointing him out to each other. Alone at the edge of the steps, the two men fell into an intense whispered argument. It looked intimate, which also surprised me. I wouldn't have thought they'd have anything to say to each other. Barclay left off shaking hands with everyone who passed him, as if he were hosting a fund-raiser, in order to join Garth and Connie, pushing his way between them.

A kind of competitive shoving match had always gone on between Barclay and Garth back at Hart High. Garth had brains, Barclay had money. For a while they were wrestling over Amanda Kean; neither one of them had kept her for long. Garth took Manhattan instead. Barclay had already married my sister, having gotten her pregnant, which none of us knew at the time of the wedding, when he inherited the family business. And Amanda married an executive at Kind Lady Cosmetics who was twice her age and who died of a heart attack within a year (I confess I did not stop myself from joining in the jokes about him at Deklerk's bar).

The birth of Barclay (Clay) Ober, Jr., was a Gloria scandal at the time; here was Barclay, heir to the Ober money and the Etten heritage, just graduated high school, marrying a cop's pregnant daughter, breaking his mother's heart. "You ruined his college experience, if not his entire future," Mrs. Ober often told my sister after Barclay flunked out of Princeton and had to go to a local college. After Gina died, Barclay married Patricia Hunt, the Philadelphia deb his mom had picked out for him in the first place. "You can't fight city hall," Pudge said of the news.

Connie led Garth and Barclay back inside the church, and I slipped through the huge doors behind them, followed them quietly as they moved along a side aisle and out the chancel door. It led to a little cloistered rose garden, now put to bed for winter. There was not much left of what had once been old Father Cooke's obsessive pride (his "vanity fair," he'd called it): dozens of different varieties of roses of all colors. It was where the priest had been found dead of a heart attack, and now it was dedicated to his memory. I cracked the door enough to peek through. On a wooden bench beside a now frozen birdbath, Garth sat studying his stretched-out legs. Barclay and Connie stood close by, both talking at once, arguing with Garth. They were too far away for me to hear what they were saying.

We all went from the cemetery to the reception at Ben's mother's house. Christmas was only a few weeks away and there were lots of Christmas cards strung on red yarn between the sunroom and the kitchen. In the living room, a large tree stood completely bare. News of Ben's death had stopped the decorating. The tree actually looked pretty with nothing on it. From the large sliders of their sunroom, you could see the white Georgian front of the Ober estate across the river, on the eastern—the society—side of the banks. The Obers, apart from Barclay and Clay, were not attending this event. There was no room for them anyhow. Certainly not around the food, two long tables full of it, everything (like the tables themselves, like the signature pink roses) from Dante's, donated by Pudge, and served by his waiters, though he kept coming back himself to make sure the heating pans stayed heaped with lasagna, cacciatore, marsala and the dozen other dishes, platters and Crock-Pots.

It was even more crowded in the kitchen, where Pudge was also working the bar; in shirtsleeves, his tie tight on his neck, his cheeks flushed and sweaty, he was opening wine bottles with a graceful speed, one after another.

A solemn reminder of the occasion in his black suit and shirt with his starched priest's collar, Connie offered me a glass of Chianti and refilled his own. We clinked our glasses. "Great eulogy."

"Thanks."

"To Ben."

"To Ben," he said and toasted the ceiling. Connie's body

was so trim and muscular (like a gymnast's) that his prematurely gray close-cropped hair looked like a strange style decision. "I feel bad for his poor girls. He was a great dad."

"Yes." I nodded. "Seems odd he was doing so badly."

"Badly?"

"In business." I gestured. "If only half the people in this house had bought insurance from Ben, why was his business failing?"

Connie shook his head. "It's easier to come to a funeral."

"Isn't that kind of cynical for a priest?"

"Who better?" He smiled. "But there's always salvation, Giovanna Ferrara. There's always the Church. Every Sunday. Eight, nine thirty and eleven A.M. It's just sitting there, waiting for you."

"Don't start, Connie. I haven't been to Mass in five years."

He laughed. "You're telling me?"

"It's just a struggle to get Dad there in the chair. And the whole thing for him was, no offense, sort of personal. He was close to Father Cooke."

"A wonderful man," Connie said, frowning at the memory of his sweet-hearted predecessor at Immaculate Conception.

We talked a while about Ben. Connie wouldn't say when he'd learned that Ben had been diagnosed with cancer, or whether he'd known if Ben and Megan were happy. A few years back there'd been another priest at Immaculate Conception, who had been a notorious gossip. Because this man's name was Weatherall, he'd been known as Father Tell-it-all. After Father Cooke died of his heart attack, the church had gotten rid of Weatherall, his presumed successor, and promoted Connie to pastor instead. Maybe that was why it was impossible to get anything out of Connie now. Keeping secrets was good for your career.

"Well, come on, Connie, at least tell me what you were arguing about afterward. You and Barclay and Garth? That argument after the service." I didn't tell him I'd followed them into the garden.

"Argument? We weren't arguing." He blinked, kept blinking. Probably wasn't aware he was doing it. Lying can't be easy on priests.

"What were you talking about?"

"Oh, I don't remember." He shrugged. "Just Ben, I guess. How hard it'll be on his kids and Megan. There was no argument." He blinked again. "Death's a part of life, but Ben was too young."

"Twenty-nine's young," I agreed. "Sometimes it doesn't feel that way. Like, look, you've got gray hair."

He rubbed his short gray cut. "Yeah, one of the parishioners pointed that out. I looked in the mirror. I couldn't believe it." He gestured at the food. "Really nice of Pudge. And all those roses at the funeral."

Debbie stepped up to us. "Those pink roses? Pudge told me he gets them wholesale from South America and they don't have any smell."

I said, "I'll tell you who had beautiful roses. Father Cooke, right, Connie? He always brought my dad some."

He smiled. "Come to church this summer; they'll be there. So, Garth's back for a while?"

"I have no idea."

"Yeah," Debbie said.

We both looked over at Garth. He was standing beside

Amanda. Okay, she was one of those perfect Grace Kelly blondes, somebody Cary Grant might call by the nickname Slim in one of the old movies my dad gets me to watch with him on cable. Both of them wore loose black jackets, as if they'd coordinated beforehand. They stood just outside the sunroom, leaning against the side of the double slider door, indifferent to the cold, shading their eyes with sunglasses in the hard December light.

Rod arrived late from his budget meeting with the chief, apologizing with a kiss. When I pointed Garth and Amanda out to him, he said, "So that's Garth."

"Yep. And Amanda."

"They look like they're posing for a Beemer ad."

I laughed. "You're right. BMWs or maybe an expensive cruise to Barbados?"

"So how long is this thing going on here? Almost over?"

Rod didn't like to stand around indoors. Cocktail parties, receptions, banquets—he didn't enjoy them. He preferred to be "doing something." It was one of the things we had in common. "I'd rather knock open a hornets' nest in a tool shed," he told me the day we met at a buffet at Chief Waige's. It wasn't that he was impatient; one of his hobbies was tying fly-fishing lures. He'd bring his kit over and work on a Davy's Caddis while I was keeping my dad company at the television. And on a stakeout Rod could sit without moving for hours. But ten minutes in this kind of crush of chatter and canapés, and he was inching toward the door.

Garth and Amanda finally came back inside.

"I guess Jim couldn't make it," Rod said to me.

I smiled, swinging an imaginary golf club at him. "Guess not." Jim Morgan was Amanda's third husband; he was retired from running Kind Lady and now compulsively devoted himself to improving his drive or his putt, or whatever golf flaw he was obsessing about whenever anyone asked him how he was doing. Either that, or he'd died suddenly, like Amanda's other two husbands.

"You want to meet Garth?"

Rod shook his head. "All I want's for that guy to go back to New York City." He brushed his lips across my hair. "You ready to go?"

"Just about."

The reception was pretty much over. But as we started out, Rod got snagged by the head of the Industrial Commission, a group of Gloria boosters eager to sell town property to developers. This man was a serious bore; I was slowly backing away from the conversation (to Rod's amusement) when I heard a bottle smash loudly off in the kitchen. It was an excuse to leave.

I pushed my way through the crush. Megan Tymosz was screaming, "*Shut up, Pudge! Just shut the stupid hell up!*"

Ben's widow stood staring down at the broken glass on the floor as if it made no sense to her, though clearly she'd either thrown it or dropped it. Three different people bent over quickly to pick up the pieces of glass. Clay watched them all with the contemptuous boredom with which teenagers view adults. Pudge tried to apologize but Megan would hear nothing of it.

"My girls are right here. They could hear you!" She pointed at her daughters, who were playing a soft uninspired duet on the white spinet in the living room, and couldn't possibly have heard Pudge. Megan wobbled fast on her stiletto heels past us out of the kitchen. Because of her recent weight gain, she was starting to look, it struck me, like a fun-house-mirror version of Amanda's blond perfection—her body shortened, wider; her face and hair distorted, badly colored.

Sam Deklerk, divorced co-owner with his sister Debbie of Deklerk's Bar, hurried out of the room after Megan. I leaned around the corner, watched him follow her down the carpeted hall and into a room at the end of the house. He closed the door behind him. That was odd.

I went back to see Pudge. Barclay and Connie stood around him now. "What's Megan's problem?" I asked. They all gave me a look. "That's stupid. I mean, I know. But why is she yelling at you, Pudge?"

He wiped his rosy face on a large cloth napkin with the Dante's *D* on it. "Because I told her somebody murdered Ben and she shouldn't let you guys in the police just drop the ball."

"For God's sake, why'd you do that? It's the funeral reception!"

"Because it's true! We've got to do something!"

Obviously Pudge had already shared his opinion with the other old members of the Killing Club, because neither Connie nor Barclay looked at all shocked by his accusation, although neither appeared to take it seriously. Barclay in fact laughed. "Pudge, drop this stupid idea."

Connie nodded. "It'll just upset her."

Even I told him, "Leave it alone for now. Why freak her out?"

Pudge shook his head at us, disappointed. "What's upsetting her is he's dead! Come on, Jamie, you read the Death Book. We're going to leave it alone that a friend of ours was maybe murdered?"

"No one but you thinks he was." Connie spoke with a calm reasonableness, even if already a little slurred of speech. His eyes were slightly bloodshot. Oddly I recalled a girl at Hart High calling him Kurt Cobain for a while because his eyes, she said, were so sad and blue. Now he'd added a decade of drink and his eyes had little pouches that hadn't been there before. Not enough drink to hurt his career. From everything I heard, he was headed big places in the Church.

Pudge, himself one of Connie's great admirers, now turned angrily to the priest. "Did you ever stop to think that this is only the beginning? That maybe we're *all* in danger? Somebody put an anonymous note in Jamie's door. What do you think it means? '*Death has come to your little town, Sheriff*'?"

Barclay laughed again. "I think it's a joke. That stupid club was back in high school! Why would somebody kill Ben now?"

"I don't know!" Pudge yanked the plastic wrap off a huge antipasto platter. "That's what the police are for!" Hoisting the tray over his head, above the crowd, he wove his way into the sunroom.

And Pudge hadn't even been told about the new nail holes I'd found in the Tymosz basement entrance. The truth was, I thought he was right. Ben had been murdered. But I was the only other person who seemed to think so.

Garth and Amanda joined us as I was talking to Debbie Deklerk, still a good friend of mine. Amanda and I hugged without meaning it. I asked how her husband was. She smiled coolly.

Clay, who'd stood alone at the food table, eating pieces

of cheese, came over beside us while Barclay was boasting to Garth about how extensively he'd managed to travel the world without ever getting jet lag because of intelligent planning and the comforts of first class. Barclay paused in his self-congratulation to improve Clay's posture by pulling on his arm. Then he told his son that his shoes were untied and that he shouldn't be wearing sneakers to a funeral anyhow. Into his teens, Clay's complexion had stayed flawless, like Gina's, but now his father's insults turned it a horrible mottled purple. Barclay didn't seem to notice as he turned back to tell Garth that he had accumulated two hundred thousand frequent flyer miles but was too busy to use them. Clay walked away. A few minutes later, I saw him out in the yard, smoking pot and taking photos with the small digital camera he carried everywhere.

For a while the group talked about the club, about Pudge's theory that Ben's death had been caused by some psychopath who'd gotten hold of copies of the old Death Books. Garth liked the idea, but admitted it was because he was in the business of selling the news and that it was a hot headline. No one else thought it made sense. I kept my mouth shut. Most people had left the reception by then. Amanda offered Garth a ride to his sister Katie's. He accepted. The fact that they were leaving together appeared to annoy the hell out of Barclay, who stomped out looking for Clay. Rod left right after Garth did. I said I'd meet him later. Megan and Sam were still missing, off in that room at the end of the hall, and I wanted to ask her some questions.

Barclay took Ben's mother into the living room, where they sat together talking on the couch. He did most of the talking while she nodded. Finally he slid a checkbook out of his jacket pocket and wrote her a check. She nodded numbly. I assumed the check was to help with the funeral expenses.

Finally the last guests wandered away, including all the members of the Killing Club who'd come together after eleven years because of the death of Ben Tymosz, whom no one but Pudge had really cared about all that much.

EVERYBODY LOVED Ben. You know that, Jamie! What enemies? He didn't have any enemies. There wasn't a mean bone in his body. People walked all over him." Megan sat on the fake French provincial couch in Ben's mother's living room. Her girls watched television in the sunroom.

I'd waited out Sam Deklerk. After he'd left the bedroom at the end of the hall, I'd knocked on the door, telling Megan I needed to talk to her. She explained that she'd been "overcome," and that Sam, a friend of Ben's, was "trying to help."

I asked her about Ben's past membership in the Killing Club. Today was the first time she'd ever heard of it.

"Pudge is crazy. I love him but he's crazy." Megan moved to a gas fireplace of plastic logs, pulled aside the chain curtain and blew the smoke from her long mentholated cigarette up the chimney. "I can't smoke in his mom's house," she explained. "You don't go for this stupid idea, do you? Somebody killed Ben?"

I'd already asked Megan if she'd really known nothing, as she'd told Rod, about Ben's illness. No; it had been a complete shock. She'd known that his cholesterol and blood pressure were through the roof, but he'd kept from her that he'd had tests done and had something as awful as pancreatic cancer. I asked her about their finances. They were fine—no, they were in terrible debt and business wasn't good. As for their happiness together, they were fine; they were fine, everything was fine. Except he hadn't told her he had cancer.

She edged away from me when I asked her more details about the last day of Ben's life. Was there anything out of the ordinary going on?

Nothing. They'd had coffee and cereal for breakfast. Ben yelled at the dog. Kristie was crying because she wanted to wear her pink jeans and they were still wet in the washing machine. Megan drove the girls to the school bus stop at the end of the street. Ben went (she assumed) to his office downtown. C. R. O'Brian Insurance. (C. R. O'Brian was Megan's father.) She had called him at the office just before noon. He'd said he was having lunch with Barclay Ober, to discuss increasing Barclay's personal insurance. He was happy about that, but Megan could give no other details. Ben didn't talk with her much about work.

She saw her husband around five thirty that evening, but only in the driveway. He was driving up as she was leaving to take the girls to their friend's birthday party. The last she saw of Ben, he had called to her to wait at the curb so Kathie and Kristie could watch the house and yard light up when he plugged in the garage outlet. He waved to them, pointing up at the reindeer rocking along the roof ledge.

Tearing up, Megan put out the cigarette in the saucer on her lap.

"And then you went to exercise at the new gym in Appleton Mall?"

"Yes." She looked furtive. "I mean, I didn't take a class or anything, just by myself."

"No, you didn't take a class. I checked."

Now Megan looked scared and indignant both; it confused her facial muscles. "You checked?"

I waited. It had turned dark outside. Ben's mother came sadly to the door, asked if we wanted anything. Christmas lights came on in the houses across the street. "Well, you didn't look to me like you'd come from a gym workout. You looked pretty dressed up." I kept waiting. Sometimes all you have to do is wait; it was a good lesson my dad had taught me about police work.

I could see guilt and the desire to give up already in her face, fighting against the secret. Sometimes you have to help. "So, how long have you and Sam Deklerk been seeing each other?"

She gave denial a try, but couldn't hang on to it for more than ten minutes of my questioning her. They'd been having an affair since the end of the summer. "It's only been a few months," she kept insisting, as if that brevity somehow made it less a betrayal of Ben. She loved Ben. I believed her when she said it. But life was too stressed and too strapped, and Sam was nice to her, and Ben was so unhappy and withdrawn and secretive (and now she knew why) and Sam was fun. And finally she admitted that she'd been with Sam at his apartment that night. She was having sex with another man at the very moment Ben died. That (curiously certain) fact was going to haunt her for the rest of her life! If she'd just come back home when she was supposed to, if she'd never gone to see her lover because he'd begged her to, her children would still have their father on Christmas morning. She flung herself on the couch beside me, whispering harshly.

"Don't tell anyone, Jamie. Please, don't let my kids find out I was cheating on Ben."

Her daughters were six and seven years old. "Jesus, Megan, I'm not going to tell your kids. But I do have to check it out."

Either her confession or this news let loose in Megan a keening so loud that her little girls ran into the living room, flinging their arms around her, crying too, shoving me to the edge of the couch as they embraced their mother.

I left them to comfort her, and drove over to Deklerk's Bar, where Sam protected Megan's reputation a lot longer than she had herself.

6

CONNIE

THE NEXT NIGHT Rod and I finally made it to the Ironworks Inn for his birthday dinner. He had what he always orders on special occasions: shrimp cocktail. Porterhouse steak, rare. The waiters put a candle in his mud pie and sang "Happy Birthday" to him. We each had a glass of champagne and toasted the holiday season. I gave him his present: tickets for the two of us to Baja, scuba diving, photographing sharks and whales, kayaking, drinking wine. We'd done two diving trips to the Caribbean already, but had never been to the West Coast. "Okay, Wolenski. Promise me, you're going to take this vacation. In the spring. No more postponements?"

"Make it a honeymoon, you got a deal. Promise. You.

Me. Ocean. Hotel. Wine. Good." He held up his hand, looking so much like an Indian agreeing to a treaty in a John Wayne movie that he made me laugh out loud.

Like always, the Ironworks was crowded with human complications, the way small towns are. Coming in, I saw the widow Megan Tymosz and her lover, Sam Deklerk, having dinner with Father Connie, who was in a sports jacket but wearing his collar and who actually had a little black missal on the table next to his scotch as if he were going to lead them in prayer. The adulterers were talking in fast urgent whispers; he was nodding sympathetically. Sort of a surf-and-turf confessional, I suppose.

On the way to our table, two different couples spoke to me about seeing me at Ben's funeral, how nice it had been. Would his family be all right?

It turns out his family would be fine. Ben had no retirement savings, but he had taken out a very nice life insurance policy on himself, as one might expect of an insurance agent (fortunately, well before he'd been diagnosed with terminal cancer); it paid off double on accidents. Rod and I talked briefly about the possibility that Megan (with or without the help of her lover, Sam) had strung a trip wire across the top of her basement steps, pushed her husband down them and then set fire to the house in order to collect that insurance.

"I don't see it happening," I admitted. "Even if she'd known he might be dying anyhow, and figured she'd get double the money if she killed him. I don't think she'd do it."

Rod nodded. "You started all this."

"I started that *somebody* killed him. I don't see it's Megan. Cheating on Ben was bad enough. She's gained ten pounds."

Rod set down his coffee cup in order to follow my logic. The man drank coffee day and night; it seemed to have no effect on his even temperament. "Okay. From guilt about the affair?"

"Look at her over there. She's eating a hot fudge sundae."

"Couldn't she be eating a sundae because she *did* kill him?"

"Go ahead. Make fun, Wolenski. How many homicides have there been in Gloria since I got promoted? Who closed every single one of them but the third one? And I still swear to God, Arthur Fishton killed his wife."

"We didn't prove it. . . . Okay, then Megan's out. She was with Sam Deklerk, just like he said."

Your lover's word was not much of an alibi, admittedly. On the other hand, Sam's condo neighbor had been nosy enough to notice Sam kissing Megan at his door at 6:15 P.M. that night, and then kissing her good-bye in the entryway again at 9:40. You have to be a lot more vigilant than they were to carry off a private affair in a town no larger than Gloria.

And speaking of adulteresses (or so I'd always supposed), Amanda Morgan (whom I hadn't seen for months and now couldn't seem to escape) came into the Ironworks with her husband, Jim, the retired CEO, just as we were leaving. She wore a sable coat that dropped in furry waves almost to her feet. That kind of coat takes guts these days. It stood out more because her husband and she were both so tan. They said they'd been on their boat in Naples, Florida. Hands jammed in his blazer, Jim gave us a long description of his birdie on the seventeenth hole of some golf course down there. Amanda looked patiently bored; she certainly had to be used to it.

"Nice to see Garth back." She smiled at me.

"Isn't it?"

Then she turned around so Rod could help her off with her sable, as her husband had made no effort to do it. He must have retired from Amanda as well as Kind Lady and anything else in his life besides golf. Rod had the height and quick reflexes to keep the heavy coat from dropping to the floor.

"So, Jamie . . ." Her smile was worth twenty thousand dollars; I'd gotten the estimate from Martha the dentist. "I hear you think somebody's killing the Killing Club. Maybe we should get in touch with Jeremy and . . . what was her name?"

"Wendy. Wendy Schumacher. I did. I tracked them down. One's in Portland, one's in Atlanta. They haven't killed anybody and nobody's killed them. Or so they say." I smiled back. It was cheaper, but all mine.

BACK HOME, my dad was watching the Yankees beat the Red Sox on ESPN Classic in some game that had been won years ago. He likes the past better; he wasn't in a wheelchair. He hit mute to ask me if I was still playing the homicide angle on Ben's house fire. I told him I wasn't sure anymore, that Rod had told me to drop it.

"Well, maybe you don't argue with the boss?"

"Why not? Didn't I argue with you?" I gave his white hair a quick rub. "Didn't I drive you crazy arguing with you?"

He grinned. "You were a pistol. Gina cried. You got mad. Here's an idea." It had occurred to my father that those cut-out letters in the envelope spelling out the line from *Halloween* had belonged to my brother Dino. Had I asked him about them? No, I hadn't seen Dino in days. I'd assumed the message from the movie had been left for me, because we'd used that line almost like a catchphrase in the Killing Club. But maybe Dino had heard the phrase on his own, and had copied it out because he was getting a stencil made for a T-shirt. He liked anything retro.

Dad told me Dino was subbing somewhere here in town tonight. As to where, all he could come up with was the name of a German airship. When I got him to the words *Graf Zeppelin,* I knew what to do. I called around town and learned that Deklerk's Bar had Dino doing Led Zeppelin covers solo because their band had bailed on them.

After changing my clothes, I drove over there around ten, taking with me a Xeroxed copy of the anonymous note. It was only five blocks from our house to Deklerk's, and as it turned out, maybe I should have walked.

SURE ENOUGH, I spotted Dino behind his double-fretted metal guitar up on a small black dais that was strung with chili pepper Christmas lights. In bell-bottoms, with his smooth, thin, bare chest exposed under a jacket embroidered with sequined flowers and birds, my brother looked about fifteen. I had to wait for his solo to end. It looked to me as if most of the other patrons at Deklerk's were doing the same thing, even though poor Dino was tamped way down on the amplifier. His long curls bouncing and sparkling with glitter, his eyes rolled back in a hazy stare, I guessed he was pretending to be Jimmy Page and in Gloria he could almost get away with it.

"Jamie, you came to hear me, that's so cool! This is my sister." He showed me off to two guys at a table near the dais; they were around his age, dressed like him, and appeared to be just as stoned. "She's a big-time cop, I swear. Don't do blow around her, she'll bust you, I swear!" They all three laughed crazily together.

Dino loved the cut-out message, *"Death has come to your little town, Sheriff,"* but he said he'd never heard it before. He hadn't noticed the envelope lying on the stoop, nor did he remember my ever talking to him about the Killing Club.

"Cool. I could put that for you know like my logo on my jacket here. I'll tell you one thing, this is a little town! I gotta go. I got another gig in A.C. This place sucks. I love you." He rubbed his curls in my face the way he had at three years old. A few little gold glitter specks stuck to my cheek.

Debbie Deklerk was working the bar. She had smart pale gray eyes in a wide Polish face. Just like at Hart High, Debbie wore a stud in her nose, her purplish black hair in a spiky comb-up, her nails the color of her hair and six rings in her left ear. Solid and shapely, she showed off her breasts in a tight, low-cut, apple-green pullover. Three gold necklaces fell into her cleavage. I asked her where her brother, Sam, was. In fact, I knew where he was (he'd left the Ironworks with Megan), but I just wanted to see what she would say.

"No idea," she said, preoccupied. "Jamie, I want you to stop all this Killing Club crap. It's creeping me out. You got everybody doing it now." She pointed me toward a back booth.

It was certainly my night for old club feelings. Hunched over mugs of beer in the booth, Garth sat with Connie, who was now wearing a sweater and jeans and had lost the missal. The two men looked intensely unhappy and I wondered if they were carrying on their argument from the church steps the day before. They'd never really gotten along. They'd both loved movies and never liked the same ones. They'd each thought they were smarter.

Debbie gave a long mock sigh. "That's a lot of prime beef to keep off the shelves."

"Father Connie?"

"Both of them. And don't start thinking otherwise, Jamie." Leaning over the bar, she tapped down hard on my hand with her square purple nails. "Look at me. Look at me! You know how they flash all those lights and clang those bells at an intersection when a train's coming?" She cupped her pale ear with its half dozen earrings, turning it in my direction. "That's what you're hearing, Sergeant Ferrara. *Clang clang clang!*"

I showed her my engagement ring.

"Hey, I'll take it!" She sighed. "I'm ready."

I interrupted Garth and Connie in their booth, giving a significant look at the young priest. "Hi, guys. What are you arguing about now?"

They said, "Nothing," and didn't ask me to join them.

I did anyhow. "So, Connie, I just saw you a little while ago at the Ironworks. With Megan and Sam."

The priest sidestepped me. "Rod's birthday, wasn't it? You two looked like you were having fun."

"Always. So now you're here at Deklerk's. Real night on the town for you."

Connie remained noncommittal. "For you too, I guess."

I asked them again what they'd been talking about so seriously. They told me, just politics. "Pro-Church and anti-State," Garth said.

Connie finished his beer quickly and slid out of the booth. He had to go; he had early Mass. Did Garth want that ride home to his sister's now?

Garth gave me the smile I used to live for. "How about you give me a lift, Jamie? That okay?"

Was I going to tell him no? That I didn't want to be enclosed in a small space with him even if the space was moving? I said, "Sure."

Both men were very attractive; Connie was better built, Garth had better features. Both men were hiding something from me. "So, guys." I tried again. "Who do you think murdered Ben?"

Simultaneously Connie said, "Nobody," and Garth said, "Maybe whoever killed Shawn Tarrini. Maybe Shawn was murdered." He shrugged in a take-it-or-leave-it way.

"Nobody killed Shawn Tarrini," Connie insisted. "What's wrong with you people? It was a car accident. See you around."

"Or not," Garth said.

A woman at the bar, looking for love and drunk enough to grab it as it passed her, hit on Connie. He brushed her off with a practiced kindly maneuver and walked out.

Garth wondered if our "priest buddy" ever succumbed to temptation.

I shrugged. "It's none of our business."

"Whoa. What's your problem? I just think the diocese ought to encourage him; take the press off messing up little boys." I didn't answer. Finally, pointing at the dais, he added, "Your brother's not very good, is he?"

"Dino? He's perfectly fine." Nobody was going to trash Dino but me. On the table, about six plastic straws had been intricately twisted into Celtic-looking designs, I assumed by Connie. "What's really going on with you and Connie? You two and Barclay in a huddle. You don't like Barclay. Is it something about Ben?"

Garth twisted his head back and forth a while, as if he had a crick in it. "No. Guy stuff. Like you say, none of your business."

"Fine." I looked at him for a minute. "Onto the next question. What did you mean, you came back early for me? What was that supposed to mean?"

He grinned. "I wanted to see you. See what you look like. You look great." I slid out of the booth, away from him. "Where're you going, Jamie?"

"You want that ride to Katie's now?"

"Looks like it's now or never." He said it to my back, as I was halfway to the door by then.

GARTH'S LESBIAN SISTER, Katie, had been my sister's best friend. In retrospect I wondered if Katie had ever been in love with Gina. I know she was upset Gina had married Barclay. But then so was I. Gina and Katie were always sketching and painting and sculpting together. They went to a small fine arts college nearby, though Gina quit after a year, when Clay was born. Now Katie teaches junior high art in town. After my sister died, Katie gave me a watercolor she'd painted of Gina standing in a blue forest. I had it on the wall of my bedroom.

For eight years now Katie has lived with Martha, a divorced dentist, who's a little bit older. They live down a dirt road in the woods west of town. When Garth and I got there (and we got there fast), the white pickup truck and white Volvo parked side by side meant both women were home. Behind a garden of staked teepees that in summer held up tomatoes and peas, a pyramid-shaped garage served as Katie's studio. Now it was bordered in white Christmas icicle lights. Katie's glazed psychedelic papier-mâché sculptures of nudes stood around the yard like an Amazon army at ease.

A friend of theirs had designed the house for them and they'd named it Chelsea Morning for the Joni Mitchell song. It was once considered experimental. Now it looks dated, more dated, ironically, than the eighteenth-century saltboxes on Front Street. But they loved it. Everything was built of red and orange woods. There were solar heat panels on the roof, and a long side room with nothing but a pool in it that was called, for tax purposes, a "thermal storage unit." The bedroom was a geodesic dome with a free-form stone chimney in its middle. There was too much furniture and half a dozen cats sleeping on it.

Katie hugged me, shushing me with a finger. Martha, who had one of the cats in her lap, lay asleep on the couch in front of a crackling log fire. Enya was singing softly from the stereo.

"Sweets works so hard," Katie explained. "She just conks out."

I don't know why everyone calls Martha, who is thin,

Sweets. Maybe because she tells her patients not to eat candy. True, she had her hands in other people's mouths ten hours a day, and that had to wear you out. More so than teaching teenagers to glue together collages the way Katie did? Hard to say.

Three years can make a big difference when you're two and someone else is five. One of my first memories is of five-year-old Katie lugging me around in her arms; another is of her teaching me how to make a *J* for Jamie. So I still felt about Katie McBride the way most of her students had for ten years. Even Clay told me she "wasn't too bad."

She led us back into the large, round, cinnamon-smelling kitchen. She wore big furry sheepskin boots and a red oversized hand-knit sweater with a Christmas tree on it as green as her eyes. "So, the Prince formerly known as Garth got you to drive him all the way out here?"

"No trouble. I was hoping you'd still be up."

"I'm always up. He's a celebrity. Why doesn't he rent a car? Why do we have to drive him places?"

Garth said that talking about the news late at night didn't make you a celebrity. Ask ten people in the supermarket; none of them would have heard of him. A celebrity was somebody people knew about in the supermarket.

"In Gloria, they know you in the supermarket," Katie assured him. "And in the dentist's office too."

He hugged her till she broke loose. "Okay, in Gloria I'm a celebrity."

Katie told him that his girlfriend, Ashley, had called and wanted him to turn on his cell phone. I could see that Katie didn't like Ashley. When Garth went back to the guest room to call her, she said so. "I don't like that Ashley. I liked the last one. This one I don't like." Then, alternating hands as if she were firing two guns, she shook her forefingers at me. "Do not, do not, let him get to you."

"Don't be stupid, Katie." I held up my left fist to show her the engagement ring I wore, but I admit it looked more like I was going to sock her for giving me a warning I needed.

Garth came back to the kitchen accompanied by Sweets, who claimed she was wide awake now, but then, yawning, drifted off to their bedroom ten minutes later, after asking me how my new filling was doing.

The three of us left shared a glass of wine together, catching up, reminiscing about Gloria, going back to our day-care days. A few years ago, Garth and Katie's mother had died of emphysema. "She smoked," Katie said, pointing at Garth. "Don't."

"I don't." He shrugged at me.

"Yes, you do. They fell out. I was doing your laundry."

"What are you doing my laundry for, Katie? Good God."

Taking my glass over to the big soapstone sink, where a Christmas cactus was soaking, I was about to announce my departure—I was a third wheel in their sibling spats, and could go have my own, especially with Joe Jr., whom I don't even like. Then I noticed two paper collages held by magnets of Botticelli's *Venus* to the refrigerator door; one of them had letters in it.

"Would you look at this for me?" I showed Katie the copy of the anonymous message that I'd stuffed in the pocket of my jeans. "Somebody left this at my front door."

"That's sick. What does it mean?"

"I don't know. I think it's about the Killing Club. Remember? Our old club."

Garth came over to look at the piece of paper. "It's our slogan." Rolling his eyes, he dropped his voice to a rumble. "Death has come to your little town, Sheriff."

Katie kept studying the helter-skelter letters, turning the paper this way and that, tugging at her long, straight, brown hair. "Absolut."

"What?"

"I think some of these letters are from Absolut ads. I'm always pulling pages from those glossy magazines, you know. For us to use at school for collages? This font looks like the Absolut ads. But is it a real threat?"

I told her I had no idea. The problem was, there had to be a why. For what reason would anybody decide to murder a member of the Killing Club? And I couldn't think of one.

Garth and I looked at each other. Finally he shrugged. "Still, be really funny if somebody was planning to kill us all, wouldn't it?"

"You and I always had a different idea of what was really funny."

He followed me out, trying to help me on with my ski jacket, but I was too quick for him. Treading my way through Katie's sculptures, I'd made it almost inside the Mustang when he turned me around, kissed me on the mouth, said, "Good night, Jamie," opened my car door for me and then walked away.

7

BARCLAY

BY THE END OF THE week we had confirmation that the fire at the Tymosz house had started no earlier than eight that night and no later than nine thirty. Since the nosy condo neighbor had definitely seen Megan and Sam kissing in the third-floor hall of Park Apartments at 9:40, and since this same woman had indignantly taken down the license plate number of Megan's Acura MDX at 7:50, because Megan was illegally parked in a "Residents Only" space right next to Sam's Chrysler Crossfire, it was not possible that they'd made it to Glen Valley and back in time to murder Ben. Not to mention that Sam's neighbor said she had heard (presumably by pressing her ear against the door) "disgusting noises nonstop all night."

Rod put Danny and me on a series of holdups at convenience stores. As for Ben, he said the file was closed. "Coroner's report said accident. Chief Waige's saying accident."

I didn't like Warren Waige, the longtime Gloria police chief. I couldn't imagine what Gert Anderssen saw in him—except maybe herself: He was tall, trim and white-haired. He was also more interested in keeping his job than in doing it. The result was that Rod worked all the time. "You don't even have time for a vacation, how are you going to have time for a wedding?" I asked him.

"Doesn't a wedding take only about fifteen minutes?"

"Somebody pulled the nails out of Ben's basement door."

"Ben tripped, fell, died in a fire. Just drop this whole Killing Club business."

I wondered if he really meant forget about Garth, but I didn't ask him. Anyhow, I figured Garth had gone back on the train, home to the fast-talking Ashley.

So I TRIED TO let Ben's death go.

On Sunday Rod and I did some Christmas shopping in Appleton Mall, along with half of Gloria. There was another Rotarian Santa in the plastic igloo where Ben had volunteered.

Every Sunday I visit with Clay, for Gina's sake. Often I bring him home to Dock Street for dinner with Dino and my dad. I really don't like Clay's father, Barclay, or his grandmother Meredith Ober, who arranged to replace my sister with the Philly deb. Sometimes it's a struggle even to like Clay. He's a thirteen-year-old boy, dancing in an emotional

Mixmaster. In some ways, I preferred his old preteen explosions to this new, quiet, sullen contempt. But there are times, not many anymore but still a few, when I can get him to laugh, and then I see Gina in his face.

The Ober house sloped down to the prettiest curve on the Deep Port River. The house had belonged to Barclay's mother's family for a long time. They were Ettens and very proud of the fact. Ettens had started the ironworks factory in 1799, built a ten-mile mule trans-way to lug their freshly made cannonballs to the ships in Deep Port Harbor—thereby personally winning the War of 1812, at least according to Mrs. Ober. Her family had kept the iron business going until after World War I, when a fire had burned down the old forge and the new shell-loading factory both. Rusted iron vats could still be found along the paths in Etten Park. Ettens had won state offices, had even once gone to Congress, but then had fallen into a long, slow decline. Just like their house.

By the late 1960s, the house, named River Bend, had sunk into such disrepair, it was in danger of being torn down. There'd been talk that Harry Ober, a juggernaut of a developer, who'd already covered a third of the county in cookie-cutter houses, had bought the surrounding land and was going to raze the old estate to build yet another of his subdivisions. Instead, he married Meredith Etten. She was the last of her clan and everyone said she'd married Harry Ober to save River Bend, for which she clearly had a great passion, spending the next decades meticulously restoring it to some dream of past perfection. But maybe she'd loved Harry too.

The couple spent a fortune on the place. It was an 1851

white-framed black-shuttered Georgian with six columns, four outbuildings (including a stable), three floors, two wings (both with side porches), a pool, a pond, a gazebo, a tennis court, a guest cottage and a dock with boats.

Clay stood on the dock, throwing things to or at a pair of hissing swans. From a distance, he looked like an adult; too much like his dad for me. "Where're your folks?" I called. "Are they having a party?" As I'd walked around to the front of the house from the gravel drive where I'd parked, I'd noticed five or six luxury cars angled onto the grass edge.

Clay kept his back to me and didn't answer until I was standing next to him, at which point he tossed a tray full of pricey-looking minuscule canapés into the water for the gluttonous swans. Finally he mumbled, "Inside, belting it down with the rest of the rich and full of themselves."

My sister had always been a sucker for the world of the wealthy. Before she let Barclay get her pregnant (and I guess that was the only way she could force the wedding over his mother's objections), she had practiced being rich by studying the pictures in home-decorating magazines. River Bend looked like the pictures.

"Well, here's to the poor and full of themselves, like me." I grinned at Clay and raised an imaginary glass.

He took a disheveled joint from his car-coat pocket, twisted and lit it, staring at me defiantly the whole while. I pulled the thing out of his mouth and tossed it nonchalantly at the swans. They pecked, then spit it away. Marijuana doesn't taste as good as beluga on buttered bread.

He scowled. "You can get fined a thousand dollars for littering the river like that."

I sat down on the dock's edge. "Yeah? You and me both. Did you get that from Dino?"

"Dino? Hah."

"I know what you mean. I don't want you riding around with him, okay? He speeds and he's, well . . ."

"Wasted."

"Right. You know, take the keys away from him."

"He's the grown-up!"

"Dino? Hah."

Clay sank into a slump beside me. His fancy sneakers were untied, their loose laces floating in the water. Like his chapped hands, his feet looked oddly large. He stared at them too, as if they were unfamiliar to him.

I didn't say anything. Sometimes it worked. Sometimes it didn't. But with Clay, it was the only way in.

After a while, I heard a car drive off, crunching the gravel on the other side of the house. First one, then several close together.

"My fuckin' dad's sending me to fuckin' Rowley in the fall."

"What's that mean?"

"You're a cop. You don't know anything."

"So, tell me."

Clay kicked at the swans. The two birds considered fighting back, then glided indifferently away. "It's in Vermont. It's where he wanted to go to fuck-ass boarding school and didn't get to because he was too *stupid*!"

"Whose idea is this?"

"His. Grandma too. He's such a liar. He keeps telling me he was this big Hart High football star. It's bullshit."

I couldn't argue. "Yeah, pretty much."

"He didn't win a single game. He was always sitting on the bench. Father Connie told me the only guy Hart ever had that could play was Ben Tymosz."

"Right." We'd had this conversation before.

"And so what, right? Even he couldn't win the championship. They lost the fuckin' championship, and everybody keeps lying about it!"

"True enough."

Clay shifted abruptly into his other gear; he had two—slow silence and fast rant. "I hate him. He thinks he's oh yeah macho man, dragging his buds out to pop little birds. You know what they do? They poke the doves' eyes out with pins, so the flight pattern'll be 'more interesting.'"

"I doubt it."

"Ask him. Meanwhile, you ever seen my dad's gun room? Grandma calls it the billiards room but it's all about guns. He keeps it locked up. Like that's going to keep me out of it. He's got telescopic lenses big enough you could see Osama bin Laden in a fuckin' cave in Afghanistan. He's got a scope on this big-ass crossbow so he can kill Bambi without ever looking at him! That room is like a fuckin' temple to death. Why would you want to cut off deer's heads and stick them up on your walls?"

"I don't know." I let this sit a while. "So, I take it you don't want to go to Rowley? You'd rather stay here, go to Hart High, even if they really weren't state champs?"

"You're not funny."

"Well, I try."

Clay said he didn't care one way or the other where he

went to school. When I offered to talk to Barclay about Rowley, he laughed. "Fat chance."

"Things with your dad not good?"

He said they were the same old shit. Then he added that things were actually worse for his stepmother, Tricia, than for him. He surprised me by saying that Tricia was "okay."

"You like her? It's hard for me to get a feel for her."

"She got religion so she tries to be nice. Hey, she's better than Slime and the Dragon Lady"—these were his pet names for Barclay and Meredith Ober.

Gina's mother-in-law had been her greatest enemy, preoccupying her thoughts, stirring her emotions more deeply than the son ever had. Barclay had just been their battleground. Gina won the siege against Meredith when she married the heir. She lost the war when she died young.

Clay now told me that Tricia (who three years ago had shocked the Obers and disappointed the country club by suddenly converting to Catholicism) was headed to the Holy Land right after the New Year. She was going there with a church group of women her age from Immaculate Conception led by Father Keith Connor. Father Connie was here at River Bend all the time with her and a group of other wealthy women who had turned to the church for society, or love. Clay didn't blame Tricia for leaving "this fuckin' hellhole" behind as soon as she could, even to go to stupid Jerusalem, where she'd probably be blown up.

"How did my mom ever stand Grandma? Maybe Mom died just to get away from her, you know?"

I pulled his near leg up to the dock floor; he let me tie the sneaker, for old time's sake, I guess. "Well, they sure didn't get along. But if she possibly could have, if she'd had a chance, your mom would have stayed alive. She tried as hard as she could. Because she wanted to hang around you, kid, see what you were going to be like. That's the last thing your mom ever said to me, did you know that? She said, 'I fuckin' hate it, I'm not going to watch Clay grow up, because he's going to be something else!'"

He pulled his foot away, but almost reluctantly. "She didn't say that."

"She sure did."

Clay thought about that a while. "Well, I fuckin' hate it that she died instead of Grandma."

"So did she! Totally fuckin' hated it!" I grabbed him in a hug, shook him until he laughed.

"Shit. Here they come." Clay scrambled to his feet, leaping off the side of the dock and loping along the green riverbank until he disappeared behind the guest cottage at the far end of the drive, heading toward an old, small, brick summer kitchen, long unused, that he'd turned into his own private place.

They weren't really coming toward the dock. The three—Barclay, his wife and his mother—were just standing on the terrace looking at me. So I joined them. "Happy holidays," I threw out.

Barclay's mother, the Dragon Lady, took the lead. She always had. "Jamie, why didn't you come inside? The caterers are cleaning up now; everyone's gone. Tricia's church friends." She made the word *church* sound like something stuck on the bottom of her shoe.

"I just dropped by to say hi to Clay."

"That boy." She shook her narrow head on her narrow

neck. Mrs. Ober was the thinnest human being I'd ever seen not on a respirator. In fact, she looked elegant, white hair in a pageboy, neck strung with pearls. She either had a dozen black Chanel sweaters with gold buttons, or she wore the same one all the time. "At least come look at the tree, it's beautiful this year, and have a cocktail." She lifted her martini at me. I'd known the woman, vaguely, for more than twelve years and had never seen her without a glass in her hand, although I'd never seen her intoxicated either.

Neither Barclay (who was tossing his car keys from hand to hand) nor his wife had said a word.

Tricia Ober was an attractive woman. She looked as if her mother-in-law had cloned herself in a laboratory, except she wasn't quite as thin, her hair was a honey pageboy, her Chanel sweater was pale gray and she wore a tiny gold cross.

"How you doing, Tricia? Clay tells me you're off to the Middle East with a group from Immaculate Conception. That's great."

Barclay answered for her. "After the holidays. It's one of Connie's tour-hoppers through Nazareth, Bethlehem, that kind of junk."

If Tricia was offended by her husband's description of these holy sites, she didn't say so. Instead she asked if I'd had a good talk with Clay.

I tried to bring up the boy's unhappiness at the prospect of going to boarding school.

Mrs. Ober quickly assured me that Rowley was the best thing for him. Hart High simply couldn't provide Clay with the kind of constructive structure he needed.

"I'm not sure 'constructive structure' is really what—"

Barclay jumped in, but talked to his mother, not me.

"Jamie's got this idea Clay's some perfect Wally Cleaver but wait'll she has kids of her own. If she ever does." His smile reminded me of why I'd always hated Barclay Ober. He was hateful. I didn't like anything about him, including the perfectly in-the-style-of-the-moment clothes, shoes, haircuts, watches, cars, drinks and dishes to order in restaurants. I didn't like the toothy all-American gym-built way he looked. But for some reason Gina had genuinely thought he was "a hunk."

I had to ask him. "Barclay, do you poke out the eyes of doves?"

"What?" Mrs. Ober looked assaulted, as if I'd torn her skirt off and used it to wipe up dog shit.

He looked at me, exasperated. "I hunt doves. Mourning doves, they're bred for it. It's like a mink coat. They raise them." To him it appeared to be an explanation. "Wing-shooting. I don't blind them. I've heard sometimes guides in South America do."

"Oh for heaven's sake, Barclay." Mrs. Ober was disgusted.

I laughed. "Yeah, Barclay, shoot something your own size."

Tricia glanced at me; if I hadn't known better I would have said it was a look of gratitude.

"There's nothing wrong with hunting if you follow the law." He gave Tricia a look. "Your best friend, Father Connie, comes hunting with me all the time. 'Course he's really fund-raising, right?"

Still tossing his car keys in the air, Barclay abruptly told us that he had to leave for the office for a little while; a problem had suddenly come up at Ober Land Development and Realty that he needed to get a jump on before Monday morning. The announcement seemed to surprise and disturb his mother and wife, although we all were very pleasant about saying good-bye. Minutes later, Barclay's car started up.

The two women stared at each other, then Tricia's hand flew up to her tiny cross and her eyes flickered down to study the terrace fieldstone. Her eyes looked so unhappy, it made me wonder why she was waiting till after New Year's to fly off to the other side of the world, even to a war zone.

It also made me wonder where Barclay was going. So as soon as I rounded the house, I broke into a trot. My Mustang was old but it was fast. By the time Barclay's black SL600 reached the open gates of the Ober estate, I was close enough behind him to see that he was headed into town.

The offices of Ober Land Development and Realty Company were in the opposite direction.

8

DEBBIE

THREE HUNDRED YEARS AGO, while stripping the forests and shipping the hardwood home to England, Captain Thomas Ricks had paid his respects to the mother country by laying out the north-south streets of Deep Port with the names of English counties. Kent, Norfolk, Sussex, Surrey and so on. The east-west streets had been given more practical names, usually telling you where they were (Dock, River, Hill), or what was happening in them (Miller, Forge). There weren't any millers or forges these days or even any docks on Dock Street. The names were just names now.

Deklerk's Bar sat crookedly at the corner of River and York. Barclay's SL600 drove slowly past it, found another

Mercedes parked on River and squeezed aggressively into the space behind, nudging the sedan's bumper as if to shove it out of the way. From across the street he clicked his car locked and waited while it blinked obediently back at him, then slowly closed its eyes. Deklerk's blinked its lights too, but that was because the neon sign had a sputter. The two decapitated Santa Claus heads floating in the bar window turned Barclay a dangerous red as he passed them. Tossing his keys again, he stood at the intersection, but didn't cross when the light changed. He waited there impatiently through another whole sequence of lights.

I waited too, back under the awning of Talbot and Jenkins, Antiques, so he couldn't see me. Not that he ever looked back.

Suddenly a new blue Jaguar smoothly braked right beside him. As the light turned green, Barclay jumped avidly into the passenger seat and the coupe roared away, accelerating fast. I couldn't see the license plate except to notice that it was one of the special "preserve our natural resources" plates with trees and ducks on it. But then I didn't need to see the plate. I knew it was Amanda's car.

Compared to the Saturday night crowd, Deklerk's was nearly empty now. My great-aunt Betty Wurtz stood waiting to use the pay phone, passing the time by throwing darts at a round board about ten inches away. She was so short she had to throw high over her head. She did pretty well. The man on the phone kept an eye on her. On the jukebox, the Screaming Blue Messiahs played a punk cover of a Hank Williams song but they weren't screaming very loudly because a small row of middle-aged men at the bar had the Giants-Cowboys game on the television. It was a big TV, swinging out into the room above the wall-mounted blue marlin that Sam Deklerk had caught ten years ago on a vacation to the Florida Keys. That marlin had made Sam think life was a Jimmy Buffett song; ever since, he'd worn shorts and flip-flops behind his bar all summer long.

"Where's Sam?" I asked his sister, Debbie.

Her pale face scrunched in a frown as she poured me an amaretto on the rocks without asking if I wanted it. "What? Now you're in love with Sam? Last night you asked me the same thing. How should I know where Sam is? Not here."

Tonight Debbie showed off her cleavage in a scoop-necked black T-shirt. There was more of her to show off than there used to be. You could see the elastic of her panties through her black jeans. Her eyes looked bloodshot, the skin beneath them bruised a pale purple version of her finger-nails. While I watched her pull two drafts, then slide the big beer mugs to the men at the bar, I told her that she looked tired.

"Whose fault is that? I haven't slept since Ben died and you and Pudge decided goddamn psycho Michael Myers was running around loose in Gloria, killing off the Killing Club."

I shrugged at her, mock-sheepish. "Yeah, well, maybe I'm wrong. One thing's for sure, Megan didn't do it. She was off screwing your brother."

"You asked me, I could have told you that."

I let it go. "Maybe Ben just died by stupid accident."

But, as always, Debbie refused to accept the reassurance she'd asked for. "What if he didn't? What if life really is just a cheesy horror movie like I always suspected?" Since child-hood she had dreaded, expected and taken satisfaction in the inevitable arrival of the worst. "Anyhow, if we *don't* get murdered, there's the future, so why not just step into the chain-saw?" She pointed at Betty Wurtz, who was sticking the extra darts into the floppy red wool hat she wore perched above her pink hair.

Aunt Betty thought Debbie was waving at her and came over to ask us to make the man get off the pay phone. "He's been on that telephone, for no reason, eleven and a half minutes."

"Hang on, Mrs. Wurtz," Debbie told her.

"Where's that boyfriend of yours? You ought to get married. My husband, God rest his soul, Isaac Wurtz, no legs but a good man. In his day that man sold a lot of houses. Low-end but a lot. In one day he sold five. Why don't you marry that man?"

I pointed at my chest, assuming she was talking to me. "Rod Wolenski? We're engaged." I showed her my ring.

"Never heard of him. I mean the tall one in the cemetery."

Debbie wondered who that might be. Aunt Betty couldn't tell her, just that he was putting roses on graves and he needed to get his hair cut. Just then the man hung up the pay phone, turning to give my great-aunt a cupped palm gesture with a raised arm that she apparently didn't understand since she told us, "At least he's apologizing."

After she left, Debbie said, "She mean Garth? What's the matter with you?"

"Nothing. I happened to see him at Lyall's grave."

"You happened to leave here with him last night. Were you two going back to the cemetery?"

I brushed the whole thing aside with a wave and took my drink over to a booth to think things through. Not busy, Debbie followed. As she sat down across from me, I told her,

"Something's going on that's got something to do with Garth and Connie and Barclay."

"That's a little vague. Like what?" By force of habit, she pulled napkins from the holder, wiped down the tabletop.

"I don't know." I started cleaning the table too, then stopped myself. "They're really worried about something."

Her laugh was a loud parodic "Ha!," her head bobbing up and down, bouncing the gold chains in her cleavage. "Like maybe dying?"

"Debbie, you know what I just saw? Amanda picked up Barclay in her car at the intersection here." I clicked my engagement ring against the side of my glass, emphasizing the sequence as I described it. "I'm at his house, he tells his wife and mother he's going to work, on a Sunday night. I follow him. Instead he comes here, parks down the block, waits, Amanda's Jaguar pulls up on York, zip, they're gone."

Debbie's wide face narrowed as she puckered her lips and crossed her eyes. What she said was, "Duh."

"Still? Barclay and Amanda?"

"More like 'again' than 'still.'" Then one of the TV watchers called to her from the bar for another round. She yelled back at him, "You want fast? Go to Dante's," but she stood up. Leaning over, she squeezed my chin affectionately. "Let me get this straight: You're a trained detective? That's what you do for a living?"

I jerked my head away, smiling. "I'm a specialist. Homicide. Adultery is a whole different division."

With a fluff of her spiked hair, she laughed as she turned to go. "It's gotta be a big division in Gloria. Adultery squad, that's about half the force. See ya."

But I followed her back to the bar. "I don't get it. He's an asshole, a smug, mean, conceited prick."

"I don't get it either, but it's clear some women disagree with us. And that guy'd fuck a rubber duck in his bathtub. You're the one told me he was cheating on Gina the whole time she was in ICU." I must have flinched because Debbie reached out for my hand. "Sorry." She squeezed so hard the cheap rings on her fingers pinched mine.

"Yeah," I said. "He cheated on Gina. He's cheating on Tricia. I bet that's why she joined the Catholic Church."

Debbie laughed. "Well, sex is sure why I left it." She took an order for a double scotch from someone who didn't need it. When she came back, she said, "Listen, Amanda and Barclay, it's a game. They play 'Password,' they're not going to get that word *monogamy*. Neither one of them."

"The way Barclay's face turned purple when she left Ben's reception with Garth, didn't look like he thought it was a game." But it was the Amanda part of the affair that didn't make sense to me. "Amanda's about money. Always has been."

Amanda and Debbie had once been pretty good friends, and while Amanda had long ago left Debbie behind in the dust of Deklerk's Bar, Debbie continued to stick up for her in a wry, half-hearted sort of way. Now she shrugged. "Who knows. Maybe she's lonely. She's a golf widow. I got a friend works in ob/gyn at St. Anthony's, says Amanda's in there a lot, doing all this fertility stuff."

"Jesus, remind me to pick another hospital if I want to keep my health a secret around this town."

"Hey, you want to drop dead a stranger, move to New York. Sounds like she really wants a baby."

"I don't think she married Jim Morgan for a baby. I think she married him for money."

Debbie swept up the tips, dumped them into the big cheap snifter on the counter. "I don't think so. I think it was social clout. She had plenty of money even before she bagged Jim on the eighteenth hole. Ol' Jim was just new icing on the old cake."

This fact surprised me. Amanda Kean had grown up in a North Gloria trailer park. All she had going for her was looks and willpower. It turned out to be enough. But the climb had taken her a while. Guys had slept with her, but they hadn't proposed. Not until an elderly minor executive at Kind Lady stepped up to the altar. But that man hadn't been all that rich. And her second husband, Shawn Tarrini, a sales manager at the same factory, had boasted about losing all of his savings playing the market.

"Plenty of money from where? Shawn didn't have a cent."

Debbie snickered derisively at me again. "Shawn Tarrini? He had a million-dollar life insurance policy."

That took me aback. "Amanda collected a million dollars?"

"She sure as shit did. Almost put Ben Tymosz's father-in-law out of business. Ben's the one that wrote it up for O'Brian's six months before Shawn died." Debbie took my glass from me. "Shawn hits the ramp rail on the turnpike at seventy miles an hour and Amanda's rich. Except she's miserable 'cause her husband's dead. Is life ironic or what?" She refused my twenty. "Don't try to pay me. I may need a favor."

"You never need a favor."

"You don't know. The Killing Club killer could be chas-

ing me with an ax, and I'll hit speed dial Jamie Ferrara, and
there you'll be!"

I patted her small veiny hand. "That's true, Debbie.
There I'll be."

"I know it's true. Unless he got you first." She always had
to have the last word.

BACK HOME IN BED, the past kept circling closer:
Shawn, Amanda and Ben were all members of the Killing
Club. Ben dies the way Pudge had told him to write a murder in the Death Book. A shadow moves across Ben's living
room window the morning after he died. Was the person
there taking the wire and nails out of the door jamb and I
scared him or her off? That night somebody leaves me a
quote from a horror movie, letters cut out of magazine ads,
letting me know that death is coming to my little town.

Amanda has Ben write up a huge insurance policy on
her second husband, Shawn Tarrini. Shawn makes up a story
for the Killing Club about someone who gets away with
murdering his rival by passing the homicide off as a hit-and-
run car accident. Shawn dies in a car accident.

Barclay is in his car outside Ben's house the night of the
fire. Barclay's car keys glint as he tosses them in the air on the
terrace at River Bend. He lies to his wife. The blue Jaguar
speeds away with Barclay and Amanda inside.

The night of that championship football game, I'd stood
in the parking lot with Debbie Deklerk, who'd come to the
stadium, she said, to score some pot. I was steamed about
Amanda, who was getting into Barclay's car with Garth, and
I said to Debbie, "That goddamn fucking bitch."

"Hey, that fucking bitch is my friend." Debbie grinned.

Amanda, Garth and Lyall crowded into the backseat of the car. Ben and Connie were in the front with Barclay. The next day, when Lyall was missing, all four of them had told the police, who'd interviewed them, that they'd all been "just hanging around talking" for most of the night at the Pine Barrens Playhouse, to which Ben had a key. (They didn't say we all had keys and were there all the time having meetings of the Killing Club.) They said that Lyall had wandered off and they'd figured he'd hitchhiked home. They'd never seen him again. Their stories were consistent. Lyall's suicide note was found on one of the nearby derelict warehouse docks. Ben's father was furious and changed the lock on the empty playhouse.

Now eleven years later Connie, Barclay and Garth were arguing on the church steps after Ben's funeral. Garth and Connie were arguing in the booth at Deklerk's. What were they hiding from me? Maybe it had absolutely nothing to do with Ben and the past. Maybe one of them had given the others a bad stock tip. Maybe anything. Lives had gone in their own very different directions.

But Garth was at Lyall's grave. Garth was back in Gloria. Not, he said, for Ben. Or Lyall. "I think I came back early for you." But then he'd left the funeral reception with Amanda. Barclay hadn't liked that at all. Amanda got a million dollars when Shawn died. Ben wrote up the policy for her. Amanda and Shawn and Ben.

I pushed my way back to a memory that was hard to bring into focus. Same town cemetery. Shawn Tarrini's funeral. Pudge stood next to me in the churchyard beside the raw open grave. It was raining. Connie was there but not officially. It was a secular funeral home service, with friends speaking instead of ministers. Only Shawn's brother spoke at the graveside. Pudge offered me space under his umbrella. "Ben's taking this hard." He sighed. I looked over, across the casket, at Ben and his wife, Megan. Ben's face was frozen.

Amanda, beautifully outfitted in black—from umbrella and raincoat to suit and shoes and gloves—stood in the midst of Shawn's family. She was trembling. I recall overhearing Barclay, who was standing next to me whispering to someone, but I can't remember who, "Christ almighty, she's fucking gorgeous," and I thought how he might have said the same tacky thing about another woman at his own wife's—my sister's—funeral.

Then Amanda walked over to Ben. Megan moved aside to let Ben give Amanda a kiss on the cheek. Amanda's arms suddenly went around Ben's neck and stayed there until Debbie moved next to them and tapped Ben's shoulder. Then Ben pulled Amanda's arms down, turned her into Debbie's embrace and hurried away from the small crowd. Debbie seemed to be holding Amanda up, as if she were dead weight.

I remember that Connie followed Ben, comforting him, though Ben tried to pull away. They were walking . . . where? The memory wouldn't come. I slipped out of bed, stood in my bay window, looked up at the hard December stars, thought back to that moment, made myself see it again.

Connie hurried after Ben along the gravel path and down the slope to the river's bank to Lyall Hillier's empty grave. When Amanda tried to follow them, Connie saw her and gestured to Barclay, who took her aside, putting his arm around her, hugging her to him.

A car noise outside broke into my thoughts. I heard a clatter at the door, then Dino fumbling for the light switch, banging his guitar case into the hall table, cursing. I ran down the hall stairs, whispering loudly, "Dino, be quiet. Dad's going to tear your head off!"

My brother was holding a manila envelope. "Hey, this was on the stoop, like the other one." Before I could stop him he'd pulled out the piece of paper with the letters pasted on it. They said, *"Was that the bogeyman? As a matter of fact . . . it was."* Another quote from the same horror movie. I was sure. I'd rented the video of *Halloween* and watched it twice.

9

SHAWN

MONDAY MORNING, early, everybody wanted to give me breakfast. Well, not everybody. Dino, who worked afternoons at Jonesy's Marina so he could play bad rock and roll all night, would sleep till noon. But my dad—and it was amazing, the speed with which he negotiated the kitchen in his wheelchair—scrambled some eggs with chopped peppers and scooped them into fried bologna halves. "Two Jamie Deluxes!" he called to me cheerfully. I couldn't resist them. My dad wasn't a bad cook, but he stuck to simple recipes inherited from his grandmother half a century ago—so, lots of 1950s chicken Parmesan. I am, I've been told, a really good cook, but I have my suspicions of the motives of the people who have told me so.

I filled my father in on my investigation into Ben's death.

Listening, he poured me more coffee. His coffee, which he warmed up in the microwave, was I think the worst coffee ever made by a first-generation Italian. "It comes down to this, sweetheart. If somebody killed Ben, and then sent you those notes, it's one of two reasons why."

I cut the egg-filled bologna into tiny squares. Sam, our cat, hopped on the table to try to get to my plate. My father was shocked that Sam would do such a thing—as he was always shocked, even though Sam did it all the time, probably because occasionally when he was alone my father fed him from the table. He shoved Sam onto the floor. I said, "One, the homicide's about the Killing Club. Two, it's not about the Killing Club, but somebody wants me to think it is. *Because* it's not."

"That's it. Choose. Or, three, could be somebody's yanking your chain and your imagination's running away with you." Dad poured more orange drink. "Drink your juice."

"It's not juice, Dad. It's carbonated cane syrup."

"It's orange. Drink it." He shoved *The Gloria Gazette* at me. Under Land Transactions, there was a mention of the purchase of the Pine Barrens Playhouse. Sellers: Mrs. William Tymosz and Mrs. Benjamin Tymosz. Buyer: Ober Land Development and Realty Company. Price: $225,400.

My father said, "That place is falling down. I guess Barclay's just trying to help them out. Maybe he's not so bad as we always thought, huh?"

"Maybe . . ."

. . .

Rod WAS WAITING FOR ME with a plate of sticky buns at Broad Street Bakery. "You know you're not supposed to tempt me."

Rod sighed. "For Christ sake, if anything, you're *underweight*."

"You're perfect." I kissed him. He tasted like sugar. I ate only one of the buns, and felt virtuous. He studied the copy I'd made of the second note. Forensics was working on the original.

"Baby, I still think it's a sick joke." Rod had brought me the state patrol file on Shawn Tarrini's DOA. "Just so you'll give this up. No way it was a hit-and-run." He had the emergency room report with him as well. "His head went through the windshield. A trucker headed south saw Tarrini's Chevy Tracker totally lose control, go into the embankment, solo. Poor guy was history on impact."

"Was he drinking?"

"They got a postmortem blood alcohol point oh six. Really that's not so bad. But the autopsy they did was minimal. We wouldn't go to court with it. No vitreous, no UAC. His mom was screaming for the body. Said he'd suffered enough."

"His mom? What about his wife? What about Amanda?"

Rod sat in white shirtsleeves wearing a tie with tiny blue diamonds on it that I'd given him two years ago. As chief of detectives, he felt he ought to set a tone with a jacket and tie. The jacket stayed in his office at the Dixon Building, looped over his chair. "You're going to like this, but don't go wild." He opened a folder from the Jersey highway patrol, turned it to face me. "The night Tarrini died? Two couples went to A.C. Trump Taj Mahal. There on the boardwalk?"

"I know it. Who?"

"Tarrini and his wife, Amanda. And another couple. The other couple? The Tymoszes. Your friend Ben and Megan."

Quickly I scanned the report. Amanda had told the patrolman who'd talked to her after the car crash that she'd quarreled with her husband because he was drunk. She'd declined to go home with him and he'd left the casino in a rage. Also interviewed, Ben and Megan confirmed Shawn's drinking with words like "staggering" and "smashed." In Megan's view, Shawn had drunk "more than his fair share"—whatever that would be. Ben was quoted as saying he'd offered Amanda a ride back to Gloria because he was reluctant to have her return in a car with her intoxicated husband.

Now frankly, as I tried to get Rod to agree, personally, if I'd just written up a million-dollar life insurance policy on someone who was about to drive off totally plastered onto the very fast and very busy Atlantic City Expressway, I wouldn't worry so much about giving the man's wife a lift as I would about taking his car keys away from him before he left in a drunken rage.

On the other hand, a BAC of only .06 and a big guy like Shawn Tarrini is "staggering"? I figured I'd make a few calls about that accident report.

After breakfast, Rod and I walked from the bakery back toward the Dixon Building. Heading across the green, I heard my name.

Pudge was calling out from the door of Dante's that he had some fresh almond biscotti and would make me an espresso. Okay, it would be my third breakfast, but then I did have some questions I wanted to ask Pudge. As far as Weight Watchers goes, I'd have to watch later.

Rod walked on across the green, past the shuttered and padlocked Christmas manger, swooping down occasionally with a long open swing of his arm to pick up litter along the diagonal path to Dixon. He looked like he was bowling. Two by two, a line of maybe fourth-graders skipped up the steps of the old white Federal courthouse next to the police station, to see how justice was done. Their teachers looked younger than Dino.

The day was cold but sunny. I watched the town hurry by, rushed by the fast approach of Christmas—only weeks away. I waited in a window booth in Dante's for Pudge to bring my espresso. My cell phone vibrated in my jeans pocket. Weirdly enough I knew it was Garth, just from the warm throb of the stupid phone.

"I'm leaving on the next train," he said by way of greeting.

"Isn't that a song?"

"I think the song is more, 'tonight I'm gonna stay here with you.'" He chuckled in a way that sounded like we were in bed, but maybe I was reading things into it.

"I thought you already did leave."

"Nope. Tonight, sad to say, I'll be at a press conference in the city."

"I've got to ask you. What does Ashley do?"

"*Money Matters.*"

"What?"

"She's one of the anchors. That show that hypes the stock market twenty-four-seven? *Money Matters*? They do it every day. It can't be easy. She's the early-morning anchor.

I'm the late-night news." He laughed. "I'm not sure I've ever seen her awake."

"Sounds like a basis for a relationship."

"Yeah, well . . . Anyhow, just wanted to say, I'm glad we got to see each other. And I wouldn't worry about this Ben-Shawn thing anymore. They just died. Forget about it. You and I could always get it going."

What the hell did that mean?

Garth read my mind. "I mean, the two of us, seeing murder all around. Your fiancé's right, a couple of freak accidents. Bad luck. You take it easy, Jamie. It really was, I mean it, good to see you." He asked me to promise to stay in touch. He vowed to do the same. We admitted neither of us would do so unless it turned out somebody really was trying to kill us.

I asked him if he remembered whether people in the club had ever made copies of the old Death Books. He said he did recall Xeroxing them once, but he'd thrown his copies away after Lyall died. By now no doubt everyone had tossed them.

Thinking he was still at Katie and Sweets's, and unable to stop myself, I asked, "Would you like a lift to the train station?"

"Got it covered. Left something on your desk, by the way. Take it easy. Bye." He was gone.

Dante's hadn't actually opened yet; it didn't till noon. It was strange to be there in the quiet, drinking coffee. Pudge's espresso was the best in town; even the Ironworks Inn at four dollars a single cup couldn't get the *crema* the way Dante's did.

Pudge and I talked about Ben's cancer and how Ben's father had died of cancer too—but not so horribly young. "He should have come to me and told me. Or gone to talk to Connie. Connie would have been there for him. Or gone to a shrink. Somebody. You shouldn't carry those things on your own. You need help."

"You think there's any way Ben committed suicide?"

"No way. He's not going to do that to himself. Come on, Jamie, he was Catholic."

I shrugged. "Me too. You too. You really believe you're going to damn your immortal soul if you commit suicide?"

Pudge's large eyes looked fretfully around his empty restaurant. "I guess I believe it, I don't know."

The truth is, few of us went to church anymore, yet all of us were still programmed to spook if we broke the rules. If I eat a hamburger on Friday in Lent, I'm aware of it. That imprinting comes early and it lasts.

We talked about the fact that Barclay had just bought the playhouse from Ben's widow and his mother. "Yeah, I heard that," Pudge said. "That's fine if all he wants to do is fix it up. You know how those preservationist-types like Amanda are around here. It's old, it's sacred."

I told him I thought I'd actually seen Barclay writing the check to Ben's mother.

Pudge pulled out his gold lighter, then noticed his wife come out of the kitchen and go to the cash register and he dropped it back in his pocket. "Well, he has to get past the planning board." His cheeks filled with stubbornness. "Somebody killed Ben. I know it."

"If you're worried it was Megan, don't. She's got an alibi."

When he looked at me, I could see the relief that he wasn't keeping a secret anymore. "Is the alibi Sam?"

I shrugged, not committing myself.

Pudge pushed forward the little plate stacked with biscotti. "Yeah, I knew about it. Don't blame Megan. Ben . . .

well, a while ago, he wasn't perfect in that particular department either. I know of one little fling he had early on." Was
there anybody in Gloria (besides presumably Pudge) who
wasn't cheating on a spouse?

When I didn't take a biscotti, he raised the plate, prod-
ding me. "So, ask. Why'd you want to see me, Jamie? Did I
kill Ben? No, I didn't."

"I know you didn't." I surprised him by asking if he knew
what the relationship was between Amanda and Barclay. He
said he hadn't heard that specific rumor, but she wasn't "Snow
White" and Barclay was "in a league of his own." They'd keep
it quiet if they were involved; they both had a lot at stake.

Pudge couldn't answer my second question either: Was
there something, in the recent past, or even the distant past,
that bonded Garth with Connie and Ben, maybe with Barclay as well—something they'd need to keep arguing about
over this past week? "I don't know, but I sort of think there
was something way back," Pudge said, slowly nodding. "I always thought some of those guys had something they were
keeping from the rest of us. I don't know what, it was just a
feeling, but I'd see them huddled up like that a lot back when
the club fell apart."

"So something way back in high school?"

"But I don't know what. I used to think it was serious
drugs they'd gotten into. That they were dealing or something. You know, Lyall sold everything there was, pot, blow,
uppers, downers, and where was he getting it? Maybe they
took over from him."

"It wasn't much of a business for Lyall. Wasn't it just to
friends? I remember the police searched his house but they
never found anything. 'Course, I figured the Hilliers

dumped whatever they came across so the news wouldn't get out what their son was up to."

"You thought that? I guess that's why you became a cop, huh, Jamie?"

"I guess."

We sat for a while.

He frowned. "It doesn't sound like Ben would be a part of drugs. Or Connie either. I can't see it."

"How about Shawn?"

"No way. Shawn never used drugs of any kind, absolutely not. And he was never a drinker either. Never." Pudge added that back at Hart High, Shawn had been apparently the only member of the football team who'd actually followed the coach's orders and didn't touch alcohol.

"So if he did drink, he might get wasted?" I explained why I was asking—what had happened that night in Atlantic City at the casino.

"No way. The few times I saw Shawn drink, he could definitely hold it. He didn't 'stagger' around."

"Well, his blood alcohol content on the autopsy wasn't that high. But Amanda and Ben both said he could hardly stand up. And why, if they thought he was so drunk, they let him get in a car . . ."

Pudge pulled me toward him across the booth. "Jamie, what are you thinking? That Shawn wasn't an accident either? You think somebody's murdered *two* of us?"

"Take it easy, Pudge. Let's just take it easy."

THERE WAS A DARK RED ROSE lying on top of an old vinyl record album on my desk. The album was the jazz drummer Billy Cobham's *Spectrum*. My name was carefully written on the back, Jamie Ferrara, right where I'd always signaled ownership of my albums. But the signature was not in my handwriting. Long ago, I'd accused Garth of borrowing *Spectrum* and not returning it. He'd always denied being guilty. I still didn't know whether he was lying or not.

In seven minutes, I made it to the Gloria train depot, which is where you get the local connection to Philly or Trenton so you can catch the Metroliner to New York. Parking in the taxi stand cut my time even more; one of the perks of my GPD plates.

Garth still stood there on the platform. The train was just pulling in. People gathered their luggage. The announcer called out the stops the train would make along the way. It could have been a beautiful moment. I could have been thanking Garth for remembering *Spectrum*. We could have been chatting about how we'd always shared that love of jazz and how maybe we still did like the same music or maybe we didn't anymore but maybe there were new . . .

It was a lot of maybes. None of them happened because Garth was kissing Amanda Morgan like something out of the end of a movie, his hands lost inside her mink.

10

DANNY

IF I HADN'T STUMBLED over some jerk's large duffel bag on the train platform, right where I'd have to dance sideways for ten feet to catch my balance after tripping over it; if my cell phone at that exact moment hadn't rung its ridiculous Beethoven's Ninth melody that I keep meaning to get rid of; if Garth and Amanda hadn't seen me; if Garth hadn't turned around and said, "Oh hi, Jamie," and Amanda hadn't asked, "Leaving town?" with her twenty-thousand-dollar smile; if all those things hadn't happened, I wouldn't have gotten so mad at myself that I almost rear-ended a tour bus pulling out of the train station with forty jolly women from the senior citizens center crowded onto it.

The seniors were headed up to Radio City Music Hall,

dressed warmly enough to be dropped off in Antarctica instead. My great-aunt Betty Wurtz was waving at me from the rear window, looking like a trendy Eskimo in a huge purple parka with a big fake-fur hood, and if I hadn't realized she was actually frantically warning me with her hand to hit the brakes, I might have smacked right into the bus.

Then when I arrived back at Dixon, my "partner," Danny Ventura, had angled his Corvette so it used up half my parking space at GPD and I sideswiped his bumper.

The entire rest of the week didn't get any better.

Rod said no to the court order I'd requested so I could have Shawn Tarrini's body exhumed. Rod said he couldn't justify where I was going.

Well, okay, I was going to Amanda, to the thought that she had involved Ben in some plot to kill her husband Shawn for that million-dollar insurance policy. I was thinking that maybe Ben had started feeling guilty about what they'd done. That when he'd found out he had a terminal disease, maybe it had felt like God's punishment. Learning that Megan was fooling around with Sam Deklerk might have felt like God's punishment too. Maybe the sicker Ben felt, the stronger his remorse had grown, until he'd told Amanda he was going to come talk to me about what they'd done to Shawn. Maybe Ben had been planning to tell me how Amanda and he had arranged things somehow to ensure that Shawn crashed that car in the concrete embankment on the Atlantic City Expressway.

Rod pulled open his tie and looked at his watch. They were both signs that I wasn't going to get his help in opening up a homicide case. He sighed in a way that made me want to choke him. "Are you suggesting that Ben Tymosz killed Shawn Tarrini as a favor for Amanda?"

All right, put that way it sounded a little far-fetched. "Not a favor. I think maybe Ben was in love with her."

Rod kept slowly shaking his head as if trying to follow a drunk or a child. "Amanda went over to Ben's house, rigged a wire in his basement doorway and shoved him over it down the steps and set fire to him?" The slowness of his voice made it even more infuriating. "Amanda Morgan killed her husband and then a few years later she killed her insurance agent so he wouldn't tell you about it? Then she sent you those notes? Amanda Morgan who's married to the retired CEO of Kind Lady?"

I was getting angry. "Now rich women don't kill people?"

"Amanda Morgan who's in the paper every other Sunday because she's saving this and saving that for the town?"

"Preservationists don't kill people?"

"The biggest donor to help out Deep Port River? That Amanda?"

I threw a file folder in the air. "Oh, okay! You've got your kayak, so I don't get my court order." (Rod owns his own kayak; he keeps it on top of his Jeep so he can throw it in water whenever he sees any, and every Saturday morning he's on that 140-mile section called Deep Port Scenic and Recreational River that Amanda saved for him.)

Rod crossed his arms. "Boy, you sure don't like her. Makes me wonder. Where's your friend Garth today?"

I crossed my arms too. "What? He left. He took the train back to New York this morning. What's that got to do with anything?"

Rod tilted his head to study me. "I don't know. I figure you do."

My dad used to say, "When Jamie gets steamed, her hair curls." Well, I probably looked like Little Orphan Annie by now.

"Okay, Rod, so you're saying, close this case?"

"Jamie, come on. What case? We never opened a case. Your dad invited me to dinner Sunday. Still okay if I come?"

"Did he say I was cooking?"

"Yeah. Fegato Veneziana."

"Great."

Rod walked away from me, calling over the shoulder of his crisp white "I'm Chief of Detectives" shirt. "Get the evidence. You're just fishing."

Maybe I was. Ice fishing, when you didn't know what the hell was down there, and you just had to wait. But you knew something was down there. Because fishing is what you did and you were good at it. At least that's what I was telling myself while I was picking up the papers that had flown out of the folder I'd tossed in the air.

THE FOLLOWING MORNING, our medical examiner, Gert Anderssen, agreed with Rod that there was no reason to dig up Amanda's second husband even if I could have gotten a court order, because nothing looked out of the ordinary about the autopsy report on Shawn Tarrini. As far as she could tell from reading the coroner's analysis (and the coroner, Herbert Steinway, was a friend of hers—"A good man with a head always on his shoulders"), Shawn hadn't been shot, or poisoned, or drugged or anything else suspicious before heading home on the Atlantic City Expressway.

"Why was he staggering around, Gert? He was a big man. He hadn't had that much to drink. And he wasn't a drinker."

"Ah. Aha. Aha." She tapped me with her pencil, on either shoulder as if knighting me. "This is the explanation. In Herb's report, he says there was nothing in the stomach. Your friend wasn't eating all day. So then it's not his custom, he drinks a little bit, he's blotted."

"Blotto."

"Yes. Blotto." Shawn Tarrini, she summarized, had been a healthy man, a little intoxicated, not wearing a seat belt, who'd died when his lightweight American SUV swerved into a head-on collision with a thick concrete guardrail at seventy miles an hour.

"Things should be worse than that, Jamie? Why?" Gert frowned at me, her slightly freckled skin a little wrinkled around eyes that were so azure blue they startled you. "If everyone has to be always one of your homicides, what a sad world, *ja*? Leave this alone."

I trusted Gert. And here she was, siding with Rod.

Finally I stomped back to my cubicle and changed Beethoven's Ninth to a phone ring choice titled "Cool Jazz." The moment I did, my cell rang and it was Garth McBride in New York.

"You just left! I thought you came to the station to thank me for that album. Believe me, it wasn't easy to find a clean copy of *Spectrum*. And then, kazaam, you were gone!"

"That was days ago. I'm busy, sorry. Thank you for returning *Spectrum*. And yes, I am accusing you, once again, of stealing it. I've gotta go. Good-bye."

"Hey, hey, Jamie, hang on. Oh, I get it. Amanda. Forget it! You got the wrong idea about Amanda. Wouldn't be the first time, would it?" He laughed. Like he expected me to join in. "In all honesty, I think she's got something serious going on the side with Barclay Ober."

"In all honesty, Garth, as you would say, it's none of my business." I repeated that I was too busy to talk further and I hung up.

I canceled my Cobb salad for lunch, walked over to Dante's and ordered a ham and cheese calzone with a side order of garlic bread, like half a loaf. Pudge brought it himself. "You don't eat stuff like this."

"Yeah, well, Pudge, you don't smoke. At least as far as Eileen knows." I gave a significant look toward his wife, Eileen, behind the cash register. She had a line of customers waiting to pay her for lunch. Dante's is always jammed with the courthouse lunch-break crowd.

"You're in a mood. Is it about Ben?" Pudge sat down across from me. "I've been calling people. We're going to get together tonight and talk about this. This Killing Club stuff. Before somebody else dies."

"What people? Everybody thinks it's a stupid idea."

But to my surprise he said that Barclay, Debbie, Amanda and Connie had all four of them agreed to meet us at Dante's Saturday night at ten thirty. (Dante's closes at nine thirty on weekdays, ten on Saturdays.)

"Us?"

He'd promised I'd be here as well to talk "about the case."

"What did you tell them that for, Pudge? There is no case. As I keep being reminded. I've been told to drop it."

"Don't."

"When you said Ben had fooled around before—you told me that, Pudge, remember?—was it with Amanda? Was it around the time Shawn died?"

"Amanda? No way. Why would she get involved with Ben? He didn't have a cent."

What was it with everybody? They all seemed to think Amanda, though a heartless gold digger, was incapable of any other crime.

"What about Amanda, Pudge? Ben and Amanda get rid of Shawn to collect on the big insurance. Then she dumps Ben. He gets sick and he wants to confess. So she gets rid of him and makes it look like the Killing Club murder."

Pudge just stared at me. Finally he said, "Are you crazy? It's not Amanda!"

"Why not?"

"It's some psycho nut that found out about the club."

"Like who, Pudge? Who found out?"

He rolled his eyes. "I don't know! You're the cop!"

Eileen, a pleasant-faced plump woman with tight brown curls and a loud irresistible laugh, made a complicated series of gestures at Pudge, then pointed at a family waiting in the doorway. He signaled her back. The Salernos had a deaf child, and sometimes they used a version of sign language to talk to each other across the crowded restaurant. It was a godsend, they said, at times when even a shout wouldn't carry. "I gotta help her out. She's the best, isn't she?" Pudge adored his wife, and his children, and he wanted the world to feel the same about them.

He picked up the little empty basket where, not that long ago, there'd been two pieces of toasted buttery garlic bread. "Forget this Amanda stuff. I told everybody that you're sure Ben was murdered by some nut after the club for some reason, and you're not going to let it go till you prove it."

"Oh, that's great."

"So you be here, Jamie. If I talk about murder, it's just old class-clown Pudge, but if you say it, it's serious."

"You were the class clown? I didn't know that. I never thought you were funny."

"Ha ha. I'll bring you another order of garlic bread."

"Oh, okay, that's funny."

"You'll be here?" I nodded yes. "Good. I don't want another one of us getting killed." His large brown eyes were solemn. "Too much death."

"*Death has come to your little town, Sheriff,*" I quoted at him. "Man, when we used to say that line from the movie, it was supposed to be a joke." Taking the folded copy of the second anonymous note from my purse, I showed it to him.

"Holy shit. You got another one?" He ran his hand over the Xerox of the pasted letters. "*Was that the bogeyman? As a matter of fact . . . it was.*"

"Same movie. Same way. Somebody left the original on the front stoop. Dino found them both."

"Why the hell do this?"

"I have no idea. But we all do need to be careful, Pudge. That's what I'm going to say to the rest tonight. Be careful." I took back the note. "Unless maybe one of them did it."

"That's nuts. Don't go there. It's an outsider."

The truth is, I couldn't see Amanda shoving Ben down those steps either. But I could see her talking some man into doing it for her. Some man she was sleeping with all of sudden, even though they were both married. Like Barclay. Barclay, who'd sat there parked outside Ben's house after calling in the fire when it was too late to save Ben.

Back at GPD, Rod was pleasant but professional when he told me that Ramon Hiago at Jonesy's Marina had just filed charges against my brother Dino for taking multiple joyrides in Ramon's Ford Ranger without asking his permission. I apologized when I called Ramon. He wouldn't listen. In the end I was the one who had to (a) post bond, (b) drive Dino home and (c) despite his begging me, "Don't tell Dad," tell Dad.

THE WAY MY WEEK HAD GONE, it was no surprise I ended up treating my so-called partner, Detective Danny Ventura, to buffalo wings and what he called a "brewski" at Deklerk's on Saturday.

Well, it was a surprise to Debbie, more like a shock, since she knew my opinion of Danny, and yet here I was in her bar, smiling at him, picking up the check. Debbie caught me on the way to the ladies' room. "Jamie, first you're here hanging with Garth, now it's Danny. Aren't you supposed to be engaged to Rod Wolenski?"

"Give me a break, Debbie. I've had a rough day. See you at Dante's at ten thirty."

"That's all I need. Get off here and go play Sherlock Holmes with you guys."

"Did I just say, 'Give me a break'?"

Debbie pried a wet dollar bill up from the bar surface. She waved it in my face. "This is the tip from a guy who sat on that stool there for two solid hours, telling me his life story, which didn't even sound interesting to him. You want me to give *you* a break? Is Danny Ventura married?"

"Not at the moment. You're not that desperate, Debbie. Trust me on this."

I was treating Ventura because he'd helped me out with something I'd asked him to do, and in his world—not one I cared to live in—that meant I "owed" him, "big time." Chicken wings were not what he'd asked me for, but they're what he got.

The worst thing about Danny is that there are two of him. Well, there're not really two. But Danny has an identical twin whose name is Donny. Right. Danny and Donny. And their mother still thinks they're cute. She told me they reminded her of when Elvis played "identicals" in a movie called *Kissin' Cousins*. I had no trouble with the analogy. The twin Venturas are good-looking, with rich black hair, fleshy faces and hip-thrusting swaggers. Plus, despite the fact that one is a cop (Danny) and the other one, Donny, owns the local bedding store and volunteers as a fireman, the Ventura boys had failed to mature. Like an Elvis movie, they are all about cars, buddies, girls and what they call "messin' around," which appears to mean anything from shooting rats at the dump to chugging beer till they vomit (often on the cars and girls).

And like an Elvis movie, they are keen on practical jokes. At twenty-eight years old, Detective Danny Ventura still thinks it is funny to blind-call locals and tell them they should yank on their phone cords because there's some extra line inside their walls.

One of their favorite jokes involved me. Donny, the

bedding-store twin (who had his own ads on local TV, in which he jumped up and down on mattresses), would show up in the squad room and pretend that he was Danny the cop. The first time they did this, I fell for it. Donny ran to my cubicle, acting as if he were Danny, shouting for me to come quick down to the parking lot, there was a dead man in my Mustang. The dead man was Danny himself, draped over the steering wheel. That a cop would think this was funny taught me things.

They swore I'd left my car door unlocked but I knew I hadn't, that Danny had palmed the key, or had managed to pick the lock (with a '68 Shelby, you don't get an alarm system), and the joke left me steamed.

They'd tricked me twice more, though never as dramatically, before I figured out enough clues to tell them apart. (Danny had black flecks in his left eye, larger hands, a tiny mole near the part of his hair.) Danny still wasn't sure if I knew who was who or not.

Like now, when he pretended to be his brother Donny as he spun my swivel chair out from my desk by splaying his hand over my knee and tugging at me.

"Hey, Sweetmeat, you seen Dan around?" He always pretended to be Donny the bedding-store twin when he wanted to get gross with me.

I shook his hand off by jerking my knee up, accidentally ramming it into his groin hard enough to make sweat pop out on his upper lip. "Gee, Donny, no, I haven't seen him. But you know what a fuck-up Dan is. It's all I can do to keep them from firing his ass."

"Just messin' around," he admitted. "It's me."

"Really? I can never tell for sure."

He ran both hands through his hair to call attention to it. "So rack me up a collar. I just broke the perp on the Mobil thing."

"Hey, great. Was it Junior Overton?"

"Yeah. Spotted his Cavalier at the pump. Ironworks Road. He was in there waving a .45 around. That bad boy's going away for the grand sum of ninety-seven bucks and a big bag of Doritos." Four convenience store/service stations had been robbed in the last month. Danny and I had narrowed down a list of suspects and he was tracking their cars. Anything about cars, he was on it.

That's why I'd asked him to help me follow up on Shawn Tarrini.

That's how he knew where the New Jersey Highway Patrol towed vehicles that had been totaled in highway crashes. And how to get to the car graveyard where an insurance company for a particular car had unloaded the wreck. And he was good at guy-talking the watchman at that graveyard. The watchman was watching a NASCAR race on his little TV, and Danny could talk car racing like he'd played Dale Earnhardt in an Elvis movie.

We spent an hour stumbling through a scary junk heap of mangled and rusted metal in which people's lives had been changed forever. We were losing sunlight and just about to quit when Danny spotted what was left of Shawn Tarrini's silver Chevy Tracker.

For another hour I kept working using a two-hundred-watt Maglite, crawling all over that SUV, while Danny and the watchman sat in the little trailer near the entrance and watched NASCAR from Miami together. It was a lot warmer in Miami (and in that trailer) than it was in a junkyard on a winter night in New Jersey.

Long ago my dad gave up trying to punish me by making me sit on a chair in the kitchen. I'd just sit there. He gave up trying to get me to go to sleep before I'd finished all my homework. I'd just work under my coverlet with a flashlight. He gave up trying to lift me out of the YMCA pool before I'd swum the number of laps I needed to get promoted from "Flying Fish" to "Shark," even though I was convulsively shaking and turning blue.

"Baby, goddamn you," my father said, rubbing me with a towel. "You don't quit. You just don't quit." Then he hugged me, rubbing harder.

I paid the watchman twenty bucks for the flattened corroded remains of Shawn Tarrini's right front tire. It had a bullet in it.

Danny said, "Okay." From him it was the equivalent of handing me the Nobel Prize. He hadn't expected anything. He'd come along to help out on a cold case—that had never been a case to begin with—mostly just because he was in a good mood after closing the armed robberies, and there was nothing else happening at GPD that afternoon, and also because he liked to do things he wasn't supposed to do (and I'd told him not to tell Rod where we were going). And—while I don't believe Danny actually thinks that in a million years I might ever "come across" in exchange for a favor—he likes to pretend that we both think it's possible.

But now I'd gotten him interested. We took a lot of pictures before we pulled the tire. We threw it in the trunk of Danny's Corvette and drove back to the accident site on the

ACE where the highway forks and the alternate ramp curves near an overpass. There were no traces of Shawn's accident still visible, except that the concrete embankment looked new. Danny had a range finder with him. (He's a big deer hunter.) What looked like the most likely position for the shooter was a bridge on that overpass, about a hundred yards past the ramp if you were headed from A.C. to Gloria. We backtracked, parked on the bridge, looked around. There was nothing near the rail but crushed beer cans, a running shoe, a broken aluminum beach chair and an old, dirty, handmade red-white-and-blue banner made from a sheet and flung over the side of the bridge. It said, THESE COLORS DON'T RUN. Except they had run. And the sheet was rotted.

The head of our forensics lab told me the bullet pulled from the tire was a Hornady A-Max 175-grain spire point fired from a 7mm Remington rifle. He said, no, it wasn't possible to tell from what distance the bullet had been fired for sure, but, yes, it could be from a hundred yards, and, yes, it sure had blown out the right front tire, and, yes, that would have spun the SUV out of control, and startled the driver. He said, "Major freak, know what I mean?"

The head of our forensics lab was pretty much our whole crime scene investigation team. His name was Abu Tomkins. He was African American, young, really smart and seriously skinny, as if he'd drawn himself back in first grade when he could do only stick figures, and had added a square head. His hair stuck up straight from his head in a box shape, and his glasses had rectangular black plastic rims. He wore baggy khaki pants, a black long-sleeved T-shirt with Mickey Mouse as the sorcerer's apprentice on it, and he had a wispy goatee that he kept tugging on as if he wanted to make sure it was still there.

I showed him the digital photos I'd taken from the overpass on the ACE. "Abu, could somebody see a particular car approaching, shoot at it from this bridge here and hit the tire right when the driver's swinging onto the ramp?"

Abu pulled up his pants, which always looked well on their way to sliding down his thin hips to his knees. "Sure. Rambo could." He was unfailingly agreeable, even when he was going to have to tell you no. "Hey, know what I mean? Somebody could stand on this bridge here, drop a concrete block on a school bus, cause a ten-vehicle collision. You've seen that, right? It's a weird world of wackos out there." He pointed past the sealed windows of his clean, neat, sensible lab.

"If we found you the rifle, Abu, could ballistics get us a match?"

He took off his glasses and looked at them, like they might tell him the answer. It wasn't a good one for me. "No." He smiled apologetically. "Not gonna happen, Jamie."

"You're sure? If I brought you a Remington seven-millimeter rifle in here, and I said I could connect this guy to the victim, you couldn't do a match?"

He rolled his eyes at Danny. "I could *say* I got a match. But that bullet's like the Terminator chewed on it. I don't think so. I wouldn't be counting on that, Detectives."

I told him it was getting to the point where I didn't count on anything anymore.

Abu gave me a wise look. "That's a downer. Don't get in that place. No reason for a white girl to go there." He grinned. "Not yet." He pushed up the sleeves on his shirt; they fell back down. "You still look pretty okay. Go for it. You got time. Little time."

Danny Ventura thought Abu was hilarious. "Yeah, Abu, if she hurried up, she could have me. 'Magine that."

Abu said, "I don't want to."

"She's taking me out to dinner tonight."

"Didn't I say it was a weird world?"

BUT ROD DIDN'T BUY IT. And as it turned out, the state highway patrol had already hit a dead end on a similar shooting. There'd been another instance of a rifle being fired at a vehicle on the expressway; the shooting had happened just two months after Shawn's accident. In the second occurrence the shot had gone through the side rail of a truck and knocked a chicken crate off onto the road, causing a few fender benders. That bullet wasn't found. Rod said the state marshal to whom he'd spoken would look into it again but figured the shooter in both cases was just some sick kid getting his kicks standing on the overpass bridge, firing into the night. Rod told me flatly that I was insisting on connecting dots that weren't there.

But I kept at it. I had to put things together the right way so I wouldn't have to listen to "accident" and "coincidence" any longer. According to Megan Tymosz, Ben wouldn't have known a 7mm rifle from an Uzi machine gun. But there was one person in the club who presumably knew a lot about guns; he had a collection of them. Barclay. I didn't even want to ask Rod to help me persuade a judge to give me a warrant to check out that gun room at River Bend. So I fed Barclay some bullshit about how we were asking around about missing weapons, because someone was currently holding up convenience stores in the area with a 7mm rifle that had perhaps been stolen. Did Barclay have one? No he didn't. He had a 30.04, but he was too busy to locate it for me. And he was too busy to let me come by now to look for myself. But he invited me to a Christmas cocktail party on Monday. Of "our crowd," Connie would be there, he said. And the Morgans. And I could spend some time with Clay. I asked to speak to Clay now, but he wasn't home. I figured the teenager could check the gun room—not that I was going to tell my nephew that I was considering the possibility that his father was murdering old friends.

By the time Barclay and I finished our unsatisfying talk, Danny was waiting at the curb of my house in his Corvette, for me to take him to dinner at Deklerk's. He even got out of his car, though he didn't come up to the stoop. Just blew the car horn and then leaned on the door, which was what he did when he occasionally picked me up for work. He was wearing a huge orange Gore-Tex parka and very tight black pants. I sort of expected him to say, "Trick or treat."

Instead he said, "Giovanna Lucia. Looking good."

"Just for you, Donny. Hey, where's my partner, Dan? You kill him? I really appreciate it, I gotta tell you that. I couldn't stand him."

"Hey, you know it's me. Don't kid a kidder."

It was that sort of conversation for almost two hours.

Danny had gotten a new tattoo, I guess for Christmas, of a small eagle on his right bicep that he showed off by flexing his muscles in his tight black polo shirt.

While my "date" was in the bathroom, combing his hair

no doubt, I tried Clay at River Bend and this time reached him. "No problem" about getting into his father's gun room and checking out whether there was a 7mm rifle in Barclay's collection. He called back twenty minutes later to say there were three rifles in there but none of them was the sort I was describing. He blew up when I asked him if he was sure.

That, and paying the check, would have made my lousy day complete, except that at home, as soon as I escaped Danny's effort at my door to wrestle my keys out of my hand to show me "how you put a key in a lock, lady," my phone started playing its cool jazz melody over and over as I fumbled for my purse. The caller was Amanda Morgan.

Amanda wanted to give me a ride to Dante's later tonight. "We need to talk," she said.

11

AMANDA

I HAVE TO SAY THIS about Amanda. She is perfect. I mean physically. Perfect height, waist, bust, hips, legs, hands, feet. Perfect platinum hair (natural), perfect nose, chin, cheeks and lips and perfectly spaced large almond-tilted gray-blue eyes with long (natural) eyelashes. Okay, she had perfect taste too, from her sable hat to her sable coat to her soft leather slacks, boots and gloves, all of them creamy brown as Godiva chocolates. And according to the Gloria paper, she did good works for the preservation of the environment. And she won blue ribbons for the perfection of her high jump at the Devon Horse Fair.

Oh, one more thing. She is perfectly frank. Her directness was a real contrast to the soft, lush blandness of the

Latin light jazz on her car radio. I hadn't been swallowed up in the luxurious bucket seat of her blue Jaguar for two minutes when she smiled that flawless smile of hers and said, "We don't like each other. We never have."

"Why do you think that is, Amanda?"

On our way to Dante's, we headed into downtown, along streets flanked by plastic Christmas wreaths that hung from all the lampposts. I was impressed and surprised by how well she drove; she seemed to enjoy it. She had manual transmission and downshifted as we approached the green. "Well," she finally said, "you probably think it's because I married for money."

I laughed, not expecting this. "And isn't that what you did?"

Her summary of her marital life was brisk and so blunt that I believed her. "Bob, yes. He got me out of the trailer. My mother with me. But I made him happy. He had a bad heart. He said I kept him alive. Not long, but it was something." She made the remark without ego, just a fact.

"No," I agreed. "It wasn't long. And then Shawn was gone awfully fast too. I don't know, Amanda, maybe your third husband ought to worry. Maybe I ought to tell Jim to get regular checkups."

I hadn't told her about the bullet I'd found in the tire of Shawn's Chevy Tracker. I hadn't asked her about her relationship with Barclay.

Amanda was smiling as she said that her current husband, Jim Morgan, was fine; I needn't worry about him. She glanced at me, then back at the road. "Losing Shawn broke my heart. I loved him. I really did."

"I'm not arguing with you."

"Yes, you are."

She was right.

Then she laughed in a low conspiratorial way that was curiously intimate. "But, hey, Jamie, you didn't like me before I married for money."

"That's true."

"I know why."

"I'm sure you do."

But she gave me a real answer. I didn't expect it. "You didn't like me because you were in love with Garth McBride and I didn't like you because I was jealous of you for other reasons. So anyhow, I was just in a bad way a few days ago. When you saw us at the train station? All Garth was doing was saying, hang in there. Maybe I'm out of line here, but don't let me stop you if Rod doesn't. Besides, oh well, hell—" She stopped, shrugged, made the turn onto River Street.

I thought about claiming not to know what she meant by her disclaimer regarding Garth, but then, like her, I thought, what the hell. "Jealous of me for what other reasons?"

She thought for a while. "I guess, that different things came easy to us."

Her reply was so unexpected it took me aback. Neither of us spoke again till she had parked. She squeezed into a place in front of the restaurant, right across from the Christmas manger, where a dozen carolers were singing "Silent Night." We watched as they finished the song, then together headed into the dark stillness of Etten Green. There was a peculiar kind of closeness, sitting with Amanda in that warm closed space of her car, looking out at the colored lights on the town tree.

Finally I asked her, "What do you think came easy to me?"

Her gloved hands stroked the leather-wrapped wheel. Again she thought for a while. "You had a dad. He loved you."

Now I turned completely in the seat to look at her. Her profile was like the rest of her, perfect. "I thought *everything* came easy to you."

She laughed, honestly surprised. "Oh lord, no. Just boys."

"Just boys . . ."

Rueful, she took off the fur hat, smoothed her platinum hair. "Like that stupid Killing Club. I never knew what the fuck that was about, except it was the first thing anybody had ever asked me to join."

When she said it, I had flashes of memories of an Amanda Kean that I'd never thought about before. I saw her painstakingly applying makeup in the girls' bathroom at Hart High, copying the look from a photo in a magazine. I saw her carefully, slowly writing in her notebook in English class, pressing so hard the paper curled. Blushing when she mispronounced a word and the teacher corrected her. Trying unsuccessfully to think of a joking comeback when one of the in-crowd bitches asked her in the hallway where she'd gotten her sweater, Sam's Club?

As if she'd followed me through my memories, she said, "So anyhow . . . I learned. And now I don't make the same mistakes."

"No, you don't."

"Actually," she said with a kind of begrudging gratitude, "Barclay taught me a lot. He knows how things ought to look. I guess if you grow up in the middle of it, with a mother like that, you learn, even if you don't have any . . . talent for it." She laughed. "And now I look so 'right,' I think he'd like to hang me on that trophy wall at River Bend. You know, between the Mercedes and the whitetail deer."

I slid out of the Jaguar. I'd laughed too, and I needed some air to decide whether or not I was being seduced. I needed to get out of space that she owned.

"So is Garth what you wanted to talk to me about that was so important?" Amanda nodded yes. "Okay. Because I thought maybe it was Ben. About what happened to Ben? Were you and Ben ever involved?"

If she wasn't puzzled by my question, her expression was a good imitation of surprise. "Sexually? No way. I liked him though. I'm sorry he's dead. It looked like he was a good father." She walked nearer the manger in order to see the Christmas tree better. "Anyhow, I just wanted to tell you that about Garth. It was nothing."

"Well, that's what Garth told me too. Actually, he said he thought you'd been having an affair with Barclay."

"Did he? Barclay probably couldn't resist saying so." She smiled, pointing at the green. "Those lights on the tree are pretty. I think this is the nicest tree in a long time."

"Amanda, is there anybody in Gloria you aren't sleeping with?"

She smiled. "You." She dropped her car keys in her purse. "You'd probably be disappointed if you knew how low the numbers really were."

"Did Shawn ever *think* you and Ben were involved?"

She took the question in stride. "He never said so. And he would have, if he'd thought it. Shawn had a problem with jealousy. Real problem. But I don't think it was ever about Ben."

Amanda seemed not to mind standing out on the town green at night answering my questions. Maybe sable kept you really warm.

"How about the night he died? Did Shawn have a problem with jealousy that night? Amanda, I'm trying to get at why you and Ben let him drive off by himself if he was so drunk."

Her answer seemed both serious and regretful: The morning of the accident, Shawn and she had had a huge fight after he'd accused her of flirting with the riding instructor at the local stables. (She hadn't been, she said; she was just trying to learn how to ride.) He'd stayed angry with her all day. He'd remained angry in Atlantic City at the casino that night where they'd gone by prior arrangement with Ben and Megan Tymosz. Yes, it was possible Shawn hadn't eaten all that day. Yes, she'd been surprised that he was acting so intoxicated, but knew he'd had only two drinks and had attributed his behavior to his mood. He'd said some ugly things to her. That's why she'd let him drive off alone and that's why she had accepted a ride with the Tymoszes. "I never would have let him go if I'd thought he was drunk enough to lose control of the car. When they told me he was dead . . . I think I died too for a long time. We'd been hoping to have a baby . . ." She stopped herself. "Why are you asking me about this?"

"I'm wondering if Shawn's death is somehow connected to Ben's. You know, Pudge thinks somebody killed Ben."

She looked at me, then shrugged, lifting the shoulders of the sable effortlessly. "Do you?"

"Maybe." I turned toward her, looked at her. "Just for the record, it wasn't you, was it?"

"Oh, Jamie." She actually laughed out loud, and put her arm through mine as we crossed the street. Her boots had heels; she was a good four inches taller than I was. I felt like a child in my parka and jeans and sneakers. She added casually, "But I will tell you a crime I did commit, since we're being so chummy here."

I pulled free as we reached the curb. "A crime?" I waited to hear what she had to say before opening the door to Dante's.

"I'm the one," she confided, "who stole Mary Beth's pearls. You remember that, how she freaked when she lost them?"

I did remember. Connie's girlfriend, Mary Beth O'Faolain, had been hysterical at the loss of her confirmation pearls, which she'd claimed had been stolen from the zip pouch of her purse. They were never recovered. Almost everyone, including the school authorities, thought she'd lost them and had tried to fob off the blame on an imaginary thief.

Amanda looked into my eyes. It was a disconcertingly direct stare. "I had some fake pearls. I loved to wear them. But then Mary Beth wore hers one day. They were the first real pearls I ever saw." She reached the door to Dante's, turned back to me. "And I could tell the difference." She held open her coat for me to look at; the lining was deep green silk. "That's one thing I can say about me. I could always tell the difference. So, no, I didn't love Bob and I don't love Jim. And, between you and me, God knows I don't love Barclay Ober. But I was nuts about Shawn."

WHAT AMANDA SAID to the five of us seated at one of Pudge's large round tables was equally surprising. As

Pudge placed plates of gelato and pastries on the green-checked cloth, he told everyone that he'd spoken tonight with Wendy, who managed a "natural remedies" franchise in Portland, and with Jeremy, a cruise agent in Atlanta. He'd updated them on "the situation." They'd both said hello to us all but felt they really had nothing to add one way or the other about how Ben might have died. It was no doubt true.

Then Pudge pulled up his chair and raised his glass of wine. "Merry Christmas. Now, can we get serious?" He said he had called this meeting because not only was he certain Ben's death was a murder, but he was more and more convinced that somebody might try to kill the rest of us too, although Pudge admitted he couldn't imagine a motive except craziness. He added that I agreed with him, which he believed ought to mean something to them because I was a police detective.

"That true?" Barclay asked me with a smirk. "You really think Ben was murdered, Jamie? Because I think that's completely insane."

Debbie and Connie looked at me as if they wholeheartedly agreed with Barclay, but neither said anything.

"So why are you here then?" I asked Barclay. Actually it looked like he was here to get close to Amanda, who unobtrusively foiled every effort he made to sit next to her, or even to make eye contact.

"To support Pudge," he replied. "He's upset and we thought it would help." Debbie and Connie nodded in agreement.

Pudge then turned to Amanda, who sat with her sable flung open over her chair like she was waiting for a plane in a VIP lounge. "Come on, Amanda, you knew Ben. You and

Shawn liked him. Don't you think we ought to do something for him?"

Amanda thought about it. Then she said, "Well, I think if anybody did kill Ben, it was Lyall Hillier."

We all just stared at her. Then I pointed out that Lyall had drowned himself in the Deep Port River. He'd been dead for more than a decade.

She shrugged. "Maybe not."

12

LYALL

PUDGE'S PARTY, as Debbie oddly called the re-union at Dante's, went on until midnight. We drank two bottles of a great Torcolato wine, ate a lot of blue cheese with pears and argued with each other.

There was a kind of consensus, I suppose: Barclay, Debbie, Connie and Amanda thought it was crazy for Pudge and me to think someone might have murdered Ben. They agreed that whoever was leaving spooky movie quotes for me was sick but harmless.

If someone *had* murdered Ben, then Barclay, Debbie, Pudge, Connie and I thought it was insane of Amanda to suggest that the murderer might be Lyall, still alive after all these years and out for revenge against the Killing Club for undisclosed reasons.

Connie and Barclay were almost jostling to get next to her, both saying the idea was "nuts."

Debbie agreed. "Amanda, you were kidding, right? You don't seriously believe Lyall climbed out of the river and hung around Gloria for the next ten years without letting anybody know about it, and now he's pretending to be Michael Myers in *Halloween* and is murdering us all for no reason?"

Amanda looked at us, one by one. "I didn't say there was no reason. And I don't think Ben *was* murdered. I'm just saying, *if* he was murdered, maybe Lyall did it."

Even Pudge, already upset because no one seemed to agree with his theory that some local sociopath had fixated on the Killing Club, had gotten hold of our old murder stories and was acting them out and had sent me the notes to say so, even Pudge, impatient with no one, was impatient with Amanda. "Lyall? Oh, come on. Lyall's dead."

She pulled her long fur coat in front of her body like a shield. "Fine, guys. But nobody ever found Lyall's body, did they? And he had a lot of reasons to be pissed."

That puzzled me. "What reasons?"

Connie yanked his chair over next to Amanda and spoke to her quietly, leaning toward her the way priests get in the habit of doing, I suppose. "Lyall drowned himself in Deep Port River. It's not something we ought to joke about."

Amanda arched away from him. "I'm not joking."

I tried again. "Why do you think Lyall would want to kill us?"

For a long while, she looked at everyone, then she turned toward the front window of Dante's, where a beautiful old wood Italian crèche sat on white gauze under a sky of tiny gold electric lights. There was an odd sort of stubborn defensiveness in her voice. "People in this room know the answer to that."

"What's that supposed to mean?" As I asked Amanda the question, I was studying the familiar faces around the table. But they all looked, or pretended to look, equally puzzled by her remark.

"This whole thing is crazy." Debbie angrily took the rings off her fingers, then shoved them back on. "I don't know why you started it, Pudge. Nobody killed anybody. Ben's dead. I'm sorry. It was an accident. And Lyall's dead. A long time ago. Is everybody going insane here?"

Pudge said he was almost sorry that he'd ever called this meeting. "But somebody stuck death threats in Jamie's door! I didn't make that up. And I think the police ought to find out who it was."

"Those notes are somebody's dumb idea of a joke." Barclay pushed his expensive watch in Pudge's face as if time itself were Pudge's fault. "You know what I can't believe? I'm even wasting my time here. I was supposed to go to the *Messiah* with Tricia tonight."

Debbie snorted, looking deliberately from him to Amanda. "Right, like you're broken-hearted. You're such bullshit, Barclay."

Barclay flung himself back from the table, jabbing his arms through his elegant overcoat. "This is all totally insane. I'm out of here. Amanda, could I see you for a second?"

She turned her back on him. "Sorry, I need to make a phone call."

Barclay left but Amanda didn't make a phone call.

So, other than the Italian desserts, which everyone but Amanda ate, the evening had proved a complete bust. Everyone had talked a lot, but overall, I'd say the words most frequently spoken were *insane* and *crazy*. I had done my best. I wore my Olympic Magnum in a shoulder holster and took off my ski jacket so they could see the seriousness of the snub-nose. I told them we all should be careful. I handed out copies of the notes I'd gotten, *"Death has come to your little town, Sheriff"* and *"Was that the bogeyman? As a matter of fact . . . it was."* I told them there was physical evidence at the Tymosz house that Ben's accident had been rigged.

I also handed out copies I'd Xeroxed from the Death Books of various murders imagined by each of them during the three years of the Killing Club. I suggested they stay out of the situations they'd once created. There was uneasy laughter at the silliness of their old fantasy crimes: Debbie was going to lock the gym teacher in the steam room till she sweated to death. Amanda, who (unlike Debbie) enjoyed and excelled in sports, was going to kill any number of in-crowd girls any number of athletic ways that would look like accidents—a horse would kick them to death, an arrow would impale them, heavy free weights would fall on them, they'd be trapped under swimming pool covers and be choked by gymnast rings. Barclay was going to pass off the murder of his mother as a drowning. Pudge was going to boil Eileen's father (who hit her) in the huge deep-fat doughnut vat at the local bakery. Connie was going to inject the basketball coach (who had diabetes) with an overdose of insulin.

There appeared to be little concern now that these same homicides could happen to their imaginers. But, then, did I actually think that any of the clever undetectable household accidents that I'd planned on carrying out against my high school enemies would be inflicted on me? Would a high-volt live wire fall on my car, a gas leak spread poison through my sleeping house, cyanide be "accidentally" ingested with my antihistamines? Did I really fear those, or half a dozen other sudden deaths? Not really. Then why should my fellow club members expect to be murdered? Nor, as they certainly insisted, should they have plans to kill anyone else. Why should Lyall Hillier want to do so either?

Lyall had never talked much during Killing Club meetings at the playhouse; I remembered whole evenings of his sitting on the floor, his hands motionless on his crossed knees, without saying a word. He had a remarkable stillness to him. I could never decide what his stillness meant—that he was paralyzed with shyness? Exhausted by anxieties? Did he take as many drugs as he sold to his friends? Or was it just a kind of acceptance of his peripheral role in life, a contentment to watch?

After Lyall's suicide, I figured that what he had accepted, for whatever unspoken reason, had been despair. Looking back, I'd seen in his eyes that he was hopeless; I'd just never paid attention. We didn't know each other well; he was Garth's friend. Garth's shadow.

From childhood on, Lyall had been very thin, with long narrow features that made his jade-green eyes look larger and sadder. In high school, he wore a snake ring on his forefinger and a favorite corduroy jacket, the nutmeg color of his hair, that had a wide black plastic zipper and a decal of a Tour de France cyclist on the back. I remember that he often spoke about liking the bike-racing movie *Breaking Away*, and that Garth had referred to it at his memorial service—that Lyall had broken away from us.

When Amanda brought the gathering at Dante's to a halt by saying that Lyall might be alive and that he had reason to be pissed at us, I assumed she meant that he felt his fellow "outsiders" in the club had let him down by not being more sympathetic and supportive, that he'd killed himself because of some failure in us to stop him. Over the years since his drowning, after I'd started to deal as a police officer with teens and narcotics, I considered the possibility that the dealers Lyall had been getting his stuff from had gotten rid of him. His file made it clear the police hadn't fully pursued a homicide in relation to his death. The more likely possibilities were that he was a serious drug addict with a preexisting mood disorder—maybe he was bipolar—or that he was gay but had felt unable to come out, although there were plenty of openly gay kids in Hart High; they even had an official Gay and Lesbian Alliance and held meetings all the time. So I don't know; he was an only child with older-than-average parents who kept to themselves; maybe he thought they wouldn't be able to deal with a homosexual son. In the last Death Book, he had "murdered" both his parents in some ingenious way—so perhaps he feared the news of his drug-dealing or addiction or his sexual orientation would kill them, or perhaps he really wanted them dead.

Amanda was the most dramatic, but not the first person to bring up the possibility that Lyall was still alive. Even at the time of his suicide, there had been speculation that he hadn't actually jumped into the river, that the drowning was a hoax. It was definite that something had smashed through the thin ice spreading from the embankment over the dark fast current of Deep Port River, but in the beginning the idea had been raised that maybe it hadn't been Lyall. It was just that no one had said it in a long time, not for a decade. The case was closed.

The morning after his disappearance, the police had found his overcoat with his wallet in it under a cinderblock on the old docks. In the wallet was a letter asking his parents to forgive him. The letter looked to be in his handwriting. Nearby on the river bottom, divers found a Bass loafer identified as Lyall's. They didn't find anything else in the right place on the river bottom that might have been used to make the jagged hole in the ice. Although his body was never recovered, the coroner ruled probable suicide, concluding that Lyall had gone into the icy river on purpose. It was clear that, thin and coatless, he would have quickly succumbed to hypothermia as he was swept into the harbor by the outgoing tide. Finally the conclusion that he was dead came down to—where else could he be? If his mother and father clung to the hope that their son was playing some dreadful joke on them, they eventually gave up as well. Sure, it was possible to disappear completely. But, sadly, teen suicide was not uncommon. We had a memorial service. His parents put up a gravestone.

LYALL HILLIER
1974–1992
Beloved Son

If he was beloved, he must not have felt it. The truth is, I'd sometimes thought he was in love with Garth. But then, who wasn't?

Barclay's outburst at Pudge and his storming off had ended the get-together just before midnight, with nothing settled and no one happy. Pudge wouldn't let us help clean up, though Connie insisted on carrying glasses out to the kitchen for him anyhow. Pudge was visibly upset, his face blotchy; maybe Connie wanted to give him a chance to talk about his disappointment that no one would take his fears seriously.

Outside, the holiday lights on the streets and the green had all been turned off. It was so dark that I couldn't see the clock tower on the town hall. The stars looked small, far away and useless. As we walked toward her Jaguar, Amanda took my arm and surprised me again. "Jamie, I should have said something on the way here, because it's really been bothering me, but all of a sudden it sounded so dumb. And we were talking for the first time like people, and . . ."

I stopped her. "About Lyall?"

"Maybe. Somebody's been following me," she said. "For weeks. That's why I've been wondering if maybe Lyall isn't really dead." Somehow even fear, if that's what it was—and that's what it looked like—couldn't disturb the perfection of her features.

"What do you mean, following you?" I stopped her as we moved onto the sidewalk. "Like stalking?"

"Sort of. In a car. Staying right behind me, speeding up and then slowing down when I do. Changing lanes when I do. Then when I get home, he drives away. I don't get out of the car till he drives away."

"God, Amanda. Why *didn't* you tell me this? Can you identify the person? Or the car?"

She said the car had only followed her at night; she'd never seen the driver and really hadn't seen the car itself well either because of the blinding lights, but she thought it was large and dark-colored. She said at first she'd dismissed her suspicion as just nerves after Ben's death; later, she'd felt too foolish to mention it to others—afraid they'd think she was imagining things. "But I wasn't, Jamie. Somebody's deliberately creeping me out. But I don't know who."

I asked her if this had ever happened to her before. She said that it had, long ago, but in the past she'd assumed it was Shawn following her, out of jealousy.

"Now I know it wasn't Shawn. And I'm a little scared. I got this." She took a folded piece of paper from her very expensive handbag. It wasn't pasted letters; it was a printout. But each word was big and in a different font. There was only one line on it, one I had heard before: *"I hate a guy with a car and no sense of humor."*

"Oh, Jesus. Where did this come from, Amanda, and how long have you had it?"

She'd found it this morning under her windshield wiper, in her garage. The Morgans didn't lock their garage. Why should they? They lived on the good side of the river in an exclusive community of new six-thousand-square-foot McMansions circling a private golf course. She looked honestly baffled. "What does it mean?"

I told her it was a line from *Halloween*, just like the two notes left at my door. I didn't know what it meant specifically. Maybe it meant something in the context of the movie, which I would watch again. Wearing gloves, I folded the note and put it in my jacket. Then I made a decision to tell Amanda about the bullet Danny and I had found in Shawn's tire. When I finished, she burst into tears. It was startling, a childlike sort of crying that didn't fit at all with her flawless face. She was so upset that I found myself emphasizing to her that Rod agreed with the state patrol, who believed that the shooter had fired randomly, that no one was trying deliberately to kill Shawn.

"It's still murder!" she said.

"Yes, it is. And the New Jersey State Police are investigating it now. It's their case."

Trembling, she dropped her keys; they were on a sterling silver ring I recognized from the Tiffany's catalog. I picked them up, handed them back and she clicked the lock open on her Jaguar.

"Amanda, wait a minute. There's a chance the same guy who shot at Shawn's car is following you around now. It's a real long shot, and I don't want to scare you, but be careful, okay?" I gave her my card. "You get the slightest hint somebody's following you again, you call my cell phone."

The whole time I was talking with Amanda, I was also considering the possibility that she was suckering me, just as she had Mary Beth O'Faolain, when she'd pretended so sympathetically to search for pearls she herself had stolen. Maybe she'd typed the note herself, lied about being followed. But why would she scam me? One reason could be that she had killed Ben, because he was going to confess to me that together they'd gotten rid of Shawn. Or maybe it had been only because she needed to distract me. After all, she was having an affair with Barclay, and since they were both married and both socially prominent, they wanted to keep it very quiet.

She interrupted. "So you don't think there's a chance Lyall is alive?"

"It seems pretty unlikely." I asked her again what she'd meant by all her mysterious insinuations about Lyall's reasons to be angry with the Killing Club.

"You need to ask other people about that." She looked across the street, and said, "Oh, great."

"What other people?"

"I really don't want to talk about it, Jamie." She opened her car door. "I need to get to bed. I'm going riding very early."

I saw that she'd been watching Barclay hurry across the street toward us from the end of the block. He must have been sitting in his car, waiting for her to come out.

Maybe Barclay himself was Amanda's "stalker"—scared he was losing her to someone else. Or maybe some other man was following her around town to see if she was still seeing Barclay. Or maybe, and who could blame him, Jim Morgan had hired a private investigator to find out if his wife was cheating on him. Maybe Morgan's P.I. was tailing her.

Barclay reached us, grabbed Amanda's arm and pulled her away, but not far enough, given the decibel level of his voice. "I need to talk to you."

She flung off his arm. "It's late."

He pushed between us, ignoring me. His neck thickened as he grabbed her again. "I don't care what time it is, you bitch! You got what you wanted and now you're dumping me? I don't think so!"

She slapped him in the face. I'd actually never seen a

woman slap a man before except in the movies. Barclay's cheek immediately turned crimson. She stared at him for a minute. "I haven't made mistakes like you in a long time." Then she turned to me. "I'm very sorry, Jamie. Could you ask Pudge to take you home? Good night." She slid quickly into the Jaguar and accelerated so fast, without even fully closing the door, that Barclay had to leap away.

Without speaking to each other, we both watched the blue car make the left turn just as the light went from yellow to red.

Barclay didn't even look at me, just ran back down the street. Along the way, he furiously picked up a trash can and smashed it into a lamppost. Rubbish like soda cans and newspapers flew into the gutter.

A minute later the Mercedes turned right on River. I didn't know whether he was trying to fool me by going in the opposite direction from Amanda or he really had given up for the night.

In the window of Dante's I could see Pudge and Connie hurry to the window to see what the noise had been about. Pudge had balled the green-checked cloth off the table into a heap that he hugged to his chest.

He was happy to drive me home. But I decided to walk instead. It wasn't really that far to Dock and Fourteenth. No one walks much in Gloria anymore. I've known people to drive their cars a single block to pick up a pizza. Even at midnight there were a few people driving around in the center of town; maybe they'd stopped at Deklerk's after Christmas shopping. The temperature was falling fast but I had a good enough pace going to keep warm. The streets got darker as I moved away from downtown. There were fewer lamplights, and some weren't working. Most people had turned off their Christmas lights in the row house windows.

By Twelfth Street it was clear to me that there was a car cruising slowly after me, staying about two blocks behind. It was the first time, even after the anonymous notes, that I'd had the creepy feeling that the danger was personal, that somebody was out there, maybe Lyall, maybe someone unknown to me, plotting to murder all the members of the Killing Club, and right now, me.

When I'm scared, I fight. So now I spun around to face the car, but all I could see was its lights. The brights were on. When I turned toward it, the car stopped. Then when I resumed my walk, it followed. Stepping quickly back into an alley between two storefronts, I waited for the car to pass me. It didn't. So, pulling out my gun from the shoulder holster, figuring I'd at least scare them, I ran toward the car as fast as I could, but the dark sedan went fast into reverse, backing into the dark intersection it had just crossed; it skidded on the side street and roared away. I couldn't see the plates. I waited a while and then jogged the last two blocks home.

THAT NIGHT, WHEN I TOLD ROD what had happened as I was walking home, he asked if I wanted a squad car to check by my house every few hours. But by then I'd decided the driver was just some guy getting his kicks, trying to spook me, or hoping to pick me up or figuring any woman out on the Gloria streets at that hour wanted to be picked up.

I stayed downstairs till three A.M. with my dad and Sam the cat, watching cable. Dad loves to have somebody to

watch his old movies with and I was too rattled to sleep anyhow. Dino was gone for the night, playing stuff like Aero-
smith covers in A.C., or so he'd said on the note he'd left.
Dad and Dino weren't talking because of Dino's joyriding
conviction for "borrowing" Ramon's truck (for which he'd
also been fired by Jonesy's Marina). On my advice (more like
a threat), my brother had pleaded guilty and gotten a
thousand-dollar fine plus a hundred hours of community
service. He'd been lucky to get Judge Louise Voisey, my favorite on the bench and a woman with a sense of humor—
or maybe she just liked Joan Baez. At any rate, she'd
sentenced Dino to play "folk" music once a week at the Gloria senior citizens center. For a year. The judge had brought
along to court her own "Easy to Play Tunes" from her piano
bench, which she lent to him. The book was called "Folk Fa-
vorites for Young and Old," and included such songs as "If I
Had a Hammer" and "Shenandoah." It seemed to strike
Dino like food poisoning.

Dad and I had a good laugh about Dino's sentence. I
promised to drive my father in his wheelchair-ready van to
the center to hear the first concert. We told him we'd get
Aunt Betty to request a lot of the Kingston Trio's big hits.

Despite a late-night showing of *Bullitt*, Dad's spirits
were low, as they tended to get around Christmastime. We
both missed Gina the most then; she'd always tried so hard
to make up for the mother and wife who wasn't there—cart-
ing down all the old boxes of decorations, filling the house
with the sound of carols and the smell of baking ginger-
bread. Joe Jr.'s Christmas Eve visits with his perky wife and
sullen children were getting shorter each year, and even
though Dad said, "The shorter the better," it hurt his feel-

ings. And Dino's feckless troubles weren't helping. "I swear on my mother's grave, I'm throwing him out of the house," my father said tonight, as he watched me let the cat out the door. "Let Dino find out what it's like to live in the real world."

But we both knew he wouldn't do it. "Be sure you find Sam before you go to sleep," he added. "It's too cold for him to stay outside."

THE NEXT DAY I HAD OFF and I slept in. It was a few minutes after nine when my dad woke me, calling urgently on the intercom that I'd set up between the downstairs rooms and mine. He said that Danny Ventura was at the door and needed to see me right away. Hurrying, I pulled on a blue quilted bathrobe I'd gotten from Joe Jr.'s wife last Christmas and had never worn.

Danny wore a black parka and a black hunter's cap with the flaps tied under his chin. He was banging his hands in their thick black ski gloves together, and he didn't look happy. "Hi, Dan, what's the problem? I'm off today. Jesus, it's cold! Come on inside." I tugged at him, but he stepped back, pointing at his car at the curb. "What are you doing here Sunday morning?"

"We gotta go, Jamie. Rod's waiting at the scene."

"What scene?"

"He told me to keep calling you. He's been trying. Some college kids just found a woman's body in the woods near that new nature trail in Etten Park. Rod said you know her. So call him."

"Who is it?" My body jerked involuntarily and I hugged

myself to keep still. I thought he was going to tell me it was
Debbie's body they'd found. But he didn't. "Rod said I
should let you know. Somebody named Amanda Morgan.
Somebody got her with a crossbow."

I had trouble taking it in. "Amanda Morgan? What are
you telling me? That she's dead?"

"Oh yeah, totally. Got her right through the eye."

13

GERT

ETTEN PARK WAS two hundred fiercely protected acres of nature preserve, with the local country
club's riding stables on one side of it and the latest
Ober subdivision on the other. It had started out as a private
amusement park beside a lake, built on the site of a settle-
ment of the Absegami Indians, a local branch of the Leni-
Lenape. A 1920s bronze statue allegedly representing their
first chief (wearing the full headdress of a Crow warrior
from the Northern Great Plains) still stood in front of the
skating rink where Gert Anderssen had once amazed a group
of us from the police department with a display of figure
skating leaps and turns and spirals. By 1918, when they put

in the carousel and paddleboat rides and the long fishing pier with its dance hall, the Indians were long gone, except for a few descendants like Rod's family. The ironworks factory, whose rusted parts could still be seen in picnic tables along the trails, was gone too.

Scowling the whole way there, Danny raced his Corvette to Etten Park (ninety miles an hour on the four-lane, fifty on the gravel road into the woods) while Rod prepared me over the phone for what I was going to see. For hours after the dispatcher took the call from two college kids on a hike who had stumbled upon Amanda's body, Rod had been trying to phone my turned-off cell and our landline (Dad takes it off the hook on Saturday nights because Dino's drunk buddies have been known to ring up at five in the morning). Then he'd sent Danny over to get me. So I knew what to expect. I told myself I was ready.

Rod was waiting in the little parking lot where old snow had been plowed in mounds against the bordering logs. I could see yellow GPD tape behind the cars: two squad cars, the road rescue ambulance, Rod's Jeep, Gert Anderssen's Volvo station wagon and the new blue Jaguar with the special nature preserve plate. Danny slammed on his brakes, almost hitting a pair of bicycles hidden on the other side of the Jag. Without a word, he was out the door and running past Rod toward the crime scene, following the yellow tape. It led through thickly clustered pines around a curve on a dirt trail. When Rod and I rounded the turn, I could see the top of a huge bare oak tree where Danny was just joining some EMS medics and four of our GPD uniforms, three guys and a young woman—the only Asian on the force, Naoko

Hayakawa. They were all standing under the oak, close together, hiding the body from my view. Our one-man forensics team, Abu Tomkins, was taking digital photographs.

Next to them, and as tall as Abu, Gert stood in a thin jacket and hatless—her hair a startling white in the sun—nodding kindly as she listened to a young couple in jeans.

The oak was the oldest, largest tree in the park, and had a marker on it saying so. Now it would be even more famous. Because someone had been killed there.

The park was no longer "the" place to go for fun around Gloria, but it was still popular in summer for family camping. In winter, the lake was off-limits, but a dozen nature trails were used for hikes and for cross-country skiing if there was any snow. There wasn't much snow now, just a few spotty patches in the shade, and the ground was so frozen that new tracks were going to be hard to find.

Rod gave my shoulder a comforting squeeze as I took off my winter gloves, put on latex ones. "You ready?" he asked.

"Yeah, I'm okay."

"Normal idea would be somebody had a shot go wild, never knew he hit her. That was Gert's first thought. Or that maybe some idiot mistook her for a deer—she's got on a fur coat—shot her, then panicked and ran."

I was already trying to fix the terrain in my memory. "Well, we know the normal idea is wrong this time, don't we?"

Slowly Rod nodded. "Yeah, we do." He pointed in a wide arc at the thickly wooded area. "The arrow could have come from anywhere. Some of these crossbows, you can do twelve, fourteen hundred yards with them. But of course, makes it flukier, the trees are pretty thick."

Rod's black hair looked almost electric in the dry air and when he rubbed it, a current pulled it toward his hand. Like Gert, he was always hatless; maybe because they'd both been serious athletes, the cold didn't bother them. Plus she was from Sweden. This weather might feel like spring to her.

Ahead of us, Gert gently led the college kids away from the tree, and I saw what I'd been told to expect. When I did, I stumbled slightly, caught Rod's arm. "I'm okay."

About fifty yards off, wearing her long sable coat over some brown riding pants, Amanda stood impaled against the trunk of the oak tree, shot through the eye with a metal arrow, the kind they call a bolt, that's used in a crossbow.

True, Amanda was wearing fur that could have been mistaken for a deer. True, it was the local deer season these weeks in December. Danny Ventura had recently boasted about killing a buck on opening day. (He already had more venison in his freezer than he could eat if he stayed on the Atkins diet the rest of his life.) While hunting was illegal in Etten Park, true, people violated the rules. There were antlered deer grazing on acorns all through the surrounding woods, and we'd had maniacs shoot each other before. Last winter someone had shot a cow in a dairy pasture.

But a hunter hadn't shot Amanda. I'd known that the minute I'd spoken to Rod. Now I handed him the third Death Book. I'd brought it with me from home, grabbing it from my bedroom desk as I hurried into my clothes. The book was opened to the page with Amanda's description of how she could steal a Hart High archery set and use it to kill the student council president, passing the girl's death off as a deer-hunting accident. Rod read through the page, then rolled the notebook and stuck it in his pocket.

"Homicide," I said. I stopped him in the path. "This time you're not going to argue with me, right? Rod? Homicide."

He nodded. "Right. It looks that way. I talked to Chief Waige. He's on board. So this one's yours, Jamie. I told Danny he's second on this. He doesn't like it but that's the way it is. You use what you need."

As we slowly walked the trail, Rod went on with a steady calm flow of facts; I'd learned from him to use that tone with relatives of victims, because it made hard things easier to hear. "It's a ten-inch carbon bolt with a hundred-gram target point. Shattered the right eye socket, exited the back of the skull. The tip's two inches into the wood. My guess is a crossbow with a real power stroke, two-hundred-pound draw or more."

I kept hearing Clay describe Barclay's gunroom: "He's got a scope on this big-ass crossbow so he can kill Bambi without ever looking at him." I told Rod, "I need a search warrant for River Bend." I told him about last night, how Amanda had slapped Barclay after he'd called her a bitch and vowed it wasn't over between them.

Rod made the call to the courthouse right there.

When he finished, I said, "It's fifteen degrees. What was she doing out here?" I pulled my thick wool ski cap down over my ears.

"Well, it's actually not a bad walk, only a quarter mile, to the riding stables along this nature trail. The woman there said she liked to walk it, being on the preservation board and all, check things out, I guess. They were expecting her at the indoor ring at seven. They had her horse ready to go, but she never showed."

"The two college kids?"

"Here to bird count for the Nature Preserve. They saw her as soon as they came 'round that bend and they called 911 right away. Dispatcher logged it at 8:09. Sent the uniforms and then phoned me. We lucked out a little because Bill and Naoko happened to be doing a look 'round Etten Lake. Here's the weird thing: Amanda'd called the station just a week ago, wanting us to do something about people chopping down Christmas trees in the park. So Bill and Naoko were on the scene right away, and Gert got here by 8:45. Said she'd been dead maybe an hour and a half. Around seven."

"Wouldn't have been enough light much earlier than that. The shooter was aiming for her, so he had to be able to see her. Even with a scope, he had to have some light."

It was, Rod told me, 141 yards to the tree from the curve that masked the trail from the parking lot, a clear shot with a good enough scope. Could be the shooter even had a night scope.

"So either somebody came here with Amanda and walked away from the scene or he had his own car." My eyes were moving in careful square sections over the ground, checking ahead of me along the path, then to the left, then to the right. "Any chance of other car treads? Footprints?"

Rod shook his head. "Don't think so. Ground's so hard now. A hundred partials, but who knows how old. It's the holidays. People are out here, hiking, biking, cutting holly. Abu did a few casts near the Jag anyhow."

We'd reached the body and now I had to look. Amanda was literally held against the oak tree by the strength of the carbon arrow that had gone through her head. Its plastic feathers brushed her skin around her eye socket. That side of her face was black with blood where the bone had shattered. Her other eye was open, staring at me without interest. Blood had dried in the corner of her mouth, under her nose, and had caked her hair. The back of her skull was stuck into the tree bark by the arrow's head.

I studied her a long while. Everyone was quiet while I did. Then Gert stepped over to me and placed her hand lightly on my back. "Rod tells me you knew her. I am so sorry."

I shook my head, made myself swallow. "We weren't close."

"But such a beautiful woman. What an awful shame it is."

"Yes, it is."

Gert's eyes were kind. "It was so fast she never had any fear. And no pain. Just died right away."

"Yes, I see that. But before he shot her, we don't know what he said, or did, do we?"

Something glinted in the dead leaves at Amanda's feet, hidden half under her soft brown leather riding boot. Her keys. She must have had them in her hand, dropped them when the arrow struck her. There were five keys on the silver Tiffany ring, along with the black Jaguar computer lock. I recognized them from having picked them up when Amanda had dropped the ring on the sidewalk last night after we'd left Dante's together.

But something had been added to the ring; something that hadn't been there last night. It was a Yale key and it was tied to a red piece of yarn. It looked a lot like a key I'd seen recently taped to the Death Book: the key Connie had copied for us long ago at his father's hardware store, so all the members of the Killing Club could open the padlock on the door to the Pine Barrens Playhouse.

TWO HOURS LATER, I was still at the scene. Near noon, it was not much warmer; the sky grayer than blue. We'd sent the college students off on their bicycles. They'd told us all they knew. It wasn't much. When they'd arrived at the parking lot, there'd been no other cars there but Amanda's Jaguar. They'd seen no one else on the trail. Amanda had looked exactly as she'd looked when the police arrived. They'd touched nothing.

Gert and the EMS unit went to the morgue with the body. Gert promised to call me with any information. She hugged me with a kind rub on my back. It was interesting that neither her job nor her long affair with Chief Waige (who, as far as I could tell, had none of her compassion) had hardened her.

A tow truck showed up to take the Jaguar to our garage, where every inch of it would be studied for evidence, its carpeting vacuumed, all surfaces dusted for prints.

Rod sent Bill and Naoko off to pick up the warrant in order to search Barclay's gun room. Then he left in the other squad car to break the news to Amanda's husband, Jim Morgan.

Of the three of us still in the park, Abu Tomkins was photographing the crime scene, including any tire treads that looked recent. Danny and I were moving out from the oak tree, side by side, walking slowly, looking among dead leaves and branches and mossy earth for anything that could help us. We bagged it all, knowing almost none of it would likely prove meaningful—a beer can pop-top, cellophane from a cigarette pack, part of a broken dog collar, part of a ballpoint pen. Danny was sullen about my being senior on the case. But I was always senior on homicides. I'd made sergeant a year before he had. I'd scored 22 percent higher on the detective exam. He'd always hated that fact. This time was worse, because of the circumstances—Danny was, after all, a deer hunter who'd "bagged a twelve-point rack last winter" and who was I?

I'd been listening to his mumbling for an hour: "What do you get out of murder, Ferrara? Looking at corpses. Why don't you get married?"

"Why don't you?" We were both squatting to study a broken piece of hard plastic I'd picked out of the earth.

"You're supposed to be a girl."

"Oh, grow up." I shoved him with the heel of my palm. Off balance, he fell backward. "I'm sick of this shit from you every time we start a homicide. You need to get over the fact that I'm female."

"You sure have," he muttered. "See, you do that to me, shove me, and get away with it. Because what am I going to do? But you don't want it the other way." Brushing off his sleeves, he pulled himself to his feet.

I leaned toward him with my hands tight. "Want it the other way?" I was a Tae Kwon Do second-degree black belt and Danny had reason to know it. A year ago, he'd seen me break the arm of a guy who'd pulled a switchblade on me.

Shaking his head, he headed back toward the parking lot.

"You're an asshole, Ventura," I yelled after him.

Abu Tomkins wasn't very enthusiastic about the work either, but that was just because he hated to be outside. He hated the heat, but he hated the cold more. Wearing a one-piece neon-blue snowsuit with a bright yellow wool ski mask, he told me he was ready to leave now, he'd *been* ready. While we talked, he periodically scanned the area with binoculars, worried, he said, about trespassing deer hunters accidentally shooting him. "Only thing brown you can see on me," he said, "is my nose. I do not want some shit-assed Rambo mounting my head on his damn wall with a label on it says 'Africanus Americanus.'"

"Abu, come on. You seriously think some hunter's going to cross a crime scene tape to take a shot at you? That's not going to happen."

"I'll tell you what I do know. Nobody's going to shoot me in my lab."

At that moment Danny came running back from the woods off to the left of the parking lot. Grabbing the binoculars from Abu, he shoved them at me. He looked excited and had forgotten to be angry. "Look over there! Somebody drove a car over those bushes, like today."

I trained the glasses where he was pointing. At the far edge of the lot, where it circled back to the gravel road, a mungo pine was crushed down. The three of us hurried over. The breaks in the branches looked fresh. Danny squatted down, his face inches from a faint squiggly rectangular indentation in the dirt about four inches long. After a while he said, "That's a Pirelli high-performance tire."

I crawled over beside him. "From the Jaguar?"

"Nope. Jag had Michelins."

"Would you use those on a Mercedes SL600?"

"If I had one, I might. Take some photos, Abu." He

turned to me, his face mocking apology. "I'm sorry. Is that all right, Detective, if I ask Abu to photo that tread? I mean, you're senior."

Danny Ventura was a jerk but he knew his cars.

AT RIVER BEND, Naoko and Bill searched Barclay's gun room and found a crossbow hanging on a wall. They bagged it and brought it in. But it had dust all over it, plus it used a smaller arrow than the one that had killed Amanda. Barclay hadn't been home when they'd served the warrant. Meredith Ober had followed them into the gun room, outraged on her son's behalf to see his "private possessions" being "manhandled" by the Gloria police.

Barclay was, Meredith told us, already upset enough, having awakened to find his Mercedes SL600 stolen. He was, she told the officers, at the Dixon Building right this minute, reporting the theft.

14

MEREDITH

AFTER DANNY DROPPED ME OFF, I drove straight to River Bend while he went to the garage to help them check out Amanda's Jaguar. It was around two o'clock, clouds gathering. Barclay's mother, wife and son met me in a living room large enough to have a grand piano, three separate clusters of silk couches and chairs and a ten-foot mirror over the fireplace mantel. Of the eight high windows, two were blocked by a Christmas tree the size of the one on the town green. In an elegant wool suit similar to the one her daughter-in-law wore, Barclay's mother offered me a Bloody Mary, which I declined. No one knew where Barclay might be now, or so they said. They thought he was off somewhere in his second car, a convert-

ible BMW, looking for his first car. Clay appeared to be quietly happy about his father's difficulties. As if she were hyp-
notized by it, Tricia stared at the oil painting of Meredith
Ober that hung behind the grand piano. In the painting,
Meredith was playing the same piano, though I had never
heard her or anyone else play it in all the times I'd visited
River Bend.

My phone rang. I stepped outside on the terrace to talk
with Rod, who said that Barclay had reported the Mercedes
missing just before noon today. Rod had run the registration
and had put out an APB; now he added the BMW's numbers
to the call.

Slouched in a brocaded Chippendale chair, in clothes so
baggy he looked like the Incredible Shrinking Man, Clay actually showed a little animation when I questioned him. He
said that he'd stayed up late in his room playing video
games, and hadn't heard his father return last night. "But he
had to be totally wasted."

"Why's that?"

Clay sat up straighter. "That SL's got 'Keyless Go.' So
Dad says he figures he dropped the transponder somewhere
between the car and the cottage 'cause he couldn't find it this
morning. He went ballistic. So somebody got his car and
blasto *gone.*" The idea made Clay cheerful enough to be will-
ing to explain that a transponder was a wallet-sized card
coded with a special ID that allowed the possessor to open
the doors of the coded car and even to start its engine.

I said, "But you didn't see your dad so you don't know
he was wasted, do you?" Clay and I looked at each other.

"Barclay wasn't 'wasted,'" Meredith interjected. "I spoke
to him briefly last night and he was perfectly normal."

"Yeah, right, Grandma. Around this fuckin' shithole, wasted *is* normal."

"Do not curse in my presence." Meredith had a look that would stop a forest fire.

Clay crumpled but tried to hide it. "Fine. Like that'll make everything great."

"It will certainly make things less offensive." They glared at each other. Clay lost the standoff. Lowering his eyes, he turned to me to say that in fact he hadn't seen his father "for days, but what else is new?" The teenager himself had slept till one in the afternoon; since then he had been just hanging around because there was nothing else to do.

"What are you after Dad for?" Clay asked. When I replied, "Just a few questions," he shut down and went back to listening to his iPod. He knew I was lying.

Tricia hadn't seen much of Barclay either. She'd left at nine thirty to host a Catholic teens breakfast in the parish hall at Immaculate Conception. She'd stayed there to go to eleven o'clock Mass, the largest service and the one at which Father Connie had preached. Her husband had not appeared at church. In fact she hadn't been with him since their early dinner on Saturday night, after which she'd attended a performance of the *Messiah* with friends. Returning home, she'd retired to her room. She'd assumed that Barclay had slept in the guest cottage. Mrs. Ober kept her eyes on Tricia as the latter admitted that her husband "occasionally" did stay out in the cottage at night.

"How about you, Meredith? When did you last see Barclay?"

"Are you concerned about him?"

"Yes, I am."

"Why? Has he been in an accident?"

"No. When did you last see him, Mrs. Ober?"

Barclay's mother ate the celery in her Bloody Mary. She looked as if drink garnishes were all she ever ate. "Last night. I was still up when he came home. And yes, he went to the guest cottage because he didn't want to disturb Tricia, who had complained of a migraine." Another hard glance at the younger woman. "And this morning he slept late. He was still in bed when I brought him coffee at eleven."

I didn't believe Meredith Ober had brought anybody coffee in bed, even her son, but I didn't say so now. I told them to have Barclay call me the minute they heard from him. "We need to talk to him as soon as possible."

"I'm sure he'll be back shortly. We're having a little cocktail party tomorrow. I believe you're invited."

"I don't think I can make it."

Tricia nervously felt the small, tasteful gold cross at her neck. "What's this about, Jamie?"

"It's about Amanda Morgan being dead."

WE GOT A PRELIMINARY REPORT on the Jaguar. Among the evidence collected, there were multiple hair samples, multiple fingerprints, and there were traces of semen on the front passenger seat.

After trying for hours, I still couldn't reach Pudge. Every time I called the Salerno home, Eileen told me not to worry, that she was used to this: Because Dante's was closed on Sundays, Pudge often went to visit his older sister in Camden. His sister's husband had left her and she was lonely. They were undoubtedly out somewhere in Philly or King of

Prussia Christmas shopping now; he rarely had his cell phone with him, hated to talk on the phone anyhow because of his father's deafness (a congenital handicap inherited by their daughter). His sister didn't even have a cell phone. Eileen was glad Pudge was out shopping instead of obsessing about this morbid Killing Club stupidness. I didn't tell her about Amanda and let her go on cheerfully about how Pudge was going to surprise her with a diamond tennis bracelet for Christmas because she'd had their daughter point one out to him in a jewelry catalog.

"Eileen, just make sure Pudge calls me before he comes back to Gloria. Okay? *Before.*"

Connie and Debbie were easier to reach and they had to be told about the homicide because Channel Four was going to have it on the early news. There were already three news vans with satellite dishes atop them outside the Dixon Building and on the steps reporters moiled around like a restless pack of stray dogs. Amanda had been rich, beautiful and, as the news would describe her, "a prominent socialite, active environmentalist and prize-winning sportswoman." She would have loved the synopsis, I suspect.

I caught Connie in the parish house at Immaculate Conception. Two women parishioners appeared to be congratulating him, but I didn't know about what. I saw Debbie as she was leaving her apartment for work. Both looked shocked at the news of Amanda's death and asked for more details than I could give them. I arranged for us to meet the next day at Deklerk's, where Debbie would be bartending.

But a lot happened before I saw them again.

I had a phone call from Dino. Distracted by everything else going on, I didn't take time to argue with him when he said he was calling from a Trailways station in Virginia, having gotten a "fantastic" chance to fill in for two shows in Richmond, Virginia, as lead guitar with an "excellent" band called First Offenders. All I got to say was, "Get your ass back here, Dino! You blow off that community service and Judge Voisey will put you away. I'm not kidding and neither was she!"

"Hey, Jamie, you think I'd miss Christmas? Bye, love you." He hung up.

THE CASE TOOK A TURN on Monday when Rod suddenly got word from the New Jersey Highway Patrol that they'd just caught the "Expressway Shooter." He'd been seen with a 7mm Remington rifle and a scope on an overpass bridge only a few miles south of the bridge from which someone had blown out Shawn's tire. The shooter had been laid off from another job and dumped by another girlfriend and once again was taking it out on the world. He confessed.

So unless the man was lying, Shawn's death turned out to have been a freakish twist of malign luck, but not "personal." Not like Amanda and Ben.

I PAID A BRIEF CALL on Lyall's parents in their modest saltbox home in the first Ober subdivision—which had been named by its builder, Barclay's father, Eden (I didn't know whether he'd been a simplistic man or a megalomaniac). The Hilliers were watching a right-wing political talk show on television and didn't turn it off until I asked them to. It was difficult to believe these bland people were lying to me when they expressed astonishment at any suggestion that they'd been secretly meeting with their son Lyall for more than a decade, or, worse, that he'd been alive all those years and had never let them know. Reluctantly, they showed me his bedroom, completely untouched since his death, a kind of shrine. Textbooks still in their Hart High wrappers sat on his desk. I took *Algebra* and *World Civilizations* to have them dusted for fingerprints. My questions about Lyall's drug use produced a total shutdown except for the request that I leave their house.

Back at Dixon, I called Dad to say I wasn't going to be able to come home to eat dinner, much less cook the fegato Veneziana that kept getting postponed. He wanted to know if I'd heard from Dino. I said Dino was fine.

Rod and I ran Lyall's prints through AFIS (automated fingerprint identification system), but nothing showed up. If he was alive, he'd never been arrested or worked for the government. Dead end.

But Saturday night, Amanda had let the Killing Club know that she thought Lyall Hillier might still be alive and the next morning someone had killed her. It was enough for me to do a computer check of all drowned bodies recovered over the past eleven years within a fifty-mile radius of Gloria. There were seven of them. Only one corpse had remained unclaimed. A female prostitute in her forties with a long arrest record. Dead end.

NAOKO CAME BACK with Ben's key ring, which she had finally located in the Tymosz basement. The house, still boarded up, was now officially (to Megan's dismay) a crime scene. Ben's keys had probably been in his pants pocket; they'd been found in the area where the body had lain. Blackened, the keys were so burned that two had fused together. Megan said there'd also been a plastic disc on the key ring, with a photo in it of their daughters. The photo disc had completely melted. There was, of course, no red yarn there. But I could still tell that the Yale key on the ring matched the one on Amanda's silver hoop and the one I'd taken from the Death Book. The Killing Club key.

THE NEXT NEWS I got somehow felt the saddest. Gert called me from the autopsy room in the morgue to tell me that Amanda Morgan had been approximately eight weeks' pregnant when she died.

Gert was heading out the door from her small medical examiner's office when I walked over there to ask, "Can you test the paternity for me?"

"Medically? *Ja.* For sure we could, if we had the semen samples. Legally? That, Jamie, you would need to find out."

"I've got a semen sample for you, Gert. From the car seat. And I don't think it's Jim Morgan's either."

AT DEKLERK'S BAR that Monday night Debbie stood leaning on the counter. She looked as if all the light had gone out of her, despite the brightness of her blue bead necklace and her lime-green Lycra top. Her face was chalk-white and the circles under her eyes were black. Back in high school, Debbie had always defended Amanda. And although

Amanda hadn't given her the time of day since then, she mourned her now.

Across from her, Connie sat on a stool; he was drinking scotch, and drinking less slowly than he usually did. He looked as bad as Debbie; exhausted, though he said that of the four Masses done at Immaculate yesterday, he'd presided only over the High one at eleven. The church was packed. Christmas, he said, "brings people back."

Both of them asked a lot of questions, but had few answers for me. They'd seen neither Amanda nor Barclay (nor, for that matter, Pudge) since our meeting on Saturday night at Dante's. Connie, who'd stayed behind that night to help Pudge clean up, confirmed what Eileen had already told me—that Pudge had said he was planning to visit his sister in Camden.

I told them we were pursuing Amanda's death as a homicide and that I was 90 percent sure that, like hers, Ben's death had been a deliberate copy of the corresponding "murder" in the Killing Club Death Book. Someone (maybe even someone who'd once been in the club) had now killed two of its members.

Debbie and Connie just kept staring at me as I said we had to face the facts: Everyone in our group was not only a potential victim, but also a possible suspect. The only one of us I *knew* to be innocent was me.

Both immediately said that the same was true of them. They hadn't killed anybody, nor did they think it possible that anyone else they knew was capable of it.

"Then Pudge has to be right," Connie said. "A crazy person."

Debbie handed me an amaretto. "It can't be one of the club, it just can't be."

I pointed out that it was even conceivable that Wendy or Jeremy had flown in from Portland or Atlanta to commit the murders, though I doubted it. I doubted it was Pudge or Garth either. And that left Barclay.

"Barclay has a crossbow," Connie said.

"Saturday night," Debbie added, "Amanda kept trying to get away from him."

Connie nodded. "Pudge and I could hear him from all the way inside the restaurant."

I asked the priest again what Garth and he had been arguing about in the church garden when Barclay had joined them there.

Reluctantly he answered. "Whether Ben had committed suicide. I don't want to think so."

"You're right," I told him. "He didn't."

"Maybe Amanda was right about Lyall," Debbie finally said. "Maybe he's out there planning to murder me in one of those sick ways I dreamed up back in that crap high school."

Connie didn't see how anyone could seriously believe that. He repeated that we had to accept Pudge's theory: Somehow a disturbed outsider had gotten hold of the Death Books and was mimicking them. "Garth made copies. Remember that? Anybody could have them."

Debbie chewed at her thumbnail. "But why? Why would they choose us to kill?"

"I'll find out, Debbie."

My vow didn't seem to reassure her. "Great. I hope I'm still alive when you do. And, Jamie, you know what? I'm outta here till that happens." Debbie explained that she was leaving town. "My friend Tara? We're taking a trip to Cancún I've been planning for a year! And I don't want some psycho butchering me before I'm sitting by a pool with some Latino hunk bringing *me* a drink! Christmas Day, I'm in a bikini."

I nodded. "It's a good idea. You should leave Gloria. Both of you."

Connie held out his arms. "During the holidays? This is the busiest time of the year for me."

"Well, Connie, it won't be so busy for you if somebody shoots you full of insulin or drops an electric hair dryer in your tub or fucking crucifies you!" (All imagined murders of Connie's.)

Debbie grabbed the drink I'd almost knocked over. "Hey, Jamie, take it easy. This Amanda thing's got us all freaked."

Connie kept shaking his head. "I'm sorry. I can't leave Immaculate. We've got a dozen special services coming up this week!"

Wiping up my spill with a dirty bar apron, Debbie threw the cloth in a bin under the counter. "Well, I can leave. Screw this. Sam'll just have to double shift for a while. Or maybe he can get Megan Tymosz to help him. In fact, you know what, I'm going tonight, I'm going to go stay with Tara till we fly to Mexico. She lives—"

I stopped her. "Don't tell anyone where she lives."

Indignant, Connie turned quickly on his stool. "What does that mean? I'm a suspect too?"

"Everybody's a suspect."

. . .

MONDAY NIGHT, I was back at my desk. Every twenty minutes or so, Rod stuck his head out of his office to ask me if I was all right, if I wanted coffee or a back rub. There was no news yet on Barclay. I hadn't been able to reach Garth. I kept getting Ashley's brisk voice on the machine. "Ashley and Garth. Leave a message." My message was just, "Garth. It's Jamie. It's important. Call me." I left all my numbers.

So when my cell rang, I thought it was Garth. But it was Pudge.

"Oh, Christ Almighty, thank God. Why didn't you call me, Pudge?!"

Pudge was too steamed to answer. "I told you! You guys should have done something!" He had only now heard about Amanda; he'd called Eileen from Camden. Connie had told her, and Pudge had already spoken with Connie before calling me so he knew the details. "Didn't I tell you, didn't I warn you?"

"Pudge, maybe you should stay at your sister's till we sort this out."

"I'll tell you what I'm going to do. I'm not going to wait for you and the rest of the stupid police anymore. We all know who did this. Barclay. He was having an affair with her and she broke it off. We all saw how mad he was Saturday night. Connie and I think Barclay did it."

I was surprised that Connie had reached Pudge so quickly when I hadn't been able to.

"A while ago you and Connie thought it was a random crazy person. You can't have it both ways, Pudge. Either it's about the Killing Club or it's not. If it's about Barclay and Amanda, why would Barclay kill Ben?"

"I don't know. I'm going to find out. On my own!" He hung up.

Before I could reach Eileen to get Pudge's sister's number, Rod stuck his head out of his office again. "Hey, baby, they found the car."

"Barclay's Mercedes?"

"Yeah." Rod still had the cordless phone to his ear, listening. "You're kidding," he said to the phone. "Tell me you didn't break into the trunk, Danny. . . . Yeah? . . . " Rod had a look of victory. "Great. Bring it on, buddy. We'll be waiting down in the lab for you."

Highway patrol had spotted the luxury sedan abandoned at the first rest stop off the expressway. The dispatcher had called Danny and he'd driven out there and ID'd it. Barclay's SL600 was undamaged. There were a few mungo pine needles embedded in the Pirelli tires. In the trunk, covered by a plaid blanket, lay an Excalibur Deluxe Version 225-pound draw, 16.5-inch power stroke crossbow. According to Abu, who examined the weapon when I brought it to the lab, the highly polished bow had as many state-of-the-art accessories as the Mercedes it had been found in. It had a quick-detach sling swivel, a fiber-optic front sight, a detachable cocking aid and a scope mount. It could shoot carbon bolts with 100-gram target points at an amazing 350 feet per second. Exactly the same kind of bolt that had killed Amanda Morgan.

The crossbow, and all its accessories, had Barclay's prints on it and no one else's, though many of the prints were smeared.

The big problem for me was that of the many different fingerprints in and on the Mercedes, there was a set already on file at GPD. There were also three or more minuscule flecks of gold glitter on the headrest of the driver's seat, just like I got on my skin when my brother Dino rubbed his curls in my face and told me he loved me.

15

TRICIA

TELEVISION NEWS POUNCED on Amanda's bizarre death, devoured it and spit out the pieces on every channel. I didn't watch.

My father and I hadn't heard a word from Dino since I'd gotten his upbeat call from a bus station somewhere in Virginia. I didn't tell Dad why I was looking for my brother now; he was mad enough at Dino as it was. The Richmond police were unable to locate a rock band calling itself First Offenders. His friends from Jonesy's Marina hadn't seen him since he'd been fired. His musician friends didn't know where *they* were, much less where Dino might have gone. There was no doubt, as I admitted to Rod, that at some point he'd gone joyriding in Barclay's Mercedes, doubtless by getting access to it through Clay; maybe it had been weeks ago that they'd taken their ride. Clay denied it. Nevertheless, Dino's mug shot went out over the wire: Wanted by the Gloria, New Jersey, Police Department for questioning in a homicide.

"Rod, we know Dino didn't kill Amanda Morgan."

"Well, let him come home and say so."

"Dino carries moths back outside. He holds open the kitchen door for moths."

"Dino should stay out of other people's cars."

Repeated phone calls to River Bend had failed to produce anything useful from Clay. I needed to talk to my nephew in person. So I went, late, to the Ober cocktail party that Monday after all. I went in a squad car, with Naoko and Bill. The driveway had floodlights on it, and stepping from the car, I noticed a tiny sprig of mungo pine, which I had Naoko come spot with me before I put it in an evidence cup.

Inside River Bend, gathered around the huge Christmas tree, as if they were going to sing, stood Gloria's rich and influential; except Jim Morgan wasn't there, of course. There was no way these people didn't know about Amanda's death, but they appeared not to care much.

Meredith wasn't happy to see me back, especially when I said I'd wait after she assured me Barclay had not been heard from. But putting a brave face on things, she decided to pretend I'd come for the party and began introducing me to people I already knew, like Connie and the mayor and the president of a nearby college. I declined her offered cup of eggnog, pointedly saying I was on duty. "Congratulate Father Connie," she ordered me. "He's been nominated by his bishop to be a monsignor. That would make him a Prelate of Honor to His Holiness the Pope." I was struck by how quickly Meredith, who'd always given me the impression that she had no use for Connie or Catholicism and disliked his being at the house all the time with Tricia, had mastered the language of church hierarchy.

I said, "That's great, Connie."

"The youngest," our hostess added.

I repeated, "That's great, Connie." He appeared to think I was being sarcastic because he frowned, then smiled in mock apology. "I mean it. May you live to be a cardinal. And speaking of living and dying, did you tell Pudge you thought Barclay had murdered Amanda?"

Meredith snapped at me, "I very much doubt that."

I shrugged. "Apparently Connie and Pudge discussed it."

"Jamie, for heaven sakes!" Connie blushed, mumbling that he must have been misunderstood. A furious Meredith hustled me back into the wide center hall of the Georgian house. The floor was black and white marble. Her dress and hair matched it. Positioning me beside a round table crowded with gifts in glittering paper, she urged me to "stop hounding" them and their guests. From the ceiling hung a gargantuan brass chandelier; Barclay's mother looked like she was hoping it would fall on my head.

"Hey, Jamie. Still looking for Dad?" Halfway up the cantilevered stairs, Clay squatted on the steps. He waved down at me, curiously cheerful.

"Looking for you, too, kid," I called to him.

Meredith hissed, "Clay, go to your room." At the same moment, Tricia appeared from the rear of the house carrying a small silver tray of Christmas cookies, and just then the

front doorbell rang. Opening the door to an elderly state
senator and his wife, Meredith glanced at the GPD squad car
behind them. It looked very ominous in her combed driveway with Naoko and Bill seated inside it. Squeezing a gift
plant from the senator's wife onto the crowded table, Meredith smiled, explaining that someone had stolen Barclay's
Mercedes right out of the driveway and that's why the police
were there. The guests expressed appropriate outrage. There
was nothing else Meredith could do now but take the silver
tray from Tricia, instruct her to show me out, tell me, "Good
night, Jamie" and bustle her late-arriving guests into the
party.

Tricia didn't try to stop me when I walked up the stairs
and sat beside Clay. But she didn't leave the foyer either, just
stood there below us, motionless as a model for a painting,
and not a happy one. I watched Connie, in his black priestly
suit, join her, take her hands to comfort her. She kept nodding as they went out the front door together.

"Okay, Clay." I leaned slightly against him. "You know
what this is about?" He smelled of marijuana.

He grinned. "My dad, the town shag king? Did he kill
Amanda Morgan?"

I shrugged. "Hope not."

"That's why you were asking me about the crossbow.
Tricia hated her; maybe she killed her."

"Could be. Know where he is?"

Clay mimicked my shrug. "Nope." I cupped his chin,
but he yanked away from me. "No!"

"Actually, I want to talk to you about his Mercedes. And
Dino."

Hopping to his feet, Clay ran upstairs. I followed but he

blocked my way to his room at the far end of the hall. There was a poster of the rock band Pearl Jam on his door that his grandmother must have loved. "You can't come in here!" he growled, standing between the door and me, trying to mask his trembling.

"Probably a good thing," I nodded. "Probably have to bust you for possession if I got in that room. Or maybe the stash is all out in that summer kitchen of yours."

"Stay out of there."

I backed away, hoping he wouldn't bolt. "Clay, you need to talk to me. This is serious. You ever let Dino drive any of your dad's cars? I know you two like to go for rides together. You ever let him come over here and borrow the SL?"

"No!" He slipped behind the door, quickly turning the lock. "Dino didn't take it!"

Below us, I heard Tricia return with Connie to the front door, walk across the marble into the party. "Clay, listen to me, you got to trust me here. This isn't about hurting Dino. Tell me the last time you guys took the Mercedes. Did he come get it here last night? Tell me where he took it. Is Dino the one who dumped it at the rest stop this morning? Talk to me, Clay."

Silence. As Clay hadn't given up his father, whom he hated, it was no surprise he wouldn't give up an uncle he loved.

"Were you two following me in a car when I was walking along Dock Street, couple of nights ago? Shining your brights on me?"

"No!" was shouted through the door.

"Did you ever let Dino use any of the weapons in your dad's gun room?"

The key turned in the door lock. Clay stared out at me through the crack, his eyes anxious to find information in mine. But he didn't speak.

"Clay, if you have any way of reaching Dino, make him come home immediately. It'll get real ugly if he doesn't." Dino didn't have a cell phone because Dad was sick of paying the bills, but I thought maybe we could trace a call if he was using someone else's phone to call Clay. "I'm not playing games. Somebody killed Amanda Morgan with your dad's crossbow."

He gave a nasty laugh. "Dad gets my vote."

Tricia startled me, climbing the stairs and moving along the dark hallway so quietly that I didn't hear her. When Clay slammed his door, I turned to see her deep green dress fade into the shadowy walls. She motioned me away from Clay's door and kept gesturing me toward her, back down the stairs. I could hear voices and the clinking of glass from the living room. Only after we were standing in the foyer again did she say anything. "He took the car at nine fifteen Sunday morning. I saw him leave from my upstairs window."

I wasn't sure what she meant. "The Mercedes? Who took it? Barclay?"

She laughed in an odd, bitter way. "No, Clay took it."

"Clay? Was Dino with him?"

"Dino, your brother? No, Clay was by himself."

"The Mercedes was here Sunday morning. Had it been here all night?"

She thought a moment. "I have no idea when Barclay brought the Mercedes home. For all I know he was out in it till morning." Tricia put her large diamond wedding ring to her lips, biting at it softly. "The first time I saw the car back,

Clay was driving it away. I was about to leave for church so I looked at my watch. It was nine fifteen. What I thought was, I can't believe Clay's up that early."

"And you're saying Clay took the car? Alone?"

"Yes."

"You let a thirteen-year-old drive away in a car?" I'd had it so firmly in my head that Dino had come over here to River Bend and taken Clay for a joyride, that I had to regroup.

"It wouldn't be the first time," Tricia said.

"Clay driving off in the Mercedes?"

"Late at night or when Barclay was out of town."

"Did Barclay know?"

Tricia managed a smile. "I'm sure he didn't. Clay would be black and blue. Don't you think? And Meredith pays no attention. But I spend a lot of time in my room upstairs . . . just looking out the window." She added, almost as if she were simply asking for information, "The police think Barclay killed Amanda Morgan, don't they?"

Taken aback, I studied the sadness in her face. It was not an unattractive face, it still had the clean preppy lines of a former debutante, but looking at Tricia made you realize how really beautiful Amanda had been. "I'm the police," I finally said. "I don't know if he killed her or not. Somebody did."

Her eyes lowered, she rearranged some of the holiday gifts that guests had brought and left on the round table. "How do you know it wasn't me? Jealous wife. Cheating husband. Husband madly in love with another woman . . . even on your wedding day." She looked up at me, almost shyly. "Maybe even on your sister's wedding day."

"That's what you think? Barclay was in love with Amanda?"

"Certainly since I met him."

Tricia pointed at the closed door on the other side of the foyer. "Why don't you ask him? He's in there." She picked up a pretty silver bowl of chocolates from the table and carried it into the party.

BARCLAY WAS SITTING in the dark. I could see his silhouette, near the fireplace where a few red embers struggled not to fade away. I'd never been in the room before. It looked like something the Obers would call a library or a study—the den sort of idea, lots of books and paneling and an entertainment center.

"Barclay? It's Jamie. We need to talk about Amanda. You need to tell me if you saw her in Etten Park yesterday morning. Because your car was there."

I waited. Finally he spoke; his voice sounded hoarse, like someone with laryngitis. "I've got nothing to say to you."

Crossing the room, I stood in front of the high-backed leather chair in which he slumped, reminding me of his son, Clay. "You can talk to me here or we can go to the police station to talk."

"I'm not doing either one. Just get out."

"Can't do it." I gave him a choice. He could leave with me without disturbing his mother's party or I could bring in the two uniformed officers who were now sitting in a squad car in his driveway and the three of us could remove him from his house by force. "You pick, Barclay."

We were quiet for a while in the dark. Then he stood, looking at me as if I'd caused all his troubles. But he followed me quietly out of the house. A senator, a judge and the mayor paused with their cocktails in the doorway to the living room as I walked Barclay out of the house. Connie saw us and started forward but I waved him back. Tricia stepped next to him, reached for his arm. Barclay's mother gathered the guests to her, leading them back to where a hired waiter in a short red jacket stood waiting to serve them drinks.

THE TOWN GREEN WAS QUIET, a few shoppers pausing to look at the Christmas tree, a few teenage boys harassing the Virgin Mary and Joseph by trying to ride the plastic camel and cow in front of the manger.

The news vans had moved from the Dixon Building to Jim Morgan's house, where they were hoping to catch a glimpse of his grief. So we weren't bothered as we headed up the Dixon steps, Naoko and Bill right behind Barclay. I kept my hand near his arm, but not touching him. He hadn't said a word on the ride to town.

Suddenly, far below us on the street, a car slammed to a stop, then someone started yelling at us. I looked down to the sidewalk. Pudge, drunk, staggered out of the still-open door of his Lexus and charged up the steps toward us, shouting loudly, "You killed her! You son of a bitch! She dumped you and you killed her!"

Barclay bared his clenched teeth at me. "Back him off."

But Pudge kept coming. "I know why now, I know why you killed Ben too. You sick son of a bitch!" Midway across the green, the couple looking at the Christmas tree turned to see what was going on.

I shoved Barclay behind me as he was saying, "That fathead lays one finger on me, he's going to jail!"

Breathless and purple-faced, Pudge made it up to where we stood and threw a punch at Barclay that missed him by six feet. Grabbing Pudge from either side, Naoko and Bill hustled him all the way back to the sidewalk.

Pudge yelled up at Barclay. "I'm not leaving this alone!"

"Yes, you are," I called to him. "Get out of here, Pudge."

"Do your job, Jamie."

"Why don't you let me?"

I told Naoko and Bill to take Pudge's car keys away from him, to walk him across the green over to Dante's and to call his wife, Eileen, and tell her to come pick him up.

When I turned back to Barclay, he had a twisted grin on his face. Maybe he already knew that he would spend no more than an hour being interrogated in the Dixon Building before I was ordered to release him.

Despite the late hour, two lawyers from Ober Land Development and Realty came marching down the hall into Chief Waige's office before Barclay had finished telling me that he had nothing more to tell me. The chief had shown up in sweats and a bad mood. Maybe he'd been over at Gert's. The lawyers showed up in tuxedos, apparently having left a gala performance of *The Nutcracker* in order to come to Dixon to convince the judge—who'd left the Ober cocktail party in order to be convinced—that there were insufficient grounds to hold Barclay Ober any longer than we already had.

In the hour I'd spent with Barclay, I kept bringing him back to the fact that his Mercedes had been parked yesterday morning in Etten Park in the same lot as Amanda Morgan's Jaguar, which was 141 yards from where Amanda Morgan had been murdered with a crossbow bolt. The crossbow found in the trunk of his Mercedes shot arrows exactly like the one that had killed her. He had motive, means and opportunity. Did he kill her?

Barclay admitted the affair with Amanda. He admitted the Mercedes was his car and the crossbow was his crossbow. But he denied that he'd killed Amanda with the bow, or put it in his trunk, or knew who had put it there or knew how they'd gotten hold of the car or the crossbow either. Someone had stolen his car. Wasn't it obvious what had happened? Hadn't I told him the SL had been found abandoned in an expressway rest stop? Whoever killed her stole the car and the crossbow both.

I let his words sit for a while, just looking at him, sipping my coffee from a Styrofoam cup, hoping he would drink from the cup I'd brought for him. Then I asked, "You think it was Clay?"

"What?" His body came off the seat. "Clay? What's Clay got to do with anything?"

"Tricia says Clay drove off in your Mercedes Sunday morning. You think he might have shot Amanda with your bow? Maybe it offended him, your cheating on your wife." I didn't say that at nine fifteen, when Clay presumably had left the house with the car, Amanda had already been dead for two hours. Even so, one of our uniformed cops was now watching River Bend to make sure Clay didn't leave it.

"Clay can't drive."

"I hear otherwise."

"Because Tricia will say anything. She hates me."

I nodded. "I don't think she hates Clay."

"Maybe not." He rubbed his face and hair with both hands, like he was toweling off after a shower, like it would all go away if he did. "You're not charging him, and you're not charging me." He smiled tightly. "As you're going to find out, very soon." Picking up the Styrofoam cup I'd placed in front of him, he drank from it, making a face.

"Sorry about the coffee." I was working hard, with my voice and body language, to make us feel like family, even if conflicted family. "Barclay, you had a fight with Amanda Saturday night. I was standing there. You said, 'You got what you wanted and now you're dumping me? I don't think so!' What did Amanda get that she wanted?"

He looked strangely at me but didn't speak.

"Was she trying to get pregnant?" The question hadn't surprised him, though he pretended that it did. I kept my voice quiet, friendly even. "Maybe you arranged to meet her yesterday morning in Etten Park, or maybe you just showed up there. You'd know where she'd park when she was going riding early. Maybe you wanted to try to talk things out, see what had gone wrong between you?"

Something suddenly happened deep inside him, like a long electric shock. His whole body shuddered. He leaned over the metal table on which his cuffed hands were resting. "Jamie, what the hell?"

I put my hands on the table across from his. "I know. What the hell."

We sat there for a while, not talking.

His voice cracked quietly. "You think I want to live in a world with her wiped out of it?"

"Did you ever love Gina?"

"Not like that," he admitted.

It was the shift to something real I'd been working an

hour for. And naturally it was just at that moment that Rod knocked on the interrogation door and told me to stop asking Barclay questions.

After Barclay and Rod left the room, I slid his coffee cup into the plastic Baggie in my pocket and stuck it behind the water cooler.

I was back in the squad room when the Ober lawyers emerged with Chief Waige from his office. The chief told me Rod would explain things. Rod explained that Barclay Ober was no longer, at this time, a suspect in the Amanda Morgan homicide. He was free to go.

"That's bullshit!" I said, loud enough for Chief Waige, hurrying away with the lawyers, to hear me. None of them looked back.

The desk sergeant returned Barclay's personal effects. Barclay went through them as if he suspected us of stealing a few.

Barclay never looked at me, speaking only to Rod, as we walked him to the door. He tucked his red scarf under his thrusting chin. "Leave me and my family alone. You'll not only be out of jobs, I'll bankrupt your department."

Slowly nodding, Rod said, "Fair warning."

As Barclay strode off, his polished shoes clicking loudly on the terrazzo floor, I called after him, "Amanda was pregnant. When we find out, you want to know if the baby's yours or not?"

He ignored me, pushing into the revolving doors.

Rod and I stared at each other for a long time, and then he shook his head. "You heard the chief. Ober is not a suspect now."

"In which case? Because maybe you recall, Barclay had lunch with Ben the day he died. Barclay was parked outside the Tymosz house, he called in the fire . . . too late."

"You know what the chief means. Ober's not to be interrogated again in the Tymosz homicide, or the Morgan homicide. Not unless we've got him cold." Rod waved his arms at me in a crossing gesture. "And no Lone Ranger, Jamie, okay?" He tried to turn me toward him. "Can you get it through your head that you could be in danger too?"

I yanked away. "Fine, no Lone Ranger. Because I sure can't count on Tonto, can I?"

We argued for ten more minutes, backing each other into corners it would be hard to get out of. Finally Rod did what he always does when he's not going to talk about something anymore. He crossed his arms. "This isn't going anywhere. Follow orders or you're off the case."

Without looking at him, I walked back through the squad room. I didn't go over to the water cooler till Rod had slammed shut the door to his office. But then I found the bagged cup and took it down to Abu in the lab. Abu was watching a DVD of Denzel Washington in *The Bone Collector* on his laptop. "How'd you like to be able to move nothing but one finger on one hand?" he asked me, peering over his square-rimmed black-framed glasses.

"I wouldn't."

He hit pause. "What you bet, Denzel'll solve it anyhow. Like Mister Tibbs. Every generation we get one black man can do no wrong."

I handed him the cup. "Yep, and you're the one for my generation. Match this saliva to the semen in the Jaguar, will you, Abu? I'll love you."

"You mean it's over between you and Dan the Man Ventura?"

"Totally over. I don't know what I ever saw in him."

There was no way for Abu to know I had no right to ask him to run the tests.

16

JOE

ALL I WANTED was to go home to Fourteenth and Dock, sit on that big dumb leather couch with a glass of Gavi di Gavi and let my dad help me pull off the heavy lace-up boots I'd been wearing all day long. I wanted to hear him say it was all right for me to go ahead investigating Barclay Ober as the prime suspect in two homicides, even though I'd been officially told not to do so. Of course, I knew my father wouldn't say any of that. Joe Ferrara had been a cop all his adult life. Injured in the line of duty and forced to retire, he was still a cop. He believed that the survival of the force depended on following the chain of command. Maybe Rod was wrong, and maybe Rod was my fiancé, but, most important, Rod was a superior officer who'd given me a direct order and I had to obey it. That's what my dad would say. And that doesn't even take into account what it would do to his blood pressure if he heard that Dino Ferrara's mug shot from his joyride in Ramon's truck was on the Fugitive Apprehension Wanted lists of police departments as far south as Richmond, Virginia.

So I was half-relieved when Dad called out as I hung my coat on the rack in the hall, "Hey, sweetheart, you've got company."

In the living room, Garth sat drinking from a longneck, his legs stretched out from Dad's couch onto some magazines lying on a coffee table that had seen better decades. Sam sat on Garth's lap. It was hard to imagine more of a contrast in styles than Garth's soft charcoal sweater and slacks and my father's old plaid bathrobe and L.L.Bean sock slippers.

From her seat on one of the big leather couch pillows at the other end of the coffee table, Debbie hopped up and waved. Dad pushed toward me with one strong shove of his wheelchair. "You heard from your brother?"

"Not yet, but you know Dino."

He nodded, not wanting to discuss it in front of company. "Where's Rod?" he asked. I told him Rod was still at Dixon, where he always was. I didn't say we'd had a terrible fight and weren't talking to each other. As I leaned down to kiss my father, I pushed his wheelchair over beside the couch.

"So what are you doing here, Garth? Aren't you supposed to be in New York?"

Shooing Sam off his lap (Sam didn't like it), Garth stood, holding out his hand to me as if we were meeting for the first time. "Katie called me about Amanda. What a sad thing. My news show actually sent me down here to cover it. Funny, huh? Figured I could give it a local-boy angle. I came back to tell you that you were right and I was wrong. Ben wasn't an accident."

"I'm really sorry I'm right," I admitted. "Yes. What a sad thing." Weirdly, I shook his hand, then turned away. "Hi, Debbie." Taking a cannoli from the white cardboard box on the table, I offered her one, but she held up three fingers and touched her stomach. "I thought you'd left too."

"I'm leaving," she said. "Tomorrow this time, I'll be in Cancún slathered with coconut oil." Debbie had on a short, tight, fake-alligator jacket, unzipped to her cleavage. She had a big green clip in her purple-black spiky hair. She had very white skin and very black, thick mascara. It was hard to imagine her lying around to get a tan on a tropical beach. She pulled a cell phone from her jeans pocket—a tight squeeze—and shook it at me. "Did you get a call tonight from Pudge?"

I shook my head. "I saw him. He'd been drinking."

"I'll say." She shoved the phone back in her jeans, as if she'd made her point.

"He tried to punch out Barclay outside Dixon. Said he was going to prove Barclay had murdered Amanda. Is that what he told you?"

"No, he called and told me he knew *I'd* killed Amanda and Ben. Jamie, it was crazy. He said he knew why I'd done it and he was going to prove it. Then he hung up."

"He said *you'd* killed them?"

"I was so freaked I called him back, but Eileen told me he was gone already. They'd had a fight about how he was

acting and she'd sent him to sleep it off over at Dante's."
Debbie rubbed her arms. "So then Connie calls me and says
Pudge has phoned him, accusing him of murder too! So I
even phone fuckin' Jeremy in Atlanta and he had the same
message from Pudge on his machine!"

"What did they say—Connie and Jeremy?"

"That Pudge was whacked up. That he'd said he was
'onto' them. This is so sick. Tell me Pudge hasn't gone off the
deep end. Tell me he didn't kill Ben and Amanda, and now
he's after me?!"

"Pudge didn't kill anybody. And, Debbie, you know he
doesn't seriously think you did either. But I don't know what
he's up to. It's nuts."

"It's not nuts that two people are dead! Two people we
knew! And we could be next."

My father wheeled his chair over to her. "Your imagination's running away with you, Debbie. If somebody's killed
those two people, it's about those two people. It's not about a
high school club."

"Go to Cancún," Garth said to Debbie. Hands linked
behind his head, he joked, "Wonder why Pudge didn't call
me? I feel left out."

Debbie zipped up her jacket. "Garth, I don't know why
you think this is funny."

He shrugged. "Sorry."

I asked Garth if Pudge knew he was even in town.
Would he know how to reach him? Garth admitted Pudge
probably didn't. "Let's face it. Pudge really cared more than
we do."

"All I care is, I'm out of here!" Debbie headed for the
hallway to get her coat. She explained that she was driving to

her friend Tara's in Cherry Hill right now and that they were taking an earlier flight to Mexico.

"Garth's staying with Katie for Christmas," my father threw in as he poured me a little glass of grappa. Because of our day care at the McBride house, Dad had known Garth and Katie since they were children. He never acknowledges, when he mentions Katie, of whom he's fond, that she lives with Martha, of whom he's also fond. I didn't know if he liked Garth or not. "New Year's too," Dad added. "Right, Garth?"

I said, "Yeah, Garth seems to be in Gloria all the time. So you rented a car?"

He grinned. "I took a taxi from Katie's."

My father was flabbergasted, and had to rub Sam's back while he took this in. "A taxi? From her place? How much did that cost?"

Garth shrugged. "I don't know, thirty bucks maybe."

"Thirty bucks?" Dad couldn't believe it. Nobody took taxis in Gloria except from the airport or the train station. "You gonna take taxis till New Year's? You could buy a car."

"I don't need one, Mr. Ferrara. I live in Manhattan." Garth had a grin it was easy to imagine on TV every night. "I don't even have a valid driver's license."

Now my father looked at Garth as if this failing were the ultimate outcome of his radical politics. "You're an adult American, you have a driver's license," he said. "You lose it for drinking?"

"Nope. But President Bush did."

It seemed a good thing to stop this discussion right now. I blurted out, "What about Ashley? I mean, the holidays."

Returning from the hall with her big thrift-store rac-
coon coat, Debbie answered my question. "They broke up."

I looked from Debbie to Garth. "You and Ashley broke
up?"

He crawled out of the couch to help Debbie on with her
thick coat. "That's right. Here's the question: Will Ashley notice? To me, she's a woman in a bed with an eye mask on,
who leaves a note on the bathroom mirror that says 'DON'T
WAKE ME UP, I'VE GOT A FOUR AM CALL.'"

Lightly, Debbie smacked his cheek twice in a good-bye
gesture. "Hey, dump her. Nobody should be up at four A.M.
that didn't stay up from the night before. So, Garth, if we're
not all killed, maybe I'll see you next Christmas. Or on TV.
Maybe I'll see you when they crown Connie pope. You hear
about that monsignor thing, Jamie? Good going for the old
outcasts, right?" She pulled a thin silver box with a black rib-
bon out of her big shoulder bag. "Merry Christmas."

Debbie had said she was "too totally freaked" to spend
another night in Gloria but she'd stopped off on the way to
Cherry Hill to leave me my Christmas present. For some
reason, the incongruity started me laughing. Here she was,
hurrying out of town because there'd been two murders already and she was terrified she'd be the third, but she was
taking the time before she left to exchange gifts. Since we'd
been doing it ten years or more, I guess murder was no reason to stop.

When I told her why I was laughing, Debbie cracked up
too as she shook the silver-wrapped box at me. "And it's always a stupid silk scarf anyhow! So where are my depressing
DVDs?" My usual gift to Debbie is disaster movies; they con-

firm her view that life is a catastrophe waiting to happen when you think you're having fun—like *Titanic* and *The Towering Inferno*.

"Under the tree." Crawling under the heavy droopy boughs to find her gift, I started laughing louder. Dad and Garth both stared at us like we'd lost our minds. "We're hysterical," I explained.

AS DEBBIE LEFT with her three-pack of *Alien* movies, she pulled me aside to whisper at the door, "Don't do it."

I knew what she meant. "This is all in your mind," I told her, shoving her out.

"Yeah. Let's keep it there."

I told Garth I needed to make some calls. He didn't take the hint.

After getting the answering machine at Dante's, I called Eileen Salerno. I woke her up. Eileen was sure Pudge was asleep in his office, where he had a pull-out couch; she thought sleep was the best thing for him. "I don't know whether to hope he was drunk or worry he's lost his mind calling people, accusing them of killing their friends!"

"Eileen, Ben and Amanda *were* murdered."

After we hung up, I tried phoning Connie at Cooke House, a very nice modern apartment the church had built him over the new parish center, but I only got his machine. If he had a cell phone, I didn't know about it.

Finally, Dad announced that he was going to bed, but that he wanted me to wake him if I heard from Dino. We told each other that Dino was fine, that he always was. My father then gave me the same nightly reminders I'd gotten since I'd first started staying up later than he did: Turn off the lights, lock the doors, get the cat in. What he thought Garth was doing there so late, I didn't know. I wasn't sure myself. Just that he seemed to have no plans to leave.

AN HOUR LATER, Dad was asleep and Garth and I were well into a bottle of wine and still talking about what had happened to Amanda, about how Barclay might have murdered her and how I could possibly prove it when I'd been ordered not to try. The double homicide was not what I was used to. Not what happened in a place like Gloria. I found myself confessing to Garth, of all people, that I was scared that maybe Rod was right: Maybe I couldn't handle a case like this, not just because I was so closely tied to the victims, not because I was a possible victim myself, but because I was professionally out of my league.

Garth took my face in his hands and shook it. "You don't believe that. You think you're as smart as they come. And God knows you're stubborn enough. You're a good detective, Jamie. Your dad just told me that, and, hey, shouldn't he know?"

"My dad said that?"

"Yep. So don't sell yourself short. Talk to me." He smiled. "Just like we used to when the murders weren't real." He poured me more wine and patted the cushion of the couch beside him. Sam jumped there, rubbed himself enthusiastically against Garth's body. Whenever Garth pushed him aside, he moved back.

I said it was because the cat knew Garth didn't want him to be there. "Cats are like that. . . ." We watched Sam for a while, then Garth told me to talk to him about the case.

I said, "The problem is, this time the murders are real. So we need a real motive." I told him I was troubled by Barclay's motive for killing Amanda, and Ben too. It couldn't be, I said, because Ben knew about the secret affair with Amanda.

Garth agreed: In the twenty-first century, not even politicians killed people to keep affairs quiet. "Even if worst came to worst, and you got a messy divorce, who'd remember in a year? This is a country with the attention span of a dog on crack."

"I'm thinking Barclay killed her because she left him. That he 'loved' her."

"Something like love," Garth agreed.

It's my belief that motive is the biggest key to solving a homicide. Find the motive, find the killer. The motive had to be there for the first murder too. For Ben. And that was the problem. How to tie them together. If Ben was the motive, maybe Barclay wasn't the killer and Amanda just got in the killer's way. Could it have been her theory about Lyall that got her killed? Could Lyall *be* alive?

Garth didn't think so.

"What about those pasted notes from *Halloween*?" I reminded him. "That's a movie about a crazy killer coming back to his little town after fifteen years in a loony bin. That's a movie with a poster that says, '*The night* he *came home.*' Is that any way possible? That Lyall's out there?"

Pouring himself another glass of wine, Garth thought it over. "What are you saying, Lyall was hospitalized or in jail all this time? Wouldn't the check you ran on him have turned up something like that?"

It was possible, I argued, to disappear, to lose an identity as well as steal one. "Tell me about the night Lyall died."

He tensed. "Tell you what?"

"Do you know why he killed himself?"

"Unhappy. Drugs."

I watched his face, a very good-looking face. "How about—did it have anything to do with you guys driving away together after that football game?"

Garth looked carefully past me, stared at the Christmas tree lights blinking in the glass of the front window. A lock of his hair fell down onto his forehead and he brushed it back. It was handsome hair, but then he was the nightly news. Finally he said, "I don't know if it did or not."

I moved in front of him so he'd have to look at me. "You know what I think, Garth? You and Barclay and Connie—that's what you were talking about at Ben's funeral and at Deklerk's. It's got something to do with Ben, and it's got something to do with the night of that football game when you all went to the playhouse together and something happened and Lyall walked away from you and drowned himself."

He looked up at me, surprised, curious. "How can you know that?"

I said it was what I did for a living. "But I don't know it. I need you to tell me."

Bending forward, elbows on his knees, he ran his hands through his hair. Then he told me the story. Some version of what he said had already crossed my mind. That night, after the so-called championship game, the group of five young men (Garth, Barclay, Connie, Lyall and Ben) and one young woman (Amanda) drove out to the Pine Barrens Playhouse in Barclay's car. They sat around in the mismatched chairs collected by the Killing Club for our meetings. They got high together on cocaine provided by Lyall. At least for Garth— and he thought for some of the others—it was the first time with coke. At some point along the way, Amanda agreed (or offered) to perform oral sex on all of them as they sat in a circle on the stage. But when his turn came, Lyall was unable to get an erection. "We gave him a really rough time about it. Pulled his pants off, held him down. It was sort of like a haz-ing, I guess you could say. Lyall got all upset and walked out."

". . . Yeah, well," I said.

We were quiet for a while. Then I asked, "So what were you arguing about at Ben's funeral?"

"Whether we should tell you. Tell the police." He looked up at me. "Ben always felt so god-awful about it—"

"Good for him."

"When I saw her at the funeral reception, Amanda told me how he'd recently talked about it with her, said he'd seen a shrink about it, even confessed it at church—I guess he believed in that crap—but nothing helped. Plus, there was the cancer. And I don't know . . ." Garth sat up, fin-ished his wine. "Probably has nothing to do with anything anyhow."

"So what was the argument?"

The argument was that Garth had wanted to tell me about that night Lyall died, but Barclay and Connie had thought so ugly a moment was best left in the past. That it had nothing to do with anything.

. . .

SILENT, WE WERE STILL SITTING in that past when the doorbell rang. I hurried toward it, thinking it was Dino. It was five minutes to midnight.

But it was Rod, his suede collar pulled up against his ears. Just as he stood there, it started snowing, small sharp flakes slanting past him. He said, "I'm sorry. That got ugly at Dixon and I should have set it right with you."

"Then let me go after Barclay."

He shook his head. "You need to step away from this case, at least for a little while. Danny's going to take over."

I was surprised, hurt and angry. "Is this Waige or is this you?"

Rod didn't answer me and maybe I would have closed the door on him, but he'd walked around me into the hallway, from which he could see the living room, where Garth stood beside the Christmas tree, studying glass ornaments on it that my grandmother had brought with her from Venice.

Garth said, "Rod. Hi there."

Rod nodded at him slowly but didn't come any farther into the room. "Thought you went back to New York."

"In and out. With my sister for the holidays."

I was so mad at Rod for turning my case over to Danny that I couldn't focus on whatever was happening between Garth and him. Nobody spoke for a few seconds, then Rod just turned around and left, shutting the front door after him. Looking out the window, I watched him swipe snow off his windshield with the back of his arm.

Garth pushed Sam away from his pants leg. Indignant, the cat walked stiffly over to the Christmas tree and swatted at a red glass ball on a low bough until he knocked it off and broke it.

"Jealous type?" Garth asked. "Rod, I mean. Not Sam. Sam's sort of into one-night stands. I'm the newest."

"Rod and I are fighting about the case. It's not personal."

He smiled. It was both infuriating and charming. Some trick. But slowly the smile went away and then we were just looking at each other. I knew I should tell him to leave, that I'd drive him to Katie's, that we should go right now before the snow got worse. There were probably a lot of reasons why I didn't. Anger at Rod. Upset about Amanda and Ben (not yet thirty and, like my sister, gone for good). The feeling that life, like my mother, was nothing you could count on to stick around. But mostly I just couldn't move. I stood there as he reached for me. He pulled me gently by the hand down onto the couch, kissing me.

"I can't do this," I told him, but then I was kissing him and his hands were under my sweater, moving softly down my back, like a flame on the wick of bunched firecrackers, when it's too late to stop them from going off.

"Give me a ride to my sister's," he whispered, his lips against my neck. And I knew what he meant.

17

KATIE

O N THE WAY TO KATIE'S, Garth and I stopped by the old empty Pine Barrens Playhouse near the docks where Lyall had drowned himself. Garth broke the lock with my lug wrench, and we used my big Maglite to look around. The stage of the theater where we'd held the original meetings of the Killing Club was littered with debris and dead leaves. Nature was reclaiming it—moss and weeds growing in the walls and floorboards, cracked windows filmy with cobwebs. We found a few memories. An empty bottle of Lambrusco, a moldy Sherlock Holmes paperback. It was the first time either of us had been there since our last meeting, when we'd sat around in shock about Lyall's death.

"'Smells like Teen Spirit,'" Garth said out of the dark beside me.

"Yeah, he's dead too," I said. "Cobain. Remember how they used to say Connie had his eyes?"

"No."

"I guess it was just a girl thing."

I spotted one of the old canvas director's chairs, overturned, the seat ripped, the wood rotted. "That was a long time ago."

Garth shoved an old couch out of the way. There was a six-pack of bottled beer behind it; half the bottles had burst open and cracked from a decade of freezing cold and high heat. Garth sat on the couch; not something I'd want to do, I told him. I kept looking around.

After a while, I heard his voice. "Hard to go back. Sitting here the way we did, dreaming up murders. Outcasts of the world."

I walked back to him. "At least in our own little narcissistic minds."

"Yeah, it's hard to hang on to that much self-absorption. 'Course, I try." He grinned as I flashed the light at him. "It works on TV." Standing up, he brushed off his cashmere overcoat. "You think Barclay really has the guts to kill people for real? Connie says he's pretty ruthless in his business dealings, and I know he cheats on his wife and he's pretty nasty to his son. But can you get from that to putting an arrow into the face of somebody you were in love with? And he was, with Amanda. At least when I knew him." Garth looked around the theater. "Trust me on that. But murder and Barclay Ober?"

"I've been a cop for six years. I've seen real things real

people have done to each other that I couldn't have imagined when I was sitting here on this stage with the stupid Killing Club."

I was flashing the light around for a last look before we left. Backstage near a loading dock, the beam picked up a small section of the cement floor that looked a different color gray from the rest of the floor. The playhouse had been built in the forties; a movie house, then a theater, it had been unused (except by us) for more than a decade. The section of fresher cement was about four by four, roughly shaped. Weird looking. But maybe drainage or pipes or cable or septic, I thought. It was the sort of thing I noticed.

THE SNOW HAD CHANGED to movie snow—pretty and lazy and disappearing without trouble when it hit the canvas top of my old Mustang as we drove to Katie's. The trees were white and the highway black. Christmas snow. It was just as well the roads weren't slippery as I headed west of town onto smaller and smaller roads that led to the woods where Katie and Sweets had built their house. Because I was sliding on ice of my own, what with Garth's hand on my leg or his lips on the palm of my hand. I'm not sure what would have happened if the two women hadn't been having a party. If they'd been asleep and there'd been nothing between me and Garth's bedroom except a few cats, I think I would have gone there.

But it was after midnight and that was the name of the song Eric Clapton was singing very loudly from their stereo and they were having a party. A big cheerful holiday dance party for fifty or sixty people—mostly high school teachers, the staff from Sweets's dental practice, and some of Gloria's gay-lesbian community, which was a lot larger than my dad would have ever suspected. When Garth and I pulled into the yard it was lit up with sparkling lights in the trees, lights wrapped around the porch rails and the torsos of the big nude sculptures. There were so many old Volvos and new Saturns squeezed together in the clearing, it was hard to find a place to park. Noise burst from the house and the festivities had spilled over into the pyramid-shaped studio out back, from which laughter (and what I suspected was the haze of pot smoke) floated toward us through the snow. Gloria is a small town, but not that small; most of these partygoers had probably never met Ben or Amanda. At any rate, they weren't friends of theirs and, despite the news coverage about Amanda, their deaths had to be just abstract losses.

I left Garth outside to smoke his cigarette. "It's an outdoor sport now, you know, smoking. In New York, it's the only fresh air I get." He grinned at me, waved good-bye.

In the main house, couples of all types danced wildly on the bare floor that edged the pool in a long room that had nothing else in it but this "thermal storage unit." Tonight the pool was filled with floating candles in red poinsettias. A man and a woman, Hart High teachers, paddled around in the water, wearing floppy cloth reindeer antlers. On pulsing stereo speakers, Carole King gave way to Bonnie Raitt.

Katie spotted me in the crowd. "Welcome to Chelsea Morning," she shouted. "What are you doing here, Jamie? Chauffeuring the prince around again?" Katie wore a long, loose, green velvet dress and a crown of spangled tinsel in her braided hair. Just then Garth appeared beside his sister. She looked from him to me, grabbed my arm and pulled me away. Shoving through a mass of dancers gyrating in steps that they'd done a decade ago, we squeezed our way into her bedroom. Three cats were sleeping on the bed, as far from the party as they could get.

Katie pushed me down to the hearth of the stone fireplace free-rising in the middle of the large cluttered room. The log fire was warm on my back. Grabbing my hand, she slapped my engagement ring. "That's all I'm going to say," she muttered. "Except"—and she gave my wrist a shake with each phrase—"how many times can one intelligent woman make the same stupid mistake? Believe me, this prince isn't looking for a glass slipper." Suddenly she hugged me to her tightly. "And I'm sorry about Amanda Morgan. Go home."

"Knock knock." Sweets came into the bedroom. Tall and thin, she wore black slacks and a red satin blouse with a black scarf. "Jamie. How you doing? Sorry to bother." (Sweets was from Boston; *bother* sounded like *bahther*.) "But, Katie, didn't we buy two cases of that other Chardonnay?"

Katie explained where the wine was. Sweets turned back in the doorway to tell me that Dino had skipped his dental appointment and I should remind him he needed to get those cavities filled before the teeth abscessed. After she'd returned to the party, I told Katie that Dino had skipped more than Sweets's appointment; he'd skipped town, blowing off community service.

"What are we going to do with him?" Katie said. It had been into Katie's arms that Dino had taken his first wobbling steps. "Our Dino."

I felt so safe beside her on the hearth that I told her about the terror I hadn't yet mentioned to anyone else. The fear that Dino had gotten the Mercedes from Clay, had gotten the crossbow, had—in some freakish mishap or drugged state—ended up somehow killing Amanda. Or if he hadn't, he (and maybe Clay too) would be accused of it, or implicated in it. Perhaps accused of Ben's murder as well. I told her that the night of the fire Dino had picked up Clay at a friend's in Glen Valley, just a few blocks from where the Tymoszes lived. That I'd seen them driving around.

Katie kept stroking my hand. "But Clay didn't take the car from River Bend until two hours after they think Amanda died. You just told me that. Dino took him joyriding, they started to run out of gas, and they left the car at the rest stop. That's it."

"Unless Tricia is wrong about the time she saw Clay leave. Or lying."

"Why would she lie, Jamie? And two hours wrong?" She gave me a little shake. "Honey, you know Dino could never figure out how to use some kind of high-tech crossbow. He couldn't do it!"

Somehow she made me laugh at that. "That's better." She took my hand. "Now I'm going to tell you something, but I don't want you to flip out. That paper collage of words you showed me last week? Something about death and a sheriff in a little town?"

"Are you going to tell me Clay, Katie?" I pulled my hand back.

"Just that Clay's in my art class. And we've been making paper collages. I checked before I said anything to you. But I was right about those letters from the Absolut ads. I found the same fonts in magazines in my supplies closet. But even if

Clay and Dino did send you those notes, I'm sure it was just a stupid joke. Jamie, are you listening to me? It's nothing."

"It's not nothing if Clay's delivering death threats."

She didn't argue that. "I know he's struggling. Can you blame him? Gina dies on him. Barclay's a shit. Meredith's no help. Come on, give the kid a break. He's so smart."

"Maybe too smart," I said.

I left the house without even looking for Garth in the loud happy bedlam of the party where Bob Dylan was rocking.

As I HEADED HOME, the snow started to stick on the road but wasn't a problem yet. The longest day of my life wasn't over yet either. I called Naoko on her cell phone. She said she'd heard that I'd been yanked from the Morgan homicide. I said *yank* was a good word. She told me Chief Waige had pulled her off surveillance at River Bend so she couldn't tell me whether Barclay and Clay were home or not. I asked her to check the desk for me. Had the Richmond PD called in with any news about Dino? Naoko called back in five minutes, just as I was pulling onto Dock. There was nothing.

The Christmas tree lights still blinked merrily in our front window. I'd forgotten to turn them off. Hurrying inside, I told myself that at least Dad wouldn't notice, since he never came out of his room after retiring there at night; he could manage his bathroom and the climb into bed on his own, but it was a struggle and he almost always fell straight to sleep afterward. I peeked in his room; he was snoring.

Still bundled in my coat, I was checking to be sure I'd

locked the door behind me when I heard a rapping knock—not the bell—on the front door.

It was Danny Ventura. "I saw you come in," he said. "I didn't want to ring and wake up your dad. Listen, I got to tell you something." He had on a pilot's jacket, a black cowboy hat and black cowboy boots. He often went to Western bars to do line dances.

The truth is, I was sort of touched that Danny had come all the way over to my house, despite the hour. Because I thought it was about Rod's turning my homicide case over to him that he'd come to talk about.

"Danny, you didn't have to do this. It's okay. You didn't ask Rod to pull me off the case. Go home. I'm wiped. I'm going to bed."

He tried to say something but couldn't. Then he took a deep breath and slowly let it out. "Man, this is too much. I don't want to do this again. I know he's a friend of yours."

He was scaring me. "Who? Who's a friend?"

"They just found him at Dante's. I'm headed there now. I figure maybe you want to come too."

"Dante's?" I could see it in his eyes. "Pudge is dead."

Danny nodded. "I got the call, I came straight here. Just leave your car, we'll go in mine."

I nodded without talking, walked into the living room and turned off the tree lights.

As I pulled the front door shut behind me and locked it, I asked him, "How was he killed?"

"They're saying heart attack."

"They're wrong."

18

SWEETS

EARLIER, UNABLE TO SLEEP once I'd awakened her with my phone call, Eileen Salerno had driven to Dante's to check on Pudge, suddenly anxious after their quarrel that something was wrong with him. In fact she had started to wonder if his strange and belligerent outbursts might have been the result of a stroke. She had always worried about Pudge, who indulged in the worst possible diet for a man who, even at twenty-nine, had clogged arteries, who smoked and drank and got no exercise but the high-stressed frenzy of a busy restaurant. While the Salernos lived in the same gated community as Jim and Amanda Morgan, Pudge had never once set foot on its golf course. For years he'd promised to use his treadmill for more than a clothes rack, to lift weights, to join a gym. He never had. So, suddenly panicked about her husband's spending the night alone in his office at Dante's, Eileen phoned him, then dressed and drove into town to check on him. It was midnight.

Eileen had found Pudge in Dante's kitchen, bent over a fifty-gallon electric frying vat, with his head submerged in the boiling oil. Screaming, she'd somehow managed to haul him out but he was already dead, his face and his hair horrifically burned away. She'd told 911 that her husband had had a heart attack.

It also looked to the EMS team who arrived eight minutes later from St. Anthony's Hospital as if Pudge had had a heart attack, either before or because he fell facedown into oil boiling at 400 degrees Fahrenheit.

TELLING ME YET AGAIN that I was "just along because the guy's your buddy," Danny pulled up in front of Dante's, where the swirling blue and red lights on the ambulance and squad cars flickered eerily over the manger on the town green. The briefly falling snow had stopped long ago and was already dripping off the camel and shepherds. It would be gone by noon tomorrow.

By the time we got to the restaurant, I'd made four calls to tell the other members of the Killing Club that someone had just killed Pudge in the same way Pudge had once imagined killing Eileen's sadistic father—by boiling him in the deep-fat vat of the local bakery.

My first call was to River Bend. I was told that Barclay

wasn't at home and no one knew where he was. Debbie I reached on her cell phone. She was safely fifty miles away from Gloria, leaving at 6 A.M. for the airport. I told her not to let anyone into her friend's house, even if she knew them. I almost didn't tell her about Pudge. It confirmed her view of the world. Connie said he'd already arrived at the restaurant to be with Eileen, who'd phoned him. At Chelsea Morning, Katie couldn't find Garth anywhere in the crowd still there partying. I told her to keep looking and when she found him to tell him to stay there.

There must have been a dozen people from GPD milling around Gert and the EMTs in Dante's. Apart from them, in a shadowy corner of the room, Eileen sat with a woman I recognized as a human services worker from the Crime Victims Center. Eileen's arms were bandaged. Her hands rested on a trumpet in her lap. Gert stood beyond the yellow tape that blocked off the kitchen, talking to one of the paramedics. Connie, still in his coat and gloves, was saying something to Rod that Rod wrote in a notebook. Danny joined them, shook Connie's hand hard. Connie winced; Danny had that effect on lots of people. Rod saw me and nodded, but said nothing as I ducked under the tape and went into the kitchen.

The fifty-gallon frying vat stood near the industrial stoves. Pudge's body lay on the floor beside the vat, covered by one of his green-checked tablecloths. With Gert standing beside me, I pulled back the cloth. But his face was covered with gauze.

"The burns were bad," Gert said quietly.

"Danny said a heart attack."

"AMI. Massive, I think. They used the intravenous nitro,

and also the AED, but it was too late." She was saying that Pudge had suffered an acute myocardial infarction (a heart attack), that the emergency responders had tried to bring him back with an automatic external defibrillator and a hypodermic of nitroglycerin but were unsuccessful. "The shock, you know, of oil was severe. And then the health habits so poor," added the trim medical examiner, who had no bad habits of her own except Chief Warren Waige.

She patted my back. "Your notion there's this killer turns out to be the sad truth, *ja*? I wish you had been wrong."

"Me too."

Joining the two women still seated in the corner, I told Eileen that I felt heartbroken for her. The social worker left the two of us alone. Eileen and I sat there together for a while, until finally she said, "How am I going to let our kids know? They loved him so much."

"Everybody loved him, Eileen."

Her voice sounded numbed. "I'm glad I called and told him I was coming over and this was crazy, fighting at Christmas. I just had a sort of, like a sixth sense something was wrong. So at least the last thing was me saying I loved him."

"He knew that, Eileen. We all knew that. I'm so sorry."

Awkwardly she held up the trumpet in her bandaged hands; it was old, dented, tarnished. "He kept it here in the office. He was going to take lessons again. He was always sorry he let his music go. But we were so busy here." She gestured at the restaurant angrily, as if Dante's had killed Pudge. "You know what? He got up, got dressed. I saw on the couch he'd already put on his pajamas. But he—you know what I mean, Jamie?—he wanted to look nice for me. He always tried so hard to make everything nice for everybody."

"I know."

"Why did I get so mad at him for getting drunk?"

"Because he wasn't supposed to drink."

"He knew that, and with the smoking and the weight . . ." She stopped herself. "It was stupid. We never fight."

I nodded. "Who could fight with Pudge?" We sat there a little longer, both looking at the trumpet. "Why didn't you just tell him to come home?"

Eileen said that Pudge had wanted to relieve the day manager of the hassle of driving over in the snow at four A.M. to receive the bakery truck delivery. So he'd told the man that he'd stay overnight instead.

"That was Pudge," I said.

Eileen's eyes moved someplace past grief, and I didn't intrude any further. As I was leaving, Connie came over to tell her good-bye. He looked haggard, but his black wool overcoat was pressed neatly and his gray hair was freshly cut. There was a smell of cigarette smoke in his coat, and I wondered if the pressure had sent him back to smoking. He took me aside to say he was glad he'd been home at the rectory when Eileen phoned. He'd just been sitting in his study, trying to think things through, looking out the window at the snow falling. "Then she called, and somehow, despite everything, I couldn't believe it. Not Pudge . . ."

"I feel the same. Debbie says Pudge had called you too, saying he knew you were the killer."

Connie shook his head unhappily. "It was just craziness. It sounded like he'd been drinking."

"I tried to phone you about Pudge's call tonight, but nobody picked up. What exactly did he say to you?"

"'You killed Amanda and Ben and I can prove it.'"

"What did you think he meant by that?"

"I just told him he sounded drunk and he laughed and said he was just 'practicing,' and he hung up."

"Practicing for what?"

"I don't know."

I said that Pudge had been right that there was a killer. Somebody *was* killing the Killing Club.

"Barclay?" When I didn't answer him, he said, "That's going to be really hard on his family. I'm worried about Clay. He's been through more than he can deal with."

I said I was worried about Clay as well. "But Connie, right now, you should just go back home and lock your door. That's what I'm going to do."

He said he'd see me tomorrow at Dixon when he came by to give Rod a statement about the history of the Killing Club. "I don't know what good it's going to do," he added. "If it's Barclay, it's about Amanda."

"I suppose. So you were at the rectory all evening?" He said yes, but added that he fielded so many calls all day long from parishioners with problems that by late at night he usually let the machine answer.

"Lucky," I told him as I walked him to the door, "that you picked up for Eileen." He explained that she'd called his cell phone, a number few people knew.

I told Connie to use that cell phone to call 911 if he should run into Barclay. "And by the way, Connie, I'm sorry you decided not to let me know about that night with Amanda and all you guys at the playhouse. The night Lyall killed himself." Connie turned to stare at me. I nod-ded. "Garth told me about it. Yeah, a regular guy thing, wasn't it? Except for poor Lyall. So you made fun of him. It might have helped if you'd told me. I guess that's what Amanda was trying to say when we all met here: 'People in this room know the answer.' To why Lyall might be a little angry."

"We took a vow to keep quiet about it." His eyes sank darkening into their sockets. "We're not proud of it."

"I wouldn't think you would be. Maybe Ben wanted to get it off his chest, being sick and all. Maybe Amanda did too. Garth says you and Barclay told him to keep it quiet."

"Because it has nothing to do with anything." As he shouldered open the door to Dante's, he turned. "We all know it's Barclay. There's no chance Lyall's alive."

"You sound like you wish he were, Connie."

"Of course I do."

I watched him walk with a soldierlike erectness and regularity across the now-whitened street, past the manger and into the shadows of the green.

A white news van sped into view. They'd heard about Pudge's macabre death. They'd all be here soon.

When I closed the restaurant door and turned around, Rod was standing there. He said he knew how much I had liked Pudge and that he was sorry.

I pointed at the ABC-NEWS van pulling up at the curb. "What are you going to tell them?"

"For as long as I can that it was a heart attack."

"It's in the first Death Book, Rod."

"I figured."

"Boiling oil."

Rod explained that they had reason to think that water (the most dangerous combination with oil—and the cause, as Pudge had often told me, of most restaurant fires) had been poured into the still very hot liquid (the vat had been turned off only an hour earlier), causing an explosive burst of steam that might in itself have killed Pudge.

I thought about this. "Not by accident. And Pudge was pushed. The rim's too high. If he'd had a heart attack and fallen against it, he would have slid to the floor."

Rod nodded. "Agree. Looks like somebody dumped in some water, tipped him over into the vat and the shock caused the coronary. His wife said he had heart problems anyhow." Rod showed me a small evidence bag. "Gert found this tied around his ankle." It was a Yale key on a red piece of yarn.

I felt like I was going to vomit. "It's the first thing Pudge said when I told him about Ben. That somebody was trying to kill us, people in the club. Now three of us are dead."

He nodded again. "This is a crazy person. Or a desperate one."

"Pudge had too much to drink tonight. He started calling people, Debbie, Connie, Jeremy, I guess just everybody in the club he could reach, saying he could prove they were the killer. Maybe he was trying to bait someone. Maybe he did. One of them *was* the killer and it has to be Barclay. And, who knows where he is. Because goddamn Waige cut him loose!"

Rod's slow even voice didn't change. "Did Pudge call you and accuse you of killing them?"

"No! Of course he didn't. He knows I didn't do it."

"Did he call Garth McBride?"

"Garth says not. Besides, Garth . . ."

He nodded. "Yeah. He was with you."

The truth was, any one of the club members could have

done it. I hadn't seen Garth since we'd arrived at Katie's party—no one would have noticed if he'd taken his sister's Volvo and sped back to town in it. Connie could have walked across the green to Dante's and back. Debbie could have gone by the restaurant on her way out of town. And Barclay . . . Barclay could be anywhere. No one could find him or his BMW coupe. My suspicion was that he'd fled the jurisdiction. But had he committed his third murder before he left? Had Pudge accused him and it cost him his life?

Danny joined Rod and me. "Some scuff marks off his shoes got tracked along the floor; probably he got dragged over to the vat. This whole thing is too fuckin' freaked for me." He rocked back on his boot heels, shook his head at us, then wandered off.

Rod said, "Jamie, I'm putting protection on you, twenty-four seven."

"Put me on the case, Rod. That's all I want from you."

He stared at me sadly. "Yeah, I get that feeling." His arms crossed in that familiar gesture. "I love you. So long. Please go home when Danny leaves."

"When Danny leaves? You're not reminding me I'm off the case?"

"You're not going to quit, so you might as well help. Danny won't say so but he can use you. Find out who did this. But unofficial, okay? My ass is on the line about this."

"Okay." I touched his arm and he smiled at me. I said, "I want an APB on Barclay Ober and I want him held when we get him."

"You got the APB. Bring me something, anything, outside that Mercedes, because that car was 'stolen,' and we'll hold him."

My phone rang. It was Garth. Rod left while I was talking to him.

THE PULL-OUT COUCH in Pudge's office lay open, sheets in a tangle, oddly old-fashioned flannel pajamas tossed over on the pillows. There was a little sink against the wall. On its glass countertop sat some contact lens paraphernalia, an aspirin bottle, two drinking glasses and some dental fixative. Pulling on latex gloves, I checked the aspirin, then picked up and sniffed at the tube of fixative. Then I telephoned Chelsea Morning, where the party had quieted down, maybe from the news about Pudge—because everybody in Gloria did know Pudge—so that Sweets was able to hear me. I asked her if Pudge wore dentures. She said he wore a bridge—that she'd made it for him—and yes, it was a large one that he removed at night. And yes, usually there was a slight spillover of the fixative when bonding the bridge, and yes, whatever was in the fixative would be transmitted sublingually.

I thanked her, asked if Garth was still there. She took a moment to look around. "Yeah, I can see him through the window out by Katie's studio. He's smoking. Like she's not going to notice. You want me to get him?"

"No, that's all right. Tell him to stay there. And be careful."

"Give Pudge's family our sympathy. He was a very nice man," Sweets said as we were hanging up.

Danny stood in the doorway to Pudge's office, waiting for me.

"Come smell this," I told him, holding out the fixative tube.

He shrugged. "I got a lousy sense of smell."

I said, "You ever tasted an almond that's gone bad? Bitter?"

After he smelled the compound in the tube, I told him to go ask Gert if the bridge was back in Pudge's mouth, and if it was, she should run tests in the autopsy for cyanide.

19

ETTEN

DANNY AND I stood back from the metal table in the autopsy morgue while Gert finished her post-mortem on Pudge. Pudge had died from acute myo-cardial infarction and pulmonary edema—a massive spasm of the heart that shut down his lungs as well. But he'd been dead before his face went into the oil. Cyanide poisoning had caused the heart failure.

"Good for you, Jamie," Gert said, drying her hands at the sink. "If you look at his eyes, *ja*? You see that bright red in the retinal veins? That is a sign of the cyanide."

I didn't feel good and I didn't want to look in Pudge's eyes, but I'd been right. The lab test showed traces of the soluble salt, potassium cyanide, mixed in the fixative. Compounded with water, it had released HCN (hydrogen cyanide gas) into Pudge's system. It wasn't far from the way they killed people in gas chambers. And his symptoms could have easily been mistaken from the onset by Pudge himself for a coronary: dizziness, confusion, chest pains and shortness of breath, nausea. It wouldn't have taken long.

"And one more thing," Gert said, pulling off the lab coat, tossing it in a hamper as we left. "You sent this Styrofoam coffee cup in for the saliva test?"

"Yes. I was off the case. I know. Somebody give you a rough time?"

"To compare with the semen we got from the Mercedes car seat?"

"The chief chewed Abu out about doing it for me?"

"No." She waved good-bye to her assistant, who would finish up with Pudge and remove his body. She patted me on the back. "Your same fellow. Saliva, semen, also the paternity of the fetus we examined in Mrs. Morgan. Same. This is just preliminary, I have to say that. But there it is. Your Barclay Ober."

"Gert, thank you."

She gave me a smile of flawless white teeth. "We had a playwright in Sweden, you know him, Strindberg. Well, he said, 'To learn something makes me happy.' Also for me. It's late. Let's all go to our beds."

BACK AT DANTE'S, I'd assured Connie and Rod that I was doing just that, going home to bed. And if Rod had sent a squad car to drive by my house, the house would be dark and my Mustang would be parked right outside. But I wasn't home.

In his Corvette, as we sped east along the river, Danny managed to keep from skidding in the melting snow despite going twenty miles an hour over the speed limit. "It's in the tires and hands," he told me. "They were talking about putting tolls on this road, remember that?"

"Yeah, that'd slow you down, I guess."

He laughed. "I'd need a 'shitload of dimes.' You know that movie where all the cowboys have to pay a dime highway toll right out in the middle of the desert?"

"*Blazing Saddles.*"

"Love it."

I think Danny was trying to take my mind off Pudge but I brought him back to the case, describing how one of my murder plans in the Death Book had been to put cyanide salt in someone's antihistamines.

Danny scratched his head under his cowboy hat. "So, what's the point, just rubbing your face in this Killing Club crap? I mean, why double up? Why dump the guy in the fryer if you already brushed his false teeth with cyanide?" He glanced over at me. "Excuse me, okay. I shouldn't talk like that about your friend."

"The best thing you can do for my friend is let me help you find out who killed him."

He laughed, smacking his steering wheel. "You want to 'help' me? That's a joke. You want to run the show."

"That's true too."

By now it was past two A.M. Danny and I were on the outskirts of Gloria, climbing over the chain-link fence that locked up Ober Land Development and Realty at night. There were no dogs, no security guards; just a light at the entrance and a light over the parking area. Why should they need more protection than that? It was just a real estate office. I doubted they'd ever been broken into before. Certainly not by the Gloria police.

"You're sure?" Danny asked me again before he snipped the external wires on the alarm system. He'd found the hookup and dismantled it so quickly that I suspected (not for the first time) that Danny Ventura had turned to the law only after a teenaged life of crime.

"Danny, we've fucked the case if we get caught."

"You've gotta say these things sooner." He was shoving me through a rear window in the building. "Besides, I'll just say I'm Donny, and that Sergeant Dan's home in bed. Hey, you see Donny's new ad on TV?"

Everybody in town had seen it. If you turned on your television, it was almost impossible to avoid. "'Donny's Dreamworld'? Where he's lying on one of his mattresses dressed like Scrooge, and the three teenaged girls in bathing suits are Christmases Past, Present and Future?"

"You saw it! That was my idea!"

"Well, it's some idea."

Danny grabbed my arm. "No! That was me in the ad! Donny didn't want to do it. He thought it was dumb."

I was thinking I hadn't been fair to Donny Ventura.

Five minutes after that, we'd popped the lock to Barclay's private office ("Piece of cake," Danny had whispered), and in just a half-hour more, I'd found Barclay's motives for murder.

.   .   .

IF YOU DON'T WANT your family to find things, you don't leave them at home. So while I wasn't sure exactly what I'd learn by illegally rummaging through Barclay's office, I thought I'd find something to tie him to Ben or Amanda or Pudge in some way I could use. What I wanted was the motive for the first killing. I didn't expect to find any cyanide tablets, or instructions on crossbows, or blackmail notes about the affair with Amanda or anything of that nature. But Barclay's desk calendar did list his lunch with Ben Tymosz on the same day as Ben's death. And an unsigned real estate contract did sit right there in the bottom of the in box, with the same ominous date on it. In the contract, OLDR was offering Ben Tymosz and his mother $675,000 for the dilapidated Pine Barrens Playhouse, which they had co-owned. It was a lot more than you would have thought that rotted building was worth, until you found the surveyors' maps, blueprint plans and faxed copies of other contracts of sale for the four, also derelict, commercial docks on the Deep Port River, and for the five-block street front that ran between the docks and the theater and the half a dozen brick warehouses, also in ruins.

Danny and I studied the rolled draft papers and the blue-covered contracts that we'd pulled from files and drawers and from the top of a Shaker armoire that also held a plasma TV. Then we accessed Barclay's computer files just by turning it on. There was no ID needed to open it. Clearly Barclay wasn't worried about secrecy here at Ober Land Development and Realty. Right there on the desktop of his PC were design drawings, elevated models and construction blueprints for a "recreational, commercial and residential center," all in a folder labeled ETTEN LANDING. Danny whistled. "I'd say Barclay's planning a big demolition derby on that old stomping ground of yours. That theater, docks, warehouses. All that shit's coming down."

"They'll be 'restored.' They'll turn it into something like South Street Seaport, Penn's Landing. Look at this. Promenade, plaza. Residential lofts. Museum. That buys off the history buffs. Galleries. Restaurant and cineplex."

"In Gloria?"

We shrugged at each other.

"Too bad," Danny said. "We can't get into Barclay's e-mail."

But I thought we could.

Clay answered his cell phone, sounding wide awake despite the hour, claiming to have heard from Dino, who was on his way home. "Dino's okay," he told me.

"You tell him to turn himself in to the police, Clay."

"Yeah, like that's going to happen."

"Are you with him?"

"No way."

"Where are you?"

He said he was home on his computer, out in his hideaway, the old summer kitchen at River Bend. Maybe he was. He told me that he'd heard about Pudge and wanted to know if we'd arrested his father yet. I said we couldn't find him.

Clay's voice was so bitter it gave me a chill. "Dead mom, psycho killer dad. Guess I'm ready-made for Devo-land, whatever."

When I asked him if there was any chance he could figure out for me what Barclay's e-mail password was, he didn't even ask me why I wanted to know. "My dad's a friggin' moron. He's always asking me to tell him how to fix things on his computer. His password's Etten 3-9. Like, wow, who'd think of that—his middle name and his birthday? He's so proud he's an Etten, it's probably tattooed on his butt."

"Clay, tomorrow you and I are going to have another talk. About whether you pasted those *Halloween* notes together and had Dino stick them in our front door. And whether you put one on Amanda Morgan's windshield?"

"I don't know what you're talking about."

"I'm talking about letters cut out of magazines."

"Yeah, blame me! Maybe I killed your pals too. Maybe you're next."

"If you don't lie to me, Clay, we can get through this. But if you do? You think a prep school in Vermont will be a drag? It'll be Paradise Island compared to a youthful-offender cell block."

Clay hung up on me.

Barclay had a lot of e-mails he hadn't opened. I didn't open them either. They seemed to be mostly about his sports enthusiasms (his squash court reservation, his hunting license renewal). Or about the realty business (sales were brisk). Or his political aspirations (judging from the subject headings, Barclay spoke at a great many public events, attended a great many parties and gave away a great deal of money). The rest of the unopened e-mails were trying to sell him something. I went to "Old Mail." There were a dozen from Amanda. She wanted Barclay to leave her alone. Their affair was over. If he couldn't accept it, she was sorry, but she didn't want to divorce Jim and marry him, she didn't even want to see him anymore. She was tired of sneaking around, tired of being looked at in that way by his mother, tired herself of the "old Amanda." There was an odd sentence in one of the e-mails that became clear to me only later. Amanda said that while she was calling off their affair, she would stick by her agreement not to block his plans, adding that he was going to need more than her vote anyhow.

It made sense in relation to two interesting e-mails sent to Barclay in the past month, the only ones written by two particular people. One was from Pudge, and it predated Ben's death by a few weeks. It was very formal. Pudge was writing as Dante Salerno Jr., chair of the Gloria, New Jersey, Planning and Zoning Board, to advise Barclay Ober, applicant for construction permits, that the board had a historic interest in preserving the Pine Barrens Playhouse as well as the old town docks. It said that Ober Land Development and Realty would have to persuade the planning board that any projects OLDR had under consideration took into account the board's many questions about restoration and preservation. This e-mail was cc'd to the nine other members of the planning board. One of the members was Amanda Morgan.

The second e-mail was from Barclay's mother, Meredith, or so I assumed from the return address—M.E.Ober. There was no salutation and no signature. It was brief. It was blunt. All it said was, "Are you determined to destroy your life? Don't think she won't enforce that prenup."

Danny asked me, "What does that mean?"

"I'm not sure yet, but I bet it means that if Tricia Ober divorces Barclay for screwing around with Amanda, she's going to walk away from River Bend with a shitload of dimes."

• • •

THERE WASN'T ENOUGH snow left on the roads to keep Danny Ventura from driving the Corvette eighty miles an hour back to town. "Maybe you can keep this up, but I gotta get some sleep, Jamie. I'll meet you at Dixon at ten, okay? It's four fucking thirty A.M."

He didn't stop for more than five seconds when he let me out in front of my house. "You're okay, right?" And then he was gone, racing around the corner in the slush onto Fourteenth Street.

I didn't see until after Danny had driven off that the front door to our house was open.

The minute I stepped inside the hall, I could smell the gas.

20

DINO

NATURAL GAS DOESN'T SMELL; neither does carbon monoxide. You just get sick. And if you replace enough of your oxygen with gas, you die. So it's very useful that gas companies add an odor as a warning that there's a leak. The odor I smelled was like a houseful of rotten eggs, and it was nauseating.

Running down the hall, yelling for my father, I wrapped my scarf around my face. I threw open the door to Dad's room. I knew I shouldn't flip on a light switch, since electric current can ignite an explosion. I ran to the bed in the dark and shook my father. "Dad! Dad!"

He jolted awake, coughing. "What! Jamie? What's the matter! What the hell is that smell?"

I figured if he could curse, he wasn't dying.

"Dad, here. Keep your mouth and nose covered. It's a gas leak."

I shoved both windows wide open, already on my cell phone to 911, talking fast. "This is Sergeant Jamie Ferrara, GPD. I need an ambulance and Gas Emergency here ASAP—1419 Dock Street."

The dispatcher said, "Jamie?"

"Sarah? We've got a bad gas leak. And a handicapped person. Get somebody here!" I gave her the address again and hung up. Dad had pulled himself to the edge of the bed. I helped him into his wheelchair and raced him back down the hall and out onto the stoop. By then both of us were coughing nonstop.

On the street behind us a black Land Rover squealed out of a parking space, banging with a loud *thunk* into the car in front of it, then skidding noisily away. Even in that moment, I thought, It's River Bend. Tricia's car. It's Barclay.

"Stay here, Dad!" I pulled my flashlight out of my pocket.

"Don't go back in there!"

"I heard somebody in there!"

"Jamie, you come back here!"

My eyes were burning, hard to keep open, as I ran down the hall to the rear of the house, where I could hear someone coughing, making choking noises in the kitchen.

The beam of my flashlight caught the tight glittery bronze curls first, then the slim shape next to the gas stove. Then I saw everything at once.

I kicked the box of kitchen matches out of Dino's hand. It was the fastest thing I could do. My brother was leaning over the stove with the unlit match pinched in his other hand, all ready to strike it against the box.

With a terrified shriek, Dino fell to his knees, then looked at me as he dropped onto the floor and passed out.

"Jesus Christ, are you crazy, Dino!" Pulling him by the armpits, I dragged him to the kitchen door, slid him down the wheelchair access ramp and toppled him over onto the cold ground in the backyard. Rubbing wads of snow in his face, I slapped him a few times before he shook himself to a groggy consciousness. "I couldn't see," he mumbled. "I thought Dad had left a burner on. It was gas, right?"

"Jesus Christ, Dino!"

"Did you get Dad?"

"Yes, I got Dad!"

He rolled over and threw up. Leaving him there, I ran back into the kitchen. The stove burners weren't even on; but the source was definitely the kitchen. It had to be a leak in a pipe or a fitting. I was opening every window I passed when I heard Dad trying to wheel himself back inside the house. He was coming along the hall.

"Dad! Will you *fuckin'* get out of here?! Nine-one-one's on it!"

"Somebody in the kitchen?"

"Dino. I dragged him into the backyard. He's okay."

Strong arms pumping, Dad shot past me in the hall like he was headed for the finish line of a wheelchair marathon. "Dino? Dino!"

I let him go. The whole family was crazy.

I COULDN'T STOP THINKING "IF." If the killer hadn't thrown off the main electrical switch after uncoupling the pipe fitting, Dino might have sparked an explosion

by flipping on every light switch in the house, not under-
standing, stoned as he was, why the lights wouldn't come on.
Any more than he could figure out to get Dad first, or how to
turn off the gas burners on the stove in the kitchen (which
weren't on) without being able to see them. If the lights
weren't coming on, then he figured the only thing to do was
to light one of the matches in the box above the stove. The
whole place would have blown.

But what if Dino hadn't even come home? What if he
hadn't remembered where we kept the extra key, under the
loose brick on the steps of the stoop? What if he hadn't at
least noticed the gas smell and tried to solve the problem,
even if he didn't know how?

And what about me? If I hadn't gone with Danny to Barclay's office, if I'd gone home, would I have caught the killer?
Or would I be dead, along with my dad, and maybe Dino?

EMS gave all three of us oxygen. Then they took my father and Dino to St. Anthony's to check them for respiratory
distress. Dad wouldn't let go of Dino's hand anyhow, so they
went in the same ambulance. The gas company shut off the
gas, the neighbors left and I locked the house.

Rod had shown up right after the man from the gas
company. Sarah, the dispatcher, had called him on her own.
We followed the ambulance to the hospital ER. I kept trying
to tell him about the Land Rover, but I couldn't stop coughing. He sent a squad car out to River Bend to see if the car
was back there.

In the emergency room, Dad was rubbing Dino's curls,
telling him that he was "a stupid idiot" and that if he hadn't
come home when he did, he (Dad) would be dead now. I
couldn't stop adding my own "What if?"s to Rod as we

waited. If I hadn't come home when I did, Dad and Dino would both be dead. Or if I'd been at home, the way the killer had assumed I was (because my Mustang was parked right there in front of the row house) when he'd uncoupled the main gas pipe leading from the basement wall to the furnace, we'd all three be dead. Because there was no doubt that someone had deliberately cut through the pipe from the gas main and shoved its open end through the hole into our kitchen wall. It was one of the murders in the Death Book.

Rod asked, "Why didn't you go home to bed? Where'd you talk Danny into taking you?"

"We had a couple of leads about Barclay. I think I know why he'd want to get rid of Ben."

ST. ANTHONY'S DECIDED to keep Dino and Dad for a few more hours; they put them in a semiprivate room together. "This is so great," Dino told the nurse, who patted him sweetly. It was now Tuesday morning, two days before Christmas; everybody was postponing elective surgery, so, for a change, there were empty beds at the busy hospital.

I sat with my father till he fell asleep, brushing his hand against the oxygen tube in his nose. As he drifted off he mumbled, "You got me out of the house. You got your brother out."

"I'm sorry I wasn't home before."

"God bless you, sweetheart." And then after a while, sleepily, "Giovanna, I don't want to hear you say a word like *fucking* again. What kind of talk is that from a daughter . . . ?"

Dino was sleepy too. I brushed his hair with my hand until he opened his beautiful goofy blue eyes. "Hi, Jamie. . . . I'm sorry I screwed up."

"Dino. Talk to me just a little bit."

". . . I'm too sleepy."

"I know you are. I just need you to answer a few questions."

"Am I in trouble?" He smiled up at me, and it was the same smile he'd had a long time ago, when I'd leaned over his crib, handing him back the pacifier he'd thrown on the floor for fun.

"Shhh. You're not in trouble. Just answer my questions. First of all . . . Listen to me, Dino. When you and Clay took Barclay's Mercedes out for a drive, what did you do with the crossbow?"

"The what?"

"The crossbow. Barclay's crossbow."

He looked at me, so transparently puzzled that relief—from the tiny part of me that couldn't be sure—poured into my bones. ". . . You mean, like a bow and arrow?"

"Yeah, sort of . . ."

"You think I stole something like that?" His nose itched so he pulled out the oxygen clamp. I put it back.

"Talk to me, Dino."

It took a while before finally I had the story as straight as someone like Dino could make it. Yes, he'd known it was wrong to teach Clay to drive—when Dino didn't have a car and Clay didn't have a license. ("But Jamie, I swear, he's a great driver.") Yes, Clay had occasionally picked Dino up in the luxury cars he'd stolen from River Bend and Dino had driven them "around town" just to see what they were like. ("Everybody says, 'Hey Mercedes, hey Beemer, that's cool,' so I wanted to know. We didn't hurt them.")

Yes, Clay had met Dino in Barclay's Mercedes on Sunday sometime before noon ("Time is not really my thing") at a rest stop on the expressway. Dino had hitchhiked there with "somebody, I don't remember exactly," some other musician playing with him at one of his Atlantic City dives. But at the last minute Dino didn't return to Gloria with Clay. He had "gotten the gig" to substitute for the lead guitarist of First Offenders, ("Jamie, they are seriously big time") down in Richmond. He'd called a friend on Clay's phone and the friend had told him. He wanted Clay to drive him to Virginia. ("Come on, Clay had credit cards, plenty of cash. He just stuffed his pockets with whatever he wanted at home—purses, wallets—they just left it all lying around the house. . . . Clay? You think he's this little kid? He hands me two hundred bucks when we split up! How cool is that?")

Clay, brighter than my brother, had refused to drive him to Virginia. So Dino had caught a ride with a truck driver he'd just met in the Roy Rogers's line at the rest stop.

He didn't know what had happened to Clay. ("Doan be mad, Jamie. We split and he left. You don't get Clay! He can do anything. He said he was going home.") No, they'd never looked in the trunk of the car and seen the crossbow there. No, they'd never driven to Etten Park in the Mercedes. No, Dino had not known that the police were looking for him. There was a screwup and the band he'd gone to play with in Richmond, the First Offenders, didn't need a lead guitarist after all. But, though disappointed, Dino had met a college girl at the club who was "really nice" and whose parents had gone to London for the holidays, leaving their cars and their beach house in her care. ("I saw dolphins! I mean whole herds of them, just having a good time in the ocean.")

"How'd you get home, Dino? Who got you home?"

"I hitched. I didn't want to get in trouble with the judge. And I wanted to be with you and Dad for Christmas. I borrowed some money from this girl, she was a really nice girl, and I took the bus to A.C."

I smoothed the blanket over him. "Dino, I need you to be honest with me. This is about somebody trying to kill Dad and me. This is serious. Did you and Clay paste together those notes, like '*Death has come to your little town, Sheriff*'? Did you stick them in the door yourself?"

He shook his head vigorously, then winced as if he'd worsened a headache. "No way."

"Did Clay pick you up tonight in Tricia's Land Rover? Did he drop you off at home?"

Dino stared up at me. "Clay loves you."

"I know. Just tell me, did he bring you home in Tricia's Land Rover?" Dino nodded yes. "Did he come in the house with you?" He shook his head no. "He just dropped you off?"

"That's right. He had to get the car back . . . I'm so sleepy, Jamie. Merry Christmas. You love me, don't you? I love you."

"Go to sleep."

I TALKED THE WHOLE while Rod was driving us from the hospital to River Bend. We laid out a case against Barclay. He knew about the Death Book murders in the Killing Club and could have carried out all three homicides so that they corresponded—even planting on each victim a signature club key. He had the physical strength to bludgeon or push Ben down his basement stairs and to dunk Pudge's body into the oil vat. He owned and had in his car trunk the murder weapon (the crossbow) that had killed Amanda, and he had the hunting skill to use it. Near the times of the homicides, we could place him (a) outside the Tymosz house and on the same day that Ben had refused to sell him the Pine Barrens Playhouse, (b) in the lot at Etten Park a hundred yards from where Amanda was killed on the morning after he'd fought bitterly with her for breaking off their affair and (c) in downtown Gloria across the green from Pudge's restaurant the same night that Pudge—who had blocked his development deal—had just claimed to be able to prove that Barclay had murdered Ben and Amanda. Presumably in the beginning, he'd thought only that it would be easy to get rid of Ben, a stumbling block in his plans for building Etten Landing (and possibly even a threat to his political future if Ben—dying—felt compelled to confess an old act of group hazing that had led to a fellow club member's suicide). But then whatever fear or rage drove him to kill Amanda, he saw he could pass off her death as the second act of a crazed person mimicking the Killing Club. The same cover-up got rid of Pudge, who possibly had more direct evidence against Barclay than we knew.

It all made sense.

That Barclay had fled made the case so strong that even Chief Waige couldn't protect the Obers any longer. We had our arrest warrant.

WHEN WE TURNED at the curving brick entrance to the Ober estate, morning light had already pushed the darkness off the horizon. One of our GPD squad cars blocked the black Land Rover that sat neatly parked in the five-car garage by the guest cottage of River Bend. The fender was dented.

Meredith Ober, in a black velvet bathrobe, spoke with us in her morning room.

The strain of Barclay's disappearance was telling, even on her. Her thin china coffee cup shook slightly in its saucer, enough that she set it down on the polished table. But her cold bullying voice was as steady as ever. "I thought this invasion of our lives had been brought to a close." She pointed at me but spoke only to Rod. "I understood Jamie had been removed from this case. Why is she here?"

Rod told her simply that things had changed. "We have a warrant for your son's arrest. Do you know where he is?"

"I don't know where he is. He isn't here. Tricia's here. Asleep. My grandson, Clay, is upstairs in his room, also asleep. And I would like to go *back* to sleep myself."

True enough, Clay was in his room. He was even in his bed. But he refused to let me in. I popped open the chain on the flimsy door of his room with a sharp kick that had taken me five years of Tae Kwon Do classes to learn how to do. Flipping on his light switch, I yanked down his covers. The coverlet was blue checks, Ralph Lauren style. The whole room looked designed, and not by its occupant, but like somebody's idea of the Ivy League a hundred years ago. Clay had done what little he could to ruin the impression. Like taping posters of gangsta rap stars above the blue canvas couch.

It was obvious he'd been just lying there, in his T-shirt and underpants, wide awake. He looked very pale and thin, a fuzz of hair on his legs, but his chest still smooth as a child's.

I pulled him off the bed and over to his desk chair and pushed him down in it. "Start talking. You're going to tell me about every fucking time you stole a car from here to take Dino for a ride, including what you saw when you dropped him off at my house tonight."

"Who said I did that?"

"I saw you there, asshole."

We stared at each other a while, breathing loud enough to hear. Finally he mumbled, "I didn't see anything when I dropped him off. Except, like, just like two minutes later, I saw Danny Ventura dropping you off. So I left! I swear!"

I asked him about the morning of Amanda's death. His story was identical to Dino's. He didn't even know his father had two crossbows. The only one he'd known about was the one he'd located in the "billiards room." "Trying to help *you* out!" he yelled at me.

He didn't know anything about a Beretta pistol we now knew also to be missing from Barclay's collection.

We went over all the other "joyrides" the thirteen-year-old could remember taking.

"The only time I ever hurt a car was Tricia's, last night. And I'll pay her back, okay! I was careful. I swear!"

"Don't push me, Clay. Now think about telling me the truth about those pasted letters you stuck in my door!"

He ran back to his bed. "What's with you and these stupid movie quotes?! I don't understand what you're talking about!" He crawled completely under the coverlet, moving to the foot of his bed.

I pulled the covers off him again. "Three people have been murdered, Clay. Do you understand that, you little jerk?"

His face struggled between fear and anger.

"It's not Dino! Do you think it's Dino? He's the only friend I've got!" He jumped up and ran over to his door where the wood was splintered at the chain plate. "You can't just break down somebody's door like that!"

"Sure I can. You just saw me do it." I left him there.

CLAY'S GRANDMOTHER WAS pouring Rod coffee when I returned. She was saying that it had been difficult raising Barclay, an only son, after his father's heart attack; that sadly the same pattern had repeated itself in the next generation—she'd had to raise an only grandson after my sister had died. "I always wanted a girl," she surprisingly remarked. Then she gestured for us to sit. "All right. What is it you need to know?"

I suppose Meredith had finally decided that the best way to get Rod and me out of her house was to tell us anything she figured we already knew.

I implied that it was from Amanda that I'd learned that there was a prenuptial with Tricia whereby, if Tricia divorced Barclay "for cause," she received back, not only everything she'd brought to the marriage (enough to build Glen Valley), but half of anything Barclay was worth when he cheated on her. "Was there cause?" I asked.

Meredith's white-gray pageboy was so precisely combed that I wondered if it might be a wig. She adjusted the black velvet band in it that matched her bathrobe and decided to drop the pretense that Barclay's marriage was a "reasonably happy one." She said, "Yes, in fact I did know of my son's affair with that whore."

"By whore, you mean Amanda Morgan?" I knew that's who she meant but I wanted her to say it.

But Meredith paid me back. "Your sister," she said, "went to her death, all too aware of that woman's name. I'm sure you know who I mean."

Rod said, "There was a prenuptial agreement with his current wife regarding adultery?"

"That is a private legal matter."

Rod declined the cup of coffee she offered him. "Ma'am, in a multiple homicide investigation, there are no private matters. We'll subpoena what we need. If you don't think your son has run off because he killed three people, you want to cooperate. Anything you can tell us is just going to help him in the long run."

She studied Rod's smooth-planed face. No matter what he was doing, he always had that same calm look. "Tricia is a Catholic. She doesn't believe in divorce."

"Tell it to half my cousins," I said.

"Is Barclay your prime suspect?" Meredith asked Rod.

He nodded at her. "I'm afraid so."

At that moment we all heard a noise behind us and turned to see Tricia Ober, dressed in corduroy slacks and a thick Irish sweater, standing in the doorway with her coat on her arm. "If you're going to talk about me, why not invite me to join you?"

Meredith hurried over to her. "I thought you were asleep."

In fact Tricia looked as if she hadn't slept for days. She said she was going outside to cut some holly branches to take to Immaculate Conception for tomorrow's Christmas Eve

High Mass. Clay was coming with her. She had no idea where Barclay might have gone. She laughed without humor. "And you know what? I really don't care anymore. I'm getting an ecclesiastical annulment. Isn't this funny—there's something in the Church called 'defective marital consent,' and God knows Barclay had it when he married me." She let Meredith kiss her cheek, then walked away.

SITTING DOWN, carefully folding the pleats of her robe over her knees, Meredith said, "She's just upset. Father Connor will help her. I don't know what Tricia would do without him. He's certainly been here for her. And for Clay . . ."

I said, "An annulment's not going to kick in that prenup, is it? Much less, equitable distribution. Because adultery's grounds for divorce in New Jersey. I guess it's pretty lucky Tricia turned Catholic, after all."

Thoughtful, the white-haired woman walked over to the window and pointed at the extensively landscaped evergreens. "Just as beautiful in winter as in spring and summer. I'm very fond of evergreens. I don't really like flowers. . . . Your sister, Gina, always wanted to plant roses there along that stone wall. But I think those different shades of green there are really best."

Rod said, "I like roses."

"Most people do." She waited by the window, clearly hoping we would leave. Finally she said, "It's an odd Christmas."

"Having your son wanted for murder?" I agreed. "Yep, that's pretty odd, okay."

"Last chance. You have no idea where Barclay might be hiding?" Rod asked her quietly. "Because we have to figure he knows we're looking for him. We know he hasn't flown anywhere."

"I can't help you any further."

"If you hear from him, call us."

"Of course." She rose now, back in command. "I have no idea why you think he might murder two young men like Ben and Pudge, whom he'd known for years and actually . . . liked."

I asked her if she knew Barclay was negotiating with Ben Tymosz to buy the old theater out by the docks, that he had in fact drawn up the contract the day Ben died. For $675,000?

"That seems substantial," she said.

"Well, I'd say so too. Except Ben didn't want to sell it. But Megan and Ben's mother are easier to deal with. And for about half that amount."

Mrs. Ober said nothing.

I asked her whether she knew that Pudge Salerno, head of Gloria's planning and zoning commission, had threatened to stop Barclay's destruction of historic landmarks, like the playhouse and the docks, in order to construct "Etten Landing" on the site.

"Barclay buys a lot of things. A lot of people try to stop him." She said it with assurance, but her eyes were troubled, and her lips, old and pale in the morning light, twitched before she could cover her mouth with her hand. I suppose it was the look of someone who'd put all her assets into one stock and had just watched it tank.

I asked, "What do you mean, Meredith? People get in his way and he kills them?"

"You have to believe me. Barclay would never harm that woman." (It was apparently not possible for her to say Amanda's name.)

I said, "You think people don't kill the people they love? They do it all the time."

Rod said, "I think she means Barclay cared too much to stop seeing Amanda, despite the divorce clause in the prenuptial."

She nodded, a concession. "I begged him to break it off. I told him he was jeopardizing everything. He'd worked so hard. We all had. He had a future."

I said, "You don't mean the new development, do you? You mean politics."

"Of course I mean politics. Money is nothing. But it can change things if you know how to use it." She looked out the window at the land and buildings she'd restored so handsomely, then back at us. "I met her, of course. She came here to my home. Invited by him. She was very beautiful."

"Yes," I agreed.

"We argued. He told me he wanted her the way I wanted River Bend. That he was in love with her." Meredith Ober smiled as if it were the strangest remark she'd ever heard anyone make.

I thought about telling her that she could have had another grandchild if Amanda hadn't died.

21

ABU

ROD OFFERED ME his bed to rest in. He lived on the "wrong" side of Deep Port River, on the way to River Bend and right on the riverbank, so he could drop in his kayak as soon as he awakened. His place, gray shingles with a wide porch, had been a summer cabin that he'd started working on by winterizing when he'd bought it. He was always adding rooms in his "spare" time. So far he'd built on a garage and a sunroom. Sometimes I helped him.

"I'm not a baby."

Rod pulled up the white comforter, tucking it around my shoulders. "I'll check you later."

"Listen . . . Rod . . . About Garth?"

He touched my hand through the covers. "Jamie, you feel like you want to give me back the ring, that's your call." He turned out the bedside lamp. "I hope you won't. Go to sleep."

"I'm not going to sleep."

"Okay, that's fine." He closed the walnut shutters on the windows of his bedroom and quietly shut the door behind him.

And the next thing I knew, the loudly ticking metal clock beside his bed said three thirty. Afternoon light flared through the western windows. I walked over and opened the shutters. The sun was already heading into the lake.

A nightmare had awakened me. All the members of the Killing Club, but the ages we are now, not teenagers, were lounging around the stage floor of the Pine Barrens Playhouse, laughing together about something, but I don't know what it was. Then all the men except Pudge suddenly sidled over to Amanda and started to pull at her clothes. She screamed. Every time Pudge tried to tell them to stop, blood instead of words poured from his lips. Then I realized that Amanda was not screaming because she was being attacked, but because of something happening behind us. The doors of the loading dock banged apart with a loud wrenching noise. And Lyall, dead, dank, wet and green, with rotted weeds hanging from him, stood there. He held Barclay's crossbow to his chest. The sunlight behind him was sparking in shafts of light, blinding us. The light made a glittering square on the backstage concrete floor near the loading dock. The concrete floor. The square of lighter gray in the concrete floor.

· · ·

WHERE YOU BEEN?" Danny said when I called him. A mug of coffee in hand, I was leaning on the rail of the high stilted porch of Rod's cabin, looking down at the river.

"You guys find Barclay?" I asked.

"Are you shitting me? That guy's in fuckin' Brazil dancing the tango."

"You mean Argentina, Danny."

He snorted. "Gotcha, I'm not Danny. It's Donny the Mattress King. . . . So they're releasing your dad and Dino."

"Yeah, I just talked to my father. Sounds like they're okay. Joe Jr.'s picking them up. So at least Dad'll see him for Christmas."

"Sorry about last night. Shoulda walked you to the door."

"Aww, Donny, you're so much nicer than Dan." I ate the last bite of the prosciutto and mozzarella sandwich that Rod had left wrapped on the counter for me. "Listen, a guy loves power tools the way you do is bound to know somebody who can use a jackhammer. I need one at the Pine Barrens Playhouse as soon as you can get it there. But I need you to pick me up at Rod's house first."

"Rod's right here. You want to talk to him?"

"No. And don't tell him about the jackhammer."

"You are one weird and bossy lady."

TURNS OUT DANNY knew two guys who used jackhammers. I should have thought of the Griswald cousins myself; after all, I saw Morris and Dwight at Dixon all the time. Between them, the two men weighed five hundred pounds. They appeared to have modeled their looks on childhood illustrations of Paul Bunyan. And they did nice work paving the streets of downtown Gloria when they weren't in the holding tank on drunk and disorderly charges. That's where they happened to be when Danny cut them a deal for the holidays.

So Morris and Dwight followed us out to the playhouse in their old blue dented pickup truck with its big Christmas wreath on the front grill and on the rear bumper a sticker surprisingly asking tailgaters to PRAISE THE LORD. The truck had a very large and angry St. Bernard dog riding in the back. The dog barked the whole hour it took the Griswalds to cut open the rough square section of concrete I'd noticed at the theater when Garth and I had looked the place over. The section backstage by the loading dock where the shade of gray looked different.

The concrete flooring was only eight inches deep. The cousins sledge-hammered the broken-up chunks out of the way. Below was hard-packed dirt, and they used their shovels to move that.

"What the hell are we doing?" Danny pulled me aside to whisper. "This better be good."

"What, you don't want to look like an asshole in front of the town drunks?"

About three feet down, I yelled for the Griswalds to stop their digging. I'd seen a scrap of torn black plastic bag. I stood in the hole and took a look at the contents. Then I gestured to Danny. "You want to get them out of here?"

"Aww, this sucks," Morris told Dwight. "We're the ones dug it."

Dwight was curious. "What is it in there? It's Barclay Ober, right? I heard in the tank, you're looking for him."

But Danny forced them to drive off with their dog, who barked furiously at us as they left.

We moved aside enough dirt to push back the torn plastic and shine our flashlights on its contents.

It wasn't the body of Barclay Ober buried there, wrapped in a garbage bag, below the concrete floor. It was Lyall Hillier.

There was little left of him but pieces of flesh, bones and rags of clothes and staring empty eyes. But the wide black zipper and the polyester decal of the Tour de France cyclist had outlasted the corduroy jacket they'd been a part of. And the silver snake ring was still on his decomposed forefinger.

BACK AT THE MORGUE, Gert Anderssen told us that she was no expert. We needed a specialist, a forensic anthropologist.

"Give me a guess," Rod told her.

Her guess would be that, yes, Lyall Hillier had been dead for at least a decade. He hadn't drowned. He hadn't killed himself. He'd been struck, very hard, on the temple with a blunt instrument. His skull was cracked. The fissure was over two inches long.

As it turned out, Sweets was able to provide us with Lyall's dental records. They were still on file in the charts of the dentist from whom she'd bought her practice. They matched the teeth of the corpse. "Hardly even any cavities," she said. "Great teeth."

GERT SAID SHE HAD called "Chief Waige" (as she always called him) to tell him to put me officially back on the Killing Club homicides, since it was clear this latest discovery of mine was connected to the current murders. "He will do this," she said. "This is settled." We all pretended not to have any idea why she'd have such influence on Waige. As we left, she warned us she was going to take early retirement if things kept on this way. "In two days is Christmas, by God, and here we stand in a morgue. Night after night, I'm never home."

Rod, Dan and I tried not to look at one another, all wondering why she'd want to be home, if that's where Warren Waige was.

THE NEXT DAY, Christmas Eve, the three of us sat together in the new squad room, talking it over, eating grinders for lunch. We had copies of the original police report on Lyall's "drowning" to study.

"Did they chase after Lyall when he ran off?" I looked at the photo we'd taken of the backstage hole. "Did they kill him to stop him from telling about the hazing, bury him, then set up the fake drowning? It's not possible."

Rod agreed. The five young people had talked to the police the next morning. "They didn't have time to bury him there. The police aren't going to notice a big square of wet concrete?"

Danny suggested that maybe the loading area floor had

been wood or dirt rather than concrete back then. The truth was, I didn't remember one way or the other. But his idea didn't make sense either. Why would the area where Lyall was buried be a different color unless someone had knocked old concrete loose, buried the body, and then poured new concrete over it? And, as Rod said, that would take more time than they'd had, even if they'd all been doing it together—Barclay, Garth, Connie, Ben and Amanda.

Plus, I couldn't believe that they all had been complicit in a killing that they'd kept quiet about in some kind of conspiracy for nearly a dozen years. But if Barclay had done it alone? If it all went back to Lyall? It would explain . . .

Abu interrupted with a knock on an imaginary door. (One of the things I don't like about our modern offices is there *are* no doors to the squad room.)

As always Abu looked like he'd borrowed his clothes from somebody three times his size. The sleeve of his sweatshirt fell down his arm when he waved at me. "Hey, Jamie, I hear that Death Book killer guy tried to gas your whole damn family. I got to tell you, this is not the kind of club I would ever want to get my name on the membership of, know what I mean?" Abu was carrying two metal evidence cups. He opened them for us.

Danny said, "Looks like dirt."

Abu told him it was dirt. One container had particles of earth taken from the clothing of the corpse we'd dug up. One had earth from the surrounding area. Some of the dirt on the clothes was indigenous to the earth in which Lyall's body had been buried. But there was other dirt there, little bits of it, clinging especially to his shoes, that was very different. The second dirt had in it traces of bonemeal, fish emulsion, phosphorous, Epsom salts and other ingredients one might use in a garden to fertilize it.

"Like a flower or a vegetable garden?" Danny asked.

"Yeah, something worked on."

The additives, trapped in plastic, were still traceable.

"So the body was moved?" Rod gave Abu the victory sign that made everyone at GPD smile whenever they got one from him.

Abu smiled now. "Lieutenant Wolenski, that body was moved no more than eight years ago." He waited till we asked him how he could know that. "Because that particular cement binder that mixed up that concrete, they didn't make it till eight years ago." Abu grinned.

I said, "Could be Barclay put Lyall in the trunk of his car, drove everybody else home, then went home himself and buried him in the gardens at River Bend."

"But why move him back to the theater?" Rod asked. "Why not just leave him where he was?"

"Maybe because of all Meredith's landscaping."

Abu screwed the tops back on his metal cups. "Meanwhile, just call me the George Washington Carver of the CSI." He did a parody of a hip-hop dance step and walked away.

"Carver? Is that somebody on a TV show?" Danny asked me.

ROD LEFT TO GO TELL Lyall's parents that they could, after all these years, bury their son's body. I wondered if it would be worse, or easier, for them to know he hadn't killed himself.

I was down in Abu's lab asking him about the use of

cyanide potassium in insecticides. Could the killer have gotten the cyanide from a garden store?

Abu said, "Well, he didn't stroll on down to Solly's Drugs and say, 'Hey, there, Mr. Pharmacist, sell me some lethal cyanide salts and throw in a tube of dental fixative while you're at it.'"

The jazz melody started to play on my cell phone. At first I didn't recognize it. "I believe that's your phone," Abu told me. "Want me to customize that ring for you?"

It was a bad connection—in a lot of ways. "Jamie? It's Garth. I've got some news."

"Are you okay? Garth, where are you, New York City? We just found Lyall's body. He didn't drown. He was killed."

For a while, I didn't hear anything. I thought maybe I'd lost him. But finally he said, "I'm going to tell you something, but only you. You understand?"

"Garth, what's going on? Where are you?"

"I figure you've got a right. But you bring other cops with you, and it's off."

"What's off?"

"I'm in Sea Isle City. Leave right now. Don't talk to Rod or anybody else on your way. You've got forty minutes." He gave me the address of a restaurant on the oceanfront.

"Are you listening to me? We found Lyall!"

"I heard you. You want to arrest the guy who did it all or not?"

My heart was thudding so fast, I had to make myself breathe. Abu turned to look at me as I asked, "What are you telling me, Garth?"

He said, "Where Barclay is," and hung up.

22

ISAAC WURTZ

GARTH MCBRIDE AND I HAD almost made love once, a lifetime ago, in a small beach house in Sea Isle City. It was the summer place of Debbie Deklerk's parents, three rows back from the ocean, and it wasn't air-conditioned. The August after we'd graduated from Hart, Debbie had had her birthday party there and had invited a group of us. It was the last time the Killing Club met together—until Ben's funeral. I remember the sea breeze chilling my sunburned skin that night.

In the parking lot of a restaurant called the Deep, in Sea Isle City, Garth leaned against a big new Lincoln Town Car, a Hertz rental.

"I thought you didn't have a driver's license." I locked up my Mustang and walked over to him.

"I don't. My source rented it for me. . . . So, a lot's happened. Sad lot."

"Too much." The sun was nearly set, but the last rays forced me to shade my eyes to see him.

"I'm really sorry about Pudge."

"Me too," I said. "Nothing will make it right." We looked at each other, acknowledging that. "You've found Barclay?"

Garth rubbed his photogenic hair. "I know nobody thinks so, including me, but I am a reporter."

"Where is he?"

"My source'll take us there. She's inside."

"She?"

"Before we go in, okay? Talk to me for a second. How did Lyall die?"

I looked at him for a long time, then told him someone had hit Lyall with something hard enough to crack open his skull. Maybe a lug wrench or an iron pipe. "At GPD we've talked about the possibility that all of you there at the playhouse helped bury Lyall that night. Is that true?"

He shook his head. "Not true. You know that." He waited until I nodded at him. Then he looked out toward the ocean. "Weird to find out after all this time that it wasn't suicide. I spent a lot of years . . ." He shrugged. "I always felt guilty. Letting that hazing happen. It's the thing I guess I'll wake up in the night over, the rest of my life. I figured . . ."

"He was in love with you?"

"Yeah."

"We all thought that. Maybe he was." We headed up the

driftwood stairs to the restaurant door. "But why did Barclay kill him?"

He shrugged. "Isn't it pretty obvious Barclay's gone nuts?"

"Is he here in Sea Isle City?"

"He's got a house up the road on Daybreak Point. I waited for you."

"Why?"

"They took you off the case and it didn't seem right. I want his story. I figure you want—do you still call it a 'collar'?"

I didn't tell him that Chief Waige had been forced to return me to the investigation, so actually I wasn't off the case. However, I couldn't arrest anybody beyond the town limits of Gloria, New Jersey. Instead I just asked him how he'd located Barclay.

"*Chinatown*," he said. "Remember how Barclay loved the movie *Chinatown*?"

No, I didn't remember that. But I remembered that Garth never forgot anything.

"So I went to Harbor House—"

"The senior care center?"

"And that's where I found her. She's in here." He pushed open the door to the seafood restaurant, every inch of which was decorated for Christmas, from strings of starfish with red lights in them hung across the ceiling to big plastic elves standing guard in the windows. It was Christmas Eve and there was only one (unhappy-looking) family having an early dinner at the tables, but the bar was so crowded with holiday revelers that I didn't see Garth's source until she waved her piña colada at the bartender. She wanted her pineapple slice, which he'd forgotten to add to the big glass. It was my great-aunt Betty Wurtz.

Aunt Betty was dressed for the outing in a red polyester pants suit with a white lace blouse, but she'd kept on her fake fur parka for warmth. "You know why old people move to Florida?" she said. "They're cold. It's cold in here." She rubbed my hands between hers. "I thought you were going to marry this guy Garth but he says you're not."

"Aunt Betty, what's going on? What are you doing with Garth?"

"What are you? He says you're going to marry a cop who's a Polish Indian. Good for you, Giovanna, but you'll be thrown out of the family."

I told her I didn't think families did things like that anymore.

"Ha," she said.

We ordered drinks, and while Garth told me how he'd located my great-aunt at Harbor House, she left us to call "a friend" who was placing bets for her on some of the Bowl games.

Here's how Garth had put it together. Since Barclay and Amanda had restarted their affair in the fall (something Barclay had been trying to do for much longer than that), and since both were "public figures," at least in the small world of Gloria, New Jersey, they needed a private place in which to meet. For convenience's sake, that place couldn't be far away. Amanda had told Garth at Ben's funeral reception (when they'd stood outside together so long) that she'd been having an affair with Barclay but she was breaking up with him. She mentioned that he'd had a beach house where they met and that it was in Sea Isle and it was on the ocean and he'd bought it three or four years ago. But that's all she had told him. (It was more than she'd told anybody else.)

I interrupted. "Why would she say any of this to you?"

"I don't know," Garth admitted. "She was really upset about Ben's dying. She said it had brought back to her how she'd lost Shawn. She didn't want to mess around with her life anymore. All she wanted was a baby. Maybe I just happened to be there when she needed to say it."

I didn't tell him that she had been carrying the baby she'd wanted when she died, and that she'd broken up with Barclay because he'd served his purpose in providing her with one. As Barclay knew: That was the meaning of what I'd heard him yelling at her outside Dante's that night before she died: "You got what you wanted and now you're dumping me? I don't think so!"

And since Barclay had disappeared from Gloria after her death, and hadn't taken a plane or a train or a car that anyone could trace, it had occurred to Garth that he might be hiding out in that house of his that was on the ocean.

So Garth did the research. Barclay Ober owned no such house under his own name in Sea Isle, nor was there property in the name of Amanda Kean or any of her married names. Next, Garth started looking up ownership of every oceanfront home in Sea Isle, anything purchased three or four years ago. He called the owners and marked them off his list as he learned they had no tie to Barclay. But there was one name that sounded familiar. Isaac Wurtz. Isaac Wurtz had bought a residential property on Daybreak Point Lane four years ago. Garth remembered meeting my great-aunt Betty Wurtz in the cemetery, and her saying how her hus-

band had been in real estate but had died. That's when Garth
had thought of Barclay's fondness for the movie *Chinatown*,
in which the names of deceased residents of an old folks'
home had been used to buy L.A. real estate.

He located Aunt Betty at Harbor House. He learned
from her that shortly before Isaac's death four years ago, her
critically ill husband had bought the Sea Isle house, for cash,
and then had privately transferred its ownership to Barclay
Ober. For his efforts, Isaac had received "a nice-sized and totally legit finder's fee," which Aunt Betty had probably not
paid taxes on, and which was a big help when her husband
died. She continued to receive a small annual "gift" as his
widow from OLDR, which also sent her money every year
for taxes and insurance and "maintenance."

YOU BLABBED ALL this to Garth, Aunt Betty?"

She shrugged. "He's a good-looking guy." Obviously it
was a gene-pool sort of thing with us.

Aunt Betty said she'd driven by the Daybreak Point
house a number of times over the years, wondering if there
was a way she could get her hands on it, since officially it was
hers, but she had always been afraid of getting in trouble
with the law. It was a reasonable suspicion, I told her.

From the restaurant, she directed us along an oceanfront street of beach houses that were squeezed together side
by side but trying to ignore one another. At the outer point
of a cul de sac, I pulled into the drive of a gray-clapboard
beach house of modern design, full of angles, with its deck
flung out to the ocean. The house was built over its parking
area, and there was a car there that we later learned was reg-

istered to Amanda Tarrini Morgan. Inside the closed garage
was Barclay's BMW.

The garbage can was full.

Lights were on.

Aunt Betty went to the back door and rang the buzzer. If
Barclay answered the door, she was going to say that she was
having some trouble with the insurance company about the
house. If I saw him, I'd call the local cops.

But Barclay didn't answer the door. Sending Aunt Betty
back to wait in my car, and leaving Garth to guard the back
door, I went in through a window on the deck. Two white
fans were turning in the ceiling of the large cathedral living
room. But they couldn't hide the odor or scare off the flies.

Barclay lay on the wall-to-wall carpet with the back of
his head blown off. There was a Beretta pistol near his hand.
There was a bottle of expensive and fashionable brandy on a
table beside the couch. It was nearly empty. There was a
business card beside the brandy bottle: Barclay Ober, President, Ober Land Development and Realty. Above his addresses and phone numbers and fax numbers and e-mail
addresses, he'd written in pencil, "I'm sorry."

Barclay wore only a bathrobe, a very nice silk one. He'd
been dead for days.

23

CLAY

So that, everyone thought, was that. It was Barclay's house. The note on the card was in Barclay's handwriting. The Beretta handgun was registered to Barclay. The Sea Isle medical examiner found powder burns on his hand and face consistent with a self-inflicted gunshot through the open mouth. We all agreed he'd killed Ben to stop Ben from exposing what he'd done to Lyall. We said he'd killed Pudge to stop Pudge from exposing what he'd done to the one person he appeared to have cared about, or at least couldn't bear to lose except to death—Amanda. We said he'd killed himself because he couldn't bear the horror of all he'd done and all he'd lost. It made sense.

Garth had his story for his TV show. I had the Killing Club killer. The white news vans with their satellite dishes raced from one scene of blood or grief to the next, terrified that their rivals would get there first. But it was Garth who got there first. The problem was, we all had it wrong.

It was after eleven at night when Rod and I drove in separate cars to River Bend to tell Barclay's family that he'd killed himself. I was going to let Rod give the news to Meredith. Tricia was at church for the Christmas Eve Mass that had started at ten. Meredith would take it better from Rod than from me, because she was going to blame me for driving her son to suicide, and it would be easier for her to progress from that blame into the pain of losing her only child if I wasn't around.

Meanwhile I went looking for Clay. The first place I looked was where he was—the private hideout he'd made of the old summer kitchen, off in the dark beyond the main house among the other outbuildings.

Clay let me in, unlocking three different locks. He already knew his father was dead. A classmate, whose older brother had heard the report on the police band, had called him.

At first he pretended that he was glad—his father was a monster and Clay was glad he was dead. I sat with him while he did that. Then he pretended that he didn't care. I sat with him while he did that too.

We sat on the couch side by side for a long time before he silently cried.

At the center of the single room was a white worktable. On it sat a lot of hi-tech machinery; among the computer monitors was a small direct printer with a digital camera. And neatly stacked in rows along the end of the table were digital photos: I asked if I could look at them. He shrugged. I said, "I used to take pictures. The Hart High newspaper? I was the photographer."

"It's just junk," he told me.

But it wasn't. He was very good, much better than I'd ever been. The photos were mostly portraits, but not posed—candid shots. These people didn't know they were being photographed. And Clay was telling you exactly who they were. His grandmother, his father, his stepmother—you didn't like them. There were a dozen from Ben's funeral reception. One sweet close-up of Pudge that I asked him to give me. There were a lot of me. A lot of Connie too. Many of Connie with Tricia. At River Bend, at Immaculate Conception. One in the rose garden in summer. The roses were all different colors. And one of Connie, close-up, taken here in the summer kitchen, that scared me, even though he was smiling at the camera.

I was so focused on studying this picture that I didn't hear Clay at first. He was telling me that he knew I wouldn't believe him, but he'd found something hidden behind a shelf here in his hideout. "I know you think I'm lying, but I didn't put it there. It was just there."

He was holding ripped-out pages of magazines, with glossy Absolut ads, and stuck in their midst was a piece of paper with pasted letters on it. They spelled "Death has come . . ." Only those three words.

". . . Backup plan." It all came together for me.

"I knew you wouldn't believe me." Clay flung himself on the small cot in the corner.

"I believe you." I gave him a hard embrace. "I've got to go right now."

Clay swiped at his eyes. "Did somebody tell my grandmother and Tricia?"

"Rod's with them now."

He nodded. "I guess I better go see." He was the man of the family now and the weight of it sank onto his thin narrow shoulders.

"You're going to be all right, Clay. It's going to be okay." I brushed his unkempt hair off his forehead. His eyes, the lashes wet now, looked so much like Gina's.

"I guess."

STARLIGHT WAS SO BRIGHT I could find my way into the garden at Immaculate Conception without a flashlight. It was now after midnight and the church was empty. I knelt in the rose bed beside the stone birdbath, digging up samples of the earth to put in my evidence cup. I would take them back to the lab. But I already knew that the soil would match the dirt we'd found on the body of Lyall Hillier.

I DIDN'T HEAR HIM coming but I felt the motion in the air as he swung the shovel. Starlight glinted on the blade as it struck me on the side of my head.

24

THE KILLING CLUB

HE THOUGHT HE'D knocked me out, but I'd turned my head at the last second. Blood in my eyes blinded me and I was fighting not to lose consciousness. Lying there in the rows of dead roses, I could still see that he was motionless, looking down at me.

Connie just stood there, staring. Maybe he thought I was dead.

It was like I could feel him thinking, so intense was the silence, as he worked his way through to how I'd gotten here. What had he done wrong? He'd been so careful, backup upon backup. Barclay's "suicide" was the logical end. Why wasn't it over?

How I'd gotten here—to this rose garden in the

starlight, where years ago Father Cooke must have discovered the buried body of Lyall Hillier, and paid for his discovery with his life—had happened too slowly to save Barclay, much less Amanda or Pudge. Not until I was standing in Clay's small hideout, there in the dark at River Bend, hearing the boy beg me to believe him that he hadn't pasted the letters on the death threats, had I gotten it. Not till I was looking at Connie's awful smile in the photograph, had I suddenly seen that we'd all been wrong. A collage of images, all jumbled, out of time, had rushed at me then, more and more coming as I drove to the church on the green.

The fertilizers used for roses.

Father Cooke's bringing roses from his garden to my grieving father. In high school, Connie, a scholarship winner with a golden future, had worked at Immaculate Conception as Father Cooke's gardener.

Connie vomiting at Lyall's funeral. Not wanting anyone to talk about Lyall.

Roses at Lyall's grave.

Ben turning to the Church, to Connie.

The shape of the shadow crossing the Tymosz living room that morning when I'd come back and discovered where the nails had held the wire across the basement door entrance.

Connie going hunting with Barclay.

Connie's never taking off his gloves at Dante's after Pudge died, wincing when Danny shook his hand, not because he didn't like Danny but because his hand had been burned from the oil splatter as he'd shoved Pudge's head down into the vat.

The smell of Pudge's Marlboro cigarettes caught in the fabric of Connie's overcoat.

Connie's slip-up, telling me he was looking at the snow falling as he'd heard about Pudge's death from Eileen, when it had stopped snowing long before that, because he'd gone long before that to Dante's to murder Pudge.

Connie a constant visitor at River Bend, able to come and go as he wished. And so able to make Barclay the killer. Barclay's car, his weapon, his motive. Able to make it look as if Barclay were mimicking the Killing Club killings. The copied keys, the anonymous notes cutting up pages from magazines Clay was using in his art class; the note to Amanda, printed on Clay's printer in the summer kitchen, where Connie had planted the copies of the notes. Everything tied to River Bend, where Connie came daily, where he was Tricia's sympathetic counselor, there to help her struggle with her husband's infidelity. Everything Barclay allegedly did tied to that infidelity with Amanda.

I heard Connie say, "God, it's been a long time coming."

"Since you killed Lyall? Yes."

In the starlight, I lifted my head till our eyes met. Connie just kept looking down at me, his hair neatly trimmed, his overcoat pressed. I asked him, "Did you mean to kill Lyall on purpose or did it just happen and then you had to make it look like he killed himself?"

Connie sighed a long low sigh; it sounded strangely relieved. "Lyall? He told me he was going to go tell the school, and go tell Father Cooke. He was going to tell about what we did with Amanda and him, and the drugs and everything."

"Your life would have been different."

He shook his head. "My life was different."

I rolled over fast, raising my arm with my gun. "Step back, Connie. Just step back."

But quickly he raised the shovel high in the air. "Don't make me, Jamie!"

I shot the shovel spinning out of his hand. He screamed, grabbing his bleeding hand.

"Put your hands over your head!"

"Why did you have to do this? Why didn't you just let it go?"

"Connie. Now. Right now. Put your hands over your head."

He just kept shaking his head. Then he slowly said, "Jamie. Kill me. Please."

Fighting my way to my feet, wiping blood out of my eyes, I kept the gun on him. "You're under arrest."

"Please. I can't do it myself."

"I know you can't. You're under arrest."

He turned and ran into the dark too fast for me to fire again. I heard the door to the church bang open.

Hauling out my cell phone, calling 911, I staggered after him. The door was now locked. There was a mullioned window nearby. I kicked through it and crawled inside. The church was an endless vault of black smoky shadows. I could smell the evergreen decorations for Christmas. There would have been hundreds of people here at that Mass singing "Joy to the World" together, just hours ago.

"Connie . . ." My voice echoed through the cathedral. I felt my way along the side aisle, from pew to pew. "Connie, let's stop this. Let's get you some help. You want it to be over.

I know that. You want it to be over." I kept talking, looking, listening.

Suddenly Connie rushed out at me in a run. Silent, but his face in a scream, he was thrusting an enormous iron candelabrum at me. The three long bare spikes pointed at me. At the last second, I rolled forward, knocking Connie over onto the marble floor, just as one of the spikes tore through the sleeve of my coat.

We fought on the floor, rolling, kicking, but his coat tore loose and he got away from me.

I couldn't find him again. He knew the huge space in the dark. I didn't.

In a crouch, slowly moving aisle by aisle I inched toward the altar. My eyes adjusting to the starlight that was coming through all the arched windows. And I could hear him. I could hear his shoes on the marble, walking toward the choir screen.

Then all at once Connie lit one of the tall white candles. The light was like a nimbus around him. Then he started lighting the other candles at the altar. Walking unhurriedly, methodically from candle to candle, he lit them all, as he must have done in his teens when he'd helped Father Cooke with the services.

In that candlelight, I could see him clearly. He looked weirdly white-faced in his dark suit, like he was wearing a mask in a play. Then he stood still beneath the wooden crucifix that hung from a gold chain in the chancel.

"Connie?"

He didn't move or speak, and I said nothing else to him. I walked up the altar steps toward him, pulling the handcuffs from the belt of my jeans. "You have the right to remain silent."

"I don't want to remain silent," he said. "I'm so tired."

"Okay. It's over."

I could hear the sirens coming.

"What was worth it, Connie? Was anything worth it?"

"Nothing," he said. "But at the time you don't believe it."

"But what? The scholarship? Running this place? Single malt scotch at River Bend? Being smarter than the rest of us?"

Connie sat on the marble step, resting his head on the altar rail as if it were just too heavy to hold up. He smiled with a sorrow I'd seen on Gina's face as she was dying. "At first, I just didn't want Mary Beth not to like me. That's all. If I just could stop Lyall from leaving that night . . . that's all I was thinking. And my life changed."

"You changed it."

"Oh, yes. Free will. I know the doctrine."

Danny was in the first black and white to get there.

As he shoved Connie's head down into the backseat, Danny pointed at my car, parked in front of the church. Danny said, "I always knew a girl driving a 1968 Ford Mustang Shelby GT-500 couldn't be all bad."

25

JAMIE

GARTH DIDN'T call me until he was waiting at the train station on his way back to New York. I drove over there to tell him good-bye. While we stood on the platform, a woman asked for his autograph.

"Katie's right," I said. "You're a celebrity." The national media, covering the shocking capture of a young star of the Church as the Killing Club Killer, had turned quickly and often to Garth for inside-source interviews. Every anchor from Peter Jennings to Larry King had asked him to tell them how this horror could have happened in such a little town and to such unlikely people. According to Katie, Garth was getting offers to go national himself.

It was now early January, cold and windy. The station

announcer told us that the train to Trenton was approaching the platform and that we should step back. I already knew that.

Pulling his hands from the pockets of his loose Italian cashmere overcoat, Garth rubbed them together and then glanced at his watch. "So, guess I'll see you around. Thanks for the story."

"You're welcome," I said. "But to me it wasn't so much a story, I guess. More a heartache."

"You know what I mean. I would have looked like an idiot if I'd gone on the air saying it was Barclay." He thought a moment. "You know what? I liked Barclay better when I thought he'd killed himself. Love and loss."

"I don't like it either way."

We talked about Connie's confession, which he'd made as soon as Rod and I had sat down with him in the Dixon interrogation room. The priest, who'd heard so many other people's confessions, declined a lawyer, not wanting to carry in silence the weight of what he'd done any longer. The confession had poured out of him. His parishioners, his diocese, his friends, all were in shock. The whole town of Gloria was stunned. Nobody talked of anything else through the holidays. "The last person you'd ever . . ." "I don't believe it . . ."

Connie had confessed that he'd killed Lyall but hadn't meant to, he'd just meant to stop him from telling anyone what had happened that night at the playhouse after the game. He'd told how he'd smashed Lyall on the head with an iron pipe that he'd snatched out of the debris on the derelict dock. How, then desperate, he'd come up with a plan to disguise that death as a suicide.

How he had tied a rope around Lyall's body, dropped

him off the dock into the river, breaking a hole in the ice. Left him there while he let Barclay drive him home with the others—all of whom thought Lyall had walked back to town.

Then later that night he had hurried back to the docks in his parents' car, hauled up the body out of the river and put it in the trunk.

Had left the suicide note he'd forged under the concrete block with Lyall's coat and wallet.

Had buried Lyall's body in the beds of Father Cooke's rose garden in the Immaculate Conception cloister, where he worked every afternoon. And for years he'd thought all was well. He'd won the scholarship, he'd gone to Georgetown, then to seminary, he'd become a priest.

He'd tried to make up for Lyall by doing good.

But then Father Cooke had discovered Lyall's corpse.

Yet, somehow even that had worked out for Connie. Easy enough to give the old priest, already having a heart attack from the shock, an extra push by confessing that he himself (beloved at Immaculate Conception) had killed his friend years earlier. Or maybe he'd even put cyanide in Father Cooke's nitroglycerin tablet, but if so, that crime Connie wouldn't confess.

All those years, climbing the ladder so fast that at twenty-seven he was head pastor of the large flourishing church where once he'd mowed the lawn and cared for the plants. So fast that he was chosen to be a monsignor, the youngest in the diocese.

Everything was all right until Ben, knowing he was dying and burdened with guilt, had confessed to Connie that he was coming the next day to tell me, and so the police, how a group of them had driven Lyall to suicide.

Even then Connie hadn't panicked. Even then he'd set things up perfectly so that if we at GPD didn't rule Ben's death an accident, there'd be a backup; Connie would tie it to the Killing Club. But not to the Lyall part of the club's past. That's what Connie couldn't afford. When Amanda tried to bring us back to think about Lyall, to what had happened that night so long ago at the Pine Barrens Playhouse, Amanda had died too. Easy enough to make it look like Barclay was guilty of everything. Stalking Amanda. Following me in the car that night. The basement fire, the crossbow, the cyanide. Connie knew Barclay had every motive—greed (Ben and Pudge and Etten Landing), lust and jealousy and betrayal (Amanda), protecting the political career, hiding the domestic secret. Connie had confessed with a kind of ironic pride, "Better than anything in the Death Books, Jamie, right? But not perfect."

"Nothing human is, Connie. You know that."

GARTH AND I AGREED we'd underestimated Connie. He reminded me that back at Hart High, Connie had always been able to copy anybody's signature. He'd signed Garth's report card for him once. So it wouldn't have been hard to forge Lyall's note, or, years later, Barclay's suicidal "Sorry." "Funny, I remember," Garth said, "Connie told me once he wanted to be famous. Now he is."

"You remember everything," I said. "At least you remember the facts of everything."

He shrugged. "Well, most of the time, even those are wrong."

I said I wished these were. These facts were too sad.

He turned to watch the train come into view. Then he said, "Yeah, Ben and Amanda and Pudge and Barclay. Four people had to die but, hey, the bigger the body count, the bigger the story, right?" His smile was rueful in its cynical acknowledgment of the professional world he lived in.

"Apparently so. Well, I'll see you around." I held out my hand.

His smile was smart and sexy and had an old affection in it. "What are you so mad about?" he asked me. "You don't want me to leave?"

I stepped back so I could look at him. Yes, his smile was beautiful. I said, "No, Garth, I think I do want you to leave."

He nodded, ruffling his hair. "Okay. Fair enough, Jamie Ferrara. But I'll be back to see you in Gloria. You know that, don't you?"

"How do you know I'll still be here?"

"You, leave Gloria?" He laughed.

"Your train's here."

"Jamie, you're always telling me things I already know." Garth kissed me good-bye as the steaming train rumbled hugely into the station.

SNOW MELTED and more snow fell and turned to ice and melted and then it was Valentine's Day in Gloria, New Jersey.

White teddy bears with red hearts and boxes of candy topped with silk pink roses all went 50 percent off at Solly's

Drugs, but Christmas trees, their needles sharp as pins now, were still waiting in the gutters for pickup as we passed Dante's, closed, and the town green, and the gothic spires of Immaculate Conception, where there was a new young pastor working hard to help the parish get over Connie.

We were all on our way to Harbor House. My dad and Clay and Rod in the van with Dino. I was driving the men in my life to a free concert.

It was Sunday, and on Sunday we went to the senior care center to hear Dino play his guitar and sing to the elderly men and women (mostly women) herded together by my great-aunt Betty into the "lounge"—a homely room with lots of plastic folding chairs and tables and wheelchairs and walkers and the awful antiseptic smell. But "the old people," as Dino called them, loved my baby brother. Probably for the first time in his "career," he was a hit.

To Debbie Deklerk, my brother's success at Harbor House was just one more example of the twisted humor of whatever immortal idiot was filling in for God. Just like the fact that she'd been caught in a freak weeklong rain storm in Cancún at Christmas. Just like the fact that the only men in her life were her brother, Sam (who was marrying Megan Tymosz in the spring), and a gay guy she'd met at her Latin-dance classes.

During Dino's "concerts," Clay took digital photos of the most terminally ill, physically twisted and mentally out-of-it of the groups of old people wheeled into the lounge. Clay spent his weekends with us now. These days Clay didn't smile much, hardly ever talked. But, silent, he sat on that leather couch more than I did now, close to my father, watching old movies on television. And one night I heard him laugh with Dad at a scene in *Caddyshack*.

It was hard to tell whether Meredith was aware of her grandson's absence or not. Barclay's death seemed to be the last thing she had paid attention to. When I'd mentioned to her something about Tricia's return to Philadelphia, she'd looked around the large living room as if surprised that her daughter-in-law wasn't in it.

At Harbor House, with his sweet goofy smile and glittering curls, Dino finished "Where Have All the Flowers Gone" with a brief, incongruous guitar flourish taken from a David Bowie number that his audience probably didn't recognize. But as they were very fond of Dino, they clapped as loudly as they could manage.

With a Vanna White flourish, Aunt Betty, in her red sequined jacket with her bright blue slacks, turned the page of Dino's "fake book" on the music stand to the next song she'd chosen for him. "All You Need Is Love," he said cheerfully.

Rod, standing tall and comfortable and steady by my father's wheelchair, winked at me, pulling from his familiar old tweed jacket the plane tickets to Baja we'd ordered. We were leaving on our long-postponed vacation the next morning. Finally. Unless something awful happened in Gloria, New Jersey, that Chief Waige needed Rod to fix for him.

Dino walked up to a woman slumped over a tray in a mechanized chair with an IV pole. He kissed the thin hair on the top of her head. She looked up at him, startled. "Love is all you need," he sang, bending toward her.

"Are you my son?" she asked him, puzzled.

"'Course I am." My little brother grinned.

Rod leaned down, his hand touching Dad's shoulder, to listen to something my father was saying to him. They smiled at each other.

Okay. Love isn't all you need. But it's better than anything else.

ACKNOWLEDGMENTS

There would be no *Killing Club* without Josh Griffith. It has been a pleasure for me to make up stories all these years with so rich an imagination as his. Thank you.

There would be no Marcie Walsh, living her very full life in Llanview, without the gifted and indefatigable writers and writing staff of *One Life to Live*. Thank you.

Marcie Walsh could never be anyone other than the extraordinary Kathy Brier, who plays the role. Thank you.

At Hyperion, my especial gratitude to Gretchen Young, Bob Miller, Zareen Jaffery, Claire McKean and Rita Madrigal. Your faith, your enthusiasm and your talents made this book possible.

And, always, my thanks to Maureen Quilligan, beloved and best of readers.

—Michael Malone

My warm thanks to everyone in the Llanview Police Department who indulged me in all my questions and who forgave me all my mistakes. Especially,

Commissioner Bo Buchanan
Chief of Detectives John McBain
and Assistant District Attorney Nora Buchanan

Thanks to my father and brothers. I'm proud that we're a family.

To President Davidson of Llanview University and to all my friends there, my lifelong gratitude for your support.

Thanks as well to Michael Malone for his help and to the people at Hyperion for their encouragement. To Chip Kidd, I love the cover you created for my novel.

And most all, I want to thank Michael McBain, for believing from the beginning that I could write this book.

—Marcie Walsh